MARVEL
GUARDIANS OF THE GALAXY
GALAXY'S MOST WANTED

D0441379

MARVEL UNIVERSE GUARDIANS OF THE GALAXY: GALAXY'S MOST WANTED. Contains material originally published in magazine form as MARVEL UNIVERSE GUARDIANS OF THE GALAXY #1-4. First printing 2015. ISBN# 978-0-7851-9315-9. Published by MARVEL WORLDWIDE, INC., a subsidiary of MARVEL ENTERTAINMENT, LLC. OFFICE OF PUBLICATION: 135 West 50th Street, New York, NY 10020. Copyright © 2015 MARVEL No similarity between any of the names, characters, persons, and/or institutions in this magazine with those of any living or dead person or institution is intended, and any such similarity which may exist is purely coincidental. Printed in the U.S.A. ALAN FINE, President, Marvel Entertainment; DAN BUCKLEY, President, TV, Publishing and Brand Management; JOE QUESADA, Chief Creative Officer; TOM BREVOORT, SVP of Publishing; DAVID BOGART, SVP of Operations & Procurement, Publishing; C.B. CEBULSKI, VP of International Development & Brand Management; DAVID GABRIEL, SVP Print, Sales & Marketing; JIM O'KEEFE, VP of Operations & Logistics; DAN CARR, Executive Director of Publishing Technology; SUSAN CRESPI, Editorial Operations Manager; ALEX MORALES, Publishing Operations Manager; STAN LEE, Chairman Emeritus. For information regarding advertising in Marvel Comics or on Marvel.com, please contact Jonathan Rheingold, VP of Custom Solutions & Ad Sales, at jrheingold@marvel.com. For Marvel subscription inquiries, please call 800-217-9158. Manufactured between 5/15/2015 and 6/22/2015 by SHERIDAN BOOKS, INC, CHELSEA, MI, USA.

0 9 8 7 6 5 4 3 2 1

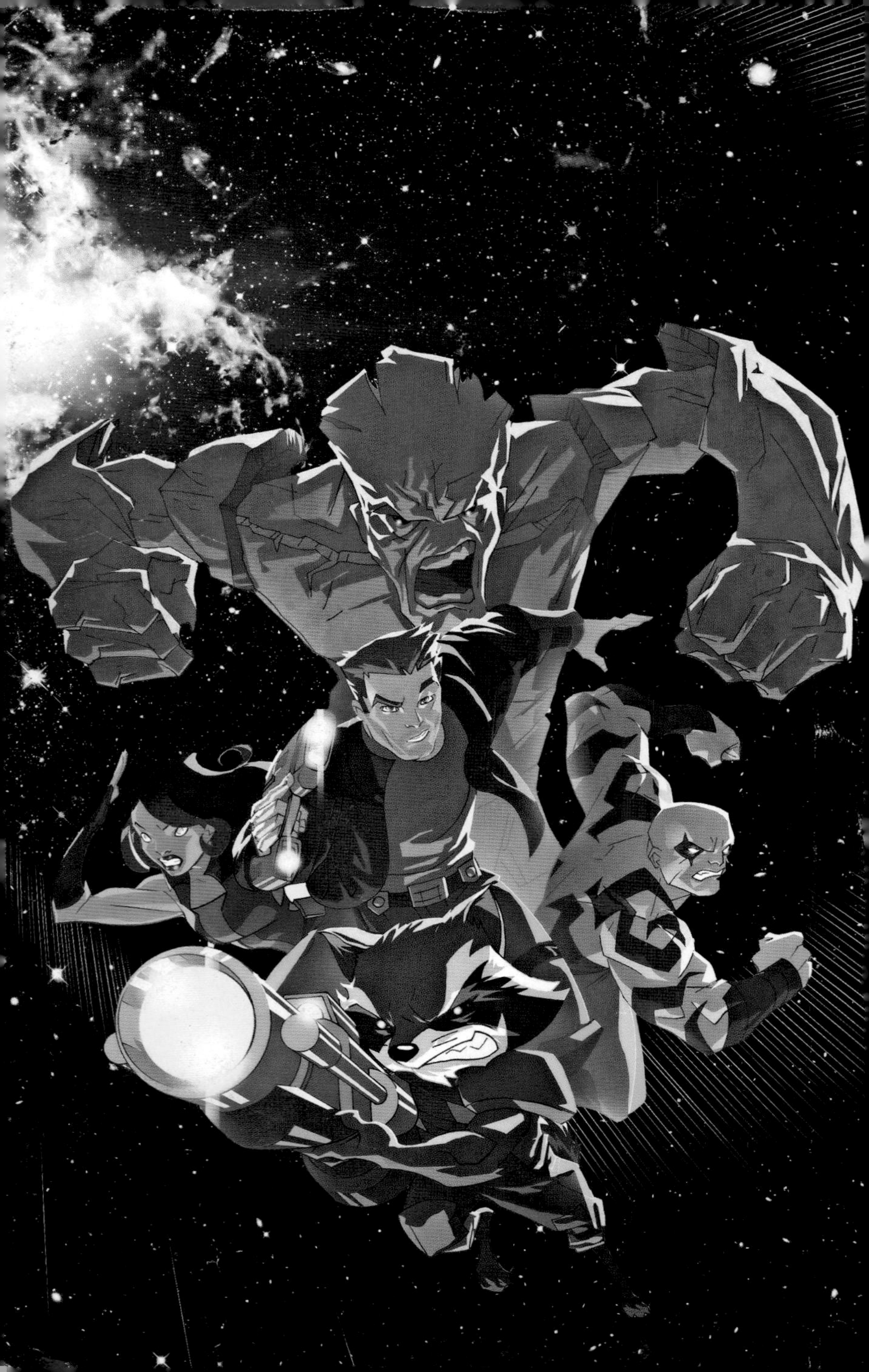

MARVEL

GUARDIANS OF THE GALAXY

GALAXY'S MOST WANTED

"SO VERY YOUNG" / *"SHOW AND TELL"*
WRITER: **MAIRGHREAD SCOTT**

"GESUNDHEIT, HANG ON TIGHT!"
WRITER: **PAUL ALLOR**

"ALL HAIL KING GROOT"
WRITER: **JOE CARAMAGNA**

ARTIST: **ADAM ARCHER**
COLORIST: **CHARLIE KIRCHOFF**
LETTERER: **VC'S JOE CARAMAGNA**

"STAR-LORD" / *"GAMORA"* / *"DRAX"* / *"GROOT & ROCKET"*
BASED ON THE TV SERIES WRITTEN BY **MARTY ISENBERG & HENRY GILROY**
DIRECTED BY **LEO RILEY**
ADAPTED BY **JOE CARAMAGNA**

COVER ART: **ADAM ARCHER (#2-3) & JEFF WAMESTER (#4)**
EDITORS: **SEBASTIAN GIRNER & JON MOISAN**
SENIOR EDITOR: **MARK PANICCIA**

SPECIAL THANKS TO HENRY ONG & PRODUCT FACTORY

COLLECTION EDITOR: **ALEX STARBUCK**
ASSISTANT EDITOR: **SARAH BRUNSTAD**
EDITORS, SPECIAL PROJECTS: **JENNIFER GRÜNWALD & MARK D. BEAZLEY**
SENIOR EDITOR, SPECIAL PROJECTS: **JEFF YOUNGQUIST**
SVP PRINT, SALES & MARKETING: **DAVID GABRIEL**

EDITOR IN CHIEF: **AXEL ALONSO**   CHIEF CREATIVE OFFICER: **JOE QUESADA**
PUBLISHER: **DAN BUCKLEY**   EXECUTIVE PRODUCER: **ALAN FINE**

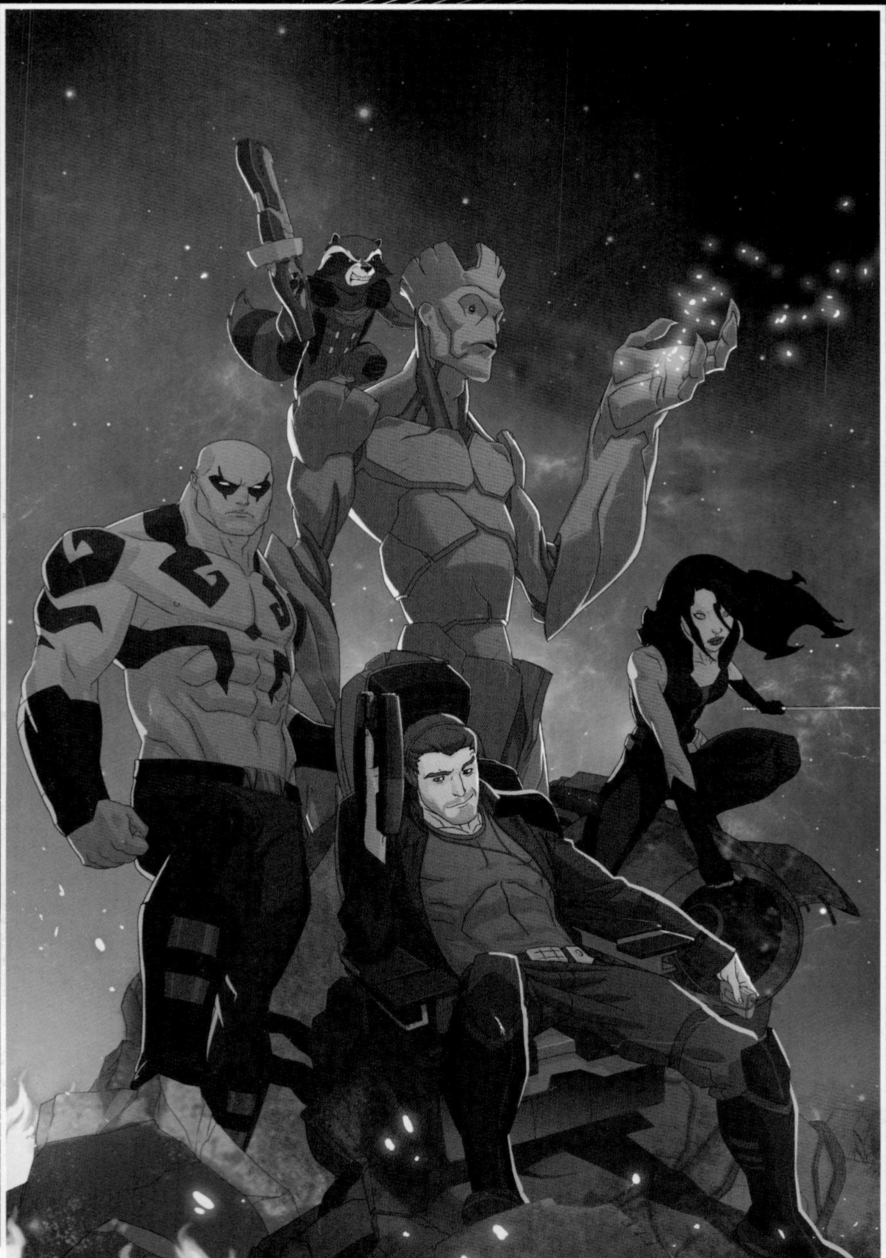

1

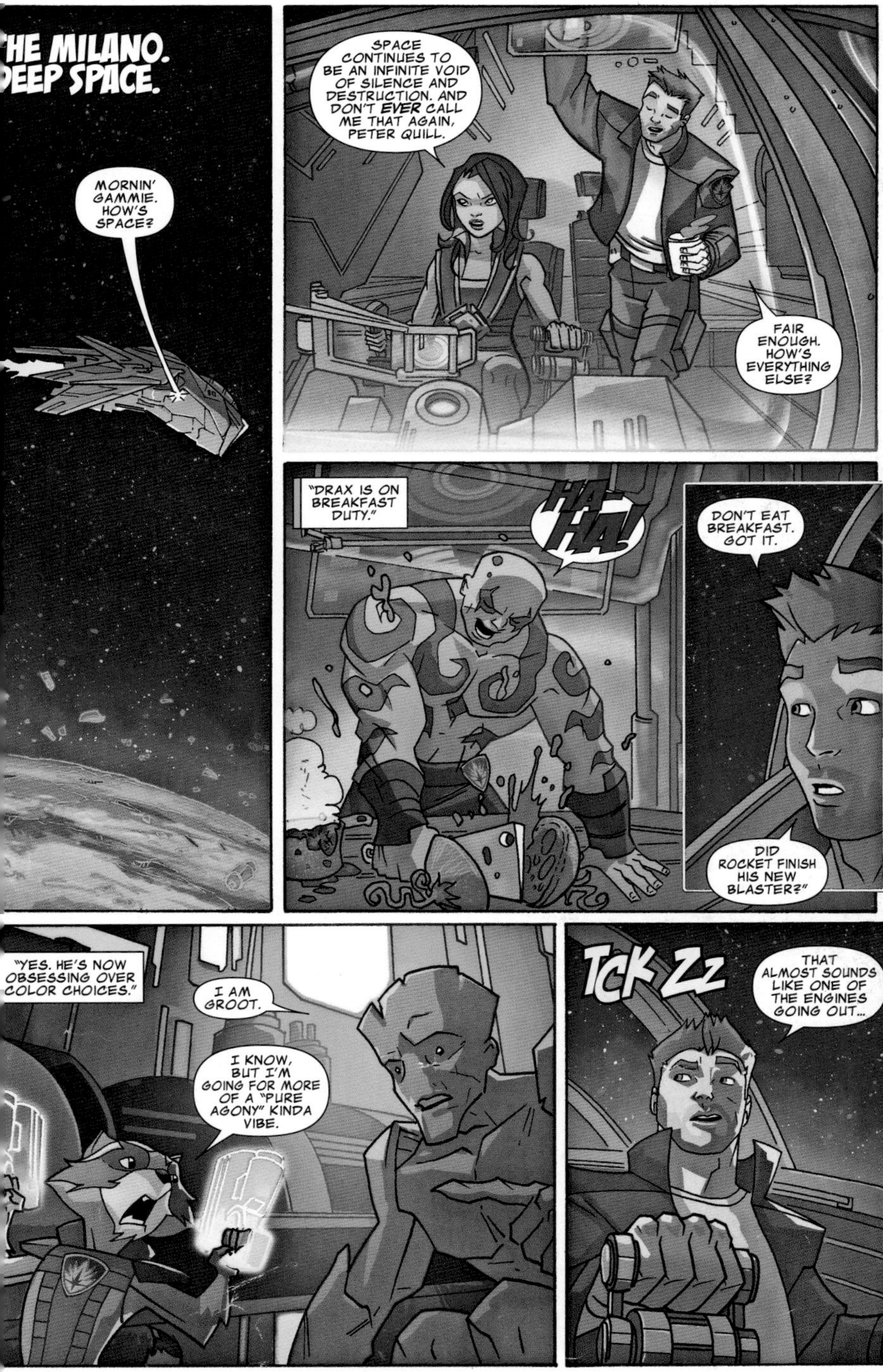

HE MILANO.
EEP SPACE.
MORNIN' GAMMIE. HOW'S SPACE?
SPACE CONTINUES TO BE AN INFINITE VOID OF SILENCE AND DESTRUCTION. AND DON'T EVER CALL ME THAT AGAIN, PETER QUILL.
FAIR ENOUGH. HOW'S EVERYTHING ELSE?
"DRAX IS ON BREAKFAST DUTY."
HA-HA!
DON'T EAT BREAKFAST. GOT IT.
DID ROCKET FINISH HIS NEW BLASTER?"
"YES. HE'S NOW OBSESSING OVER COLOR CHOICES."
I AM GROOT.
I KNOW, BUT I'M GOING FOR MORE OF A "PURE AGONY" KINDA VIBE.
TCK ZZ
THAT ALMOST SOUNDS LIKE ONE OF THE ENGINES GOING OUT...

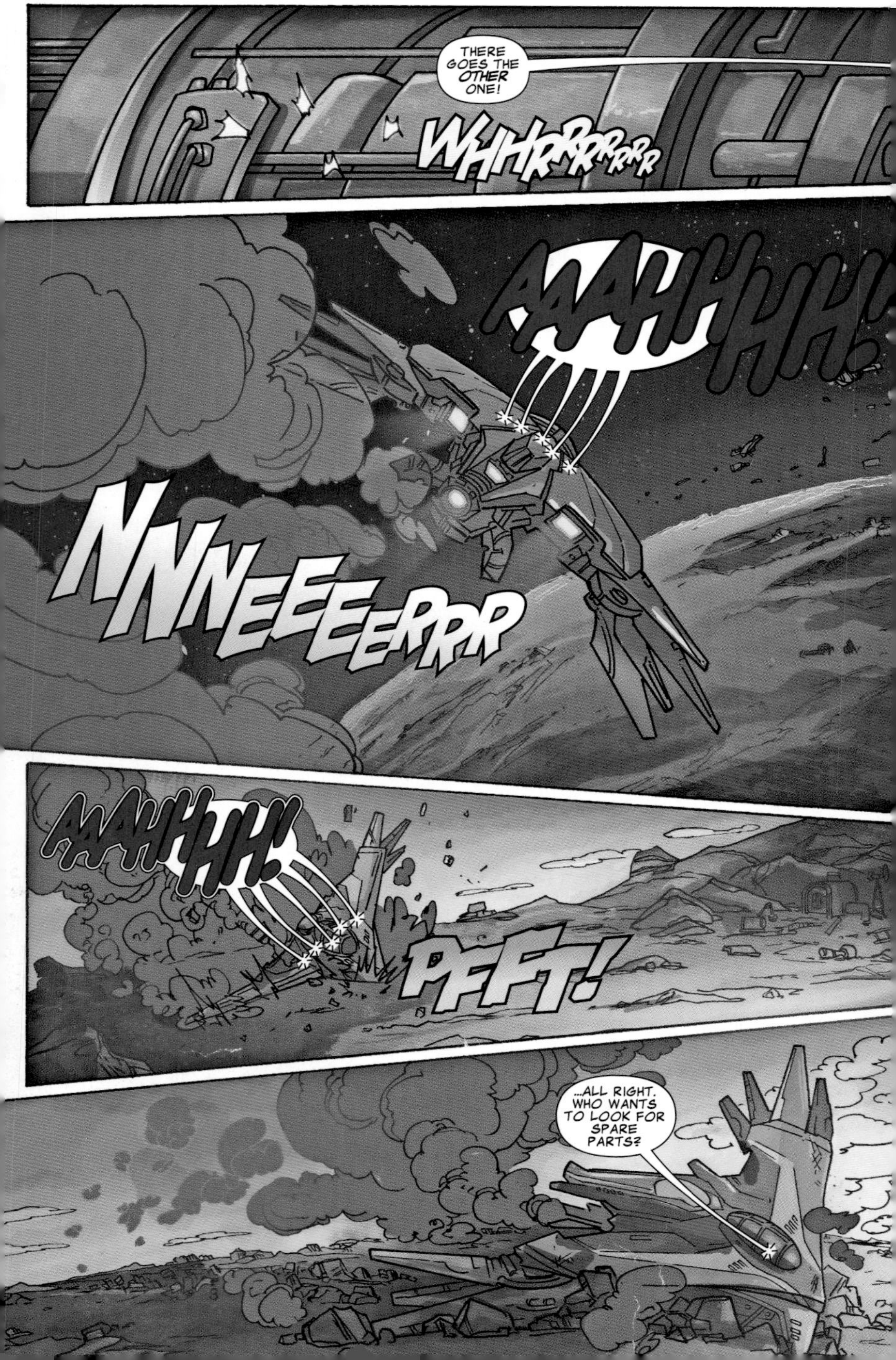
THERE GOES THE OTHER ONE!
WHHRRRRRRR
AAAHHHHH!
NNNEEEEERRR
AAAHHHH!
PFFT!
...ALL RIGHT. WHO WANTS TO LOOK FOR SPARE PARTS?

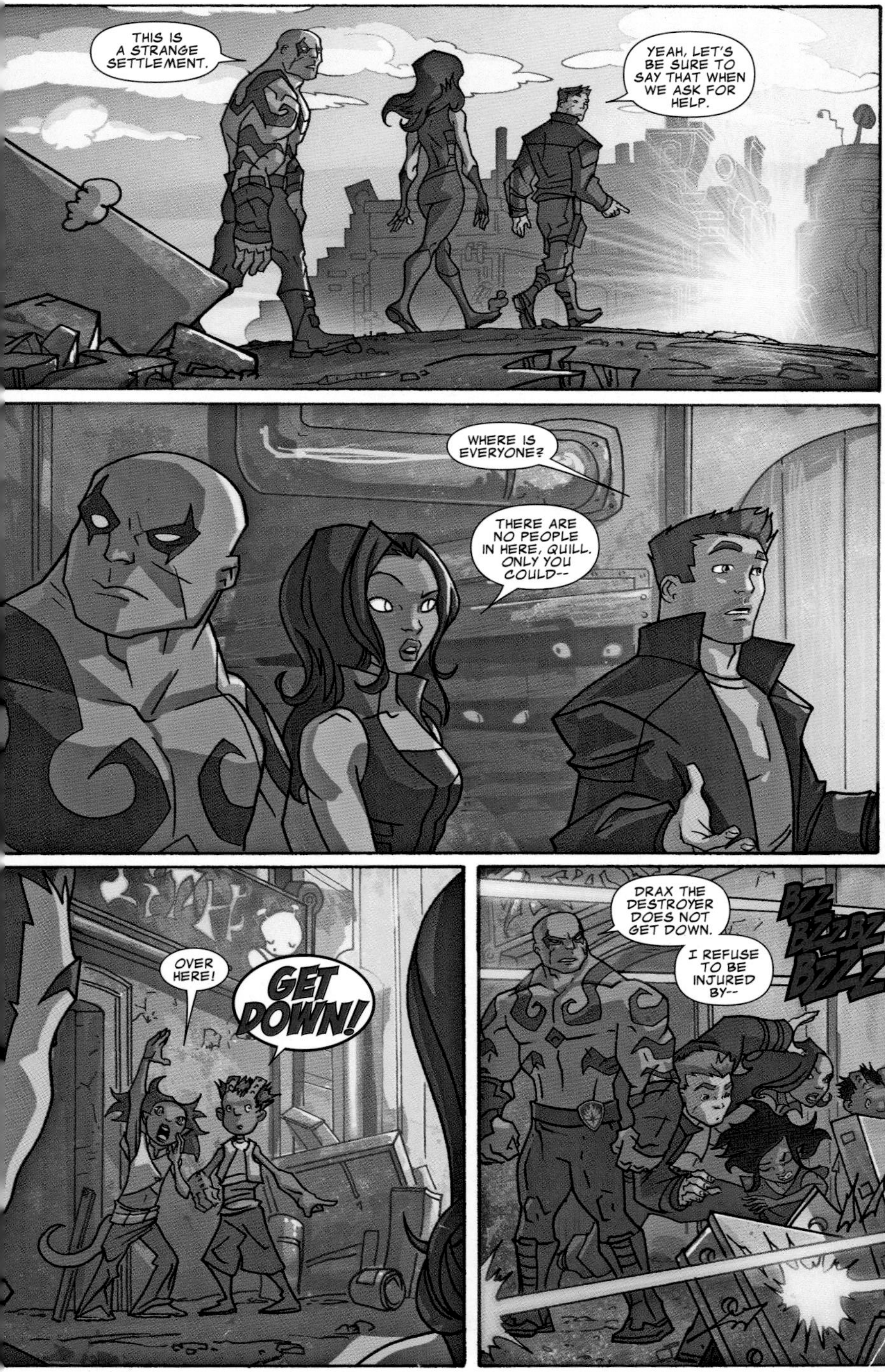
THIS IS A STRANGE SETTLEMENT.
YEAH, LET'S BE SURE TO SAY THAT WHEN WE ASK FOR HELP.
WHERE IS EVERYONE?
THERE ARE NO PEOPLE IN HERE, QUILL. ONLY YOU COULD--
OVER HERE!
GET DOWN!
DRAX THE DESTROYER DOES NOT GET DOWN.
I REFUSE TO BE INJURED BY--
BZZ BZZZBZ BZZZ

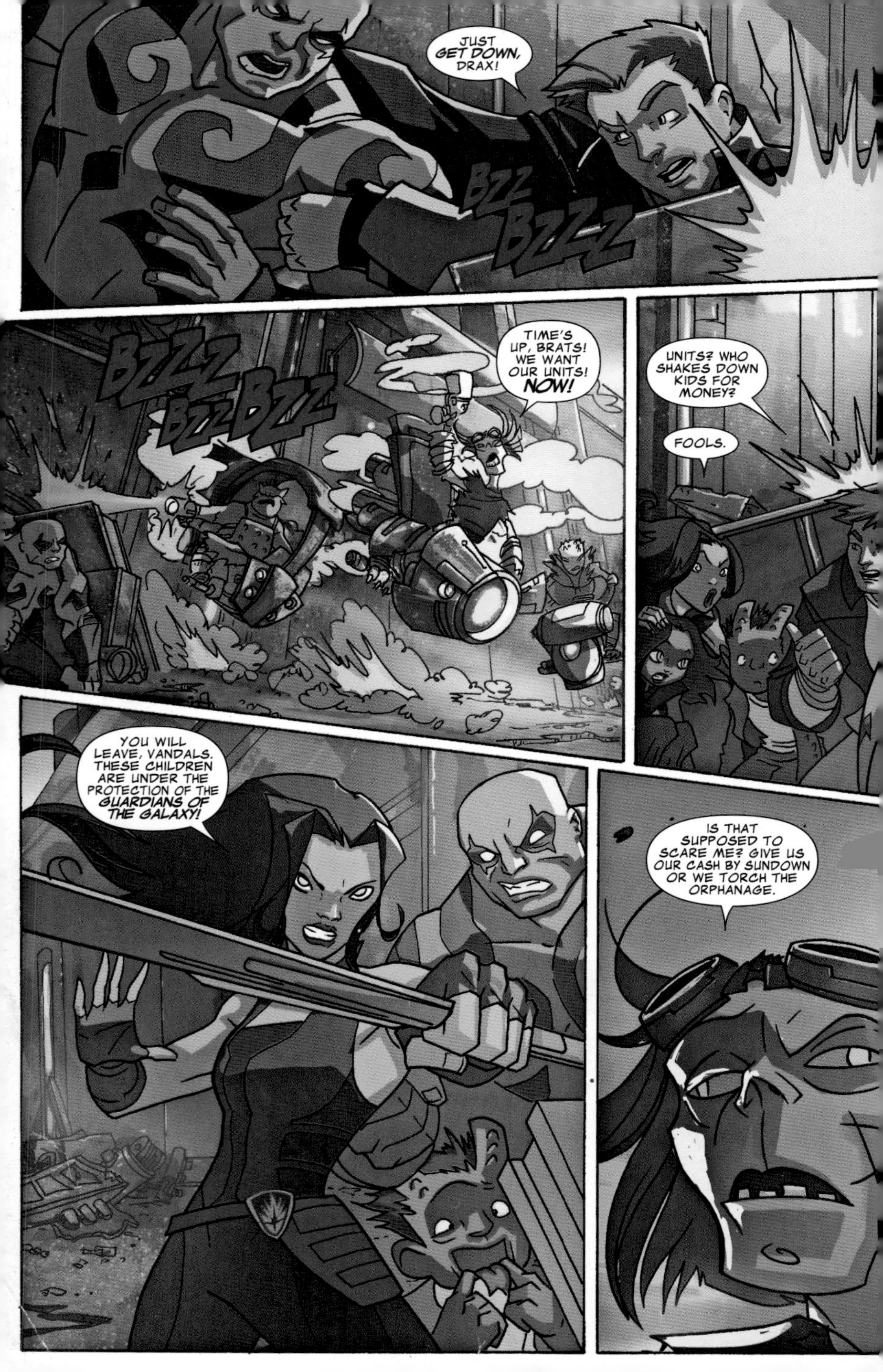
JUST GET DOWN, DRAX!
BZZ BZZZ
BZZZ BZZ BZZ
TIME'S UP, BRATS! WE WANT OUR UNITS! NOW!
UNITS? WHO SHAKES DOWN KIDS FOR MONEY?
FOOLS.
YOU WILL LEAVE, VANDALS. THESE CHILDREN ARE UNDER THE PROTECTION OF THE GUARDIANS OF THE GALAXY!
IS THAT SUPPOSED TO SCARE ME? GIVE US OUR CASH BY SUNDOWN OR WE TORCH THE ORPHANAGE.

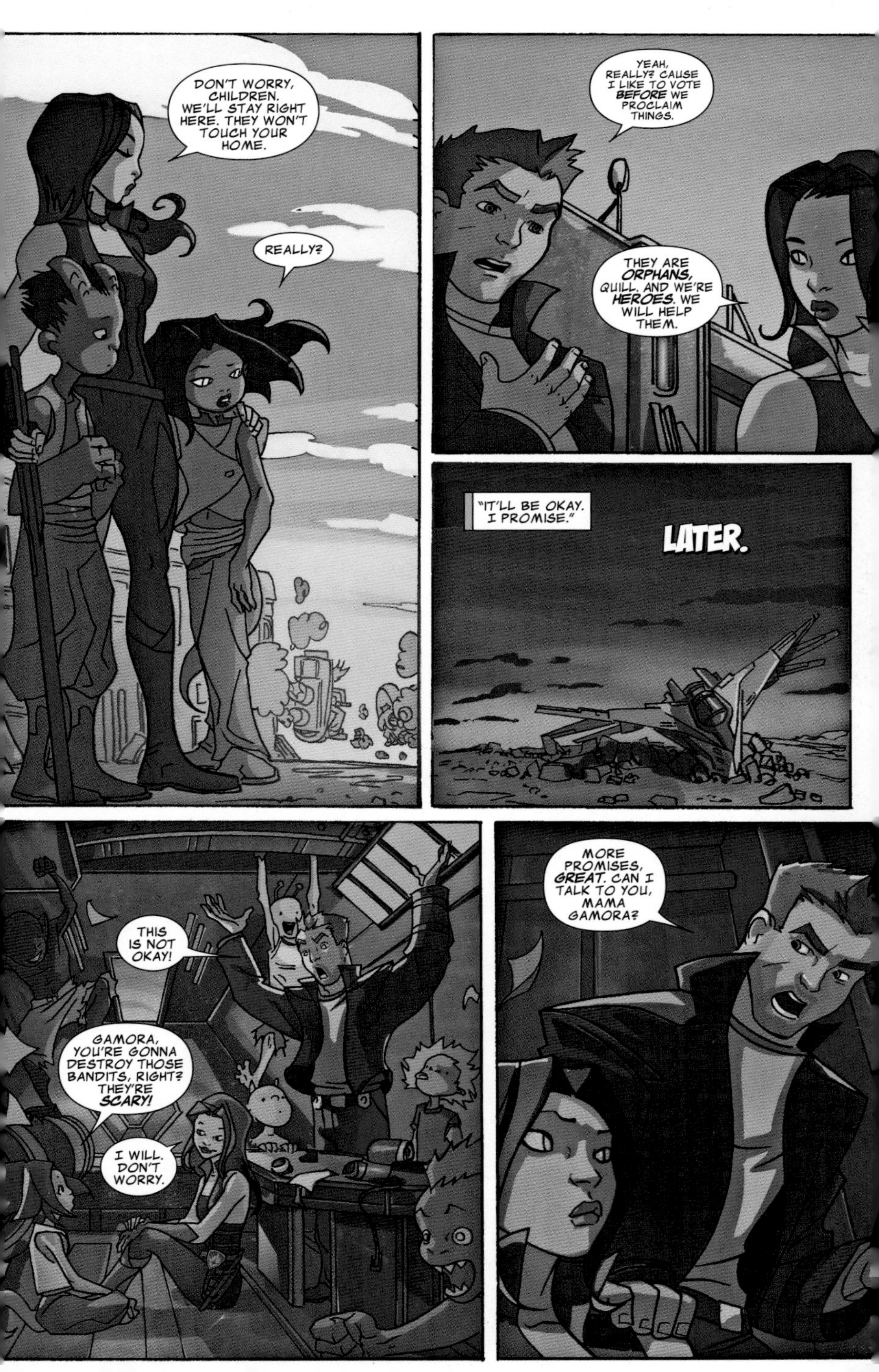
DON'T WORRY, CHILDREN. WE'LL STAY RIGHT HERE. THEY WON'T TOUCH YOUR HOME.
REALLY?
YEAH, REALLY? CAUSE I LIKE TO VOTE BEFORE WE PROCLAIM THINGS.
THEY ARE ORPHANS, QUILL. AND WE'RE HEROES. WE WILL HELP THEM.
"IT'LL BE OKAY. I PROMISE."
LATER.
THIS IS NOT OKAY!
GAMORA, YOU'RE GONNA DESTROY THOSE BANDITS, RIGHT? THEY'RE SCARY!
I WILL. DON'T WORRY.
MORE PROMISES, GREAT. CAN I TALK TO YOU, MAMA GAMORA?

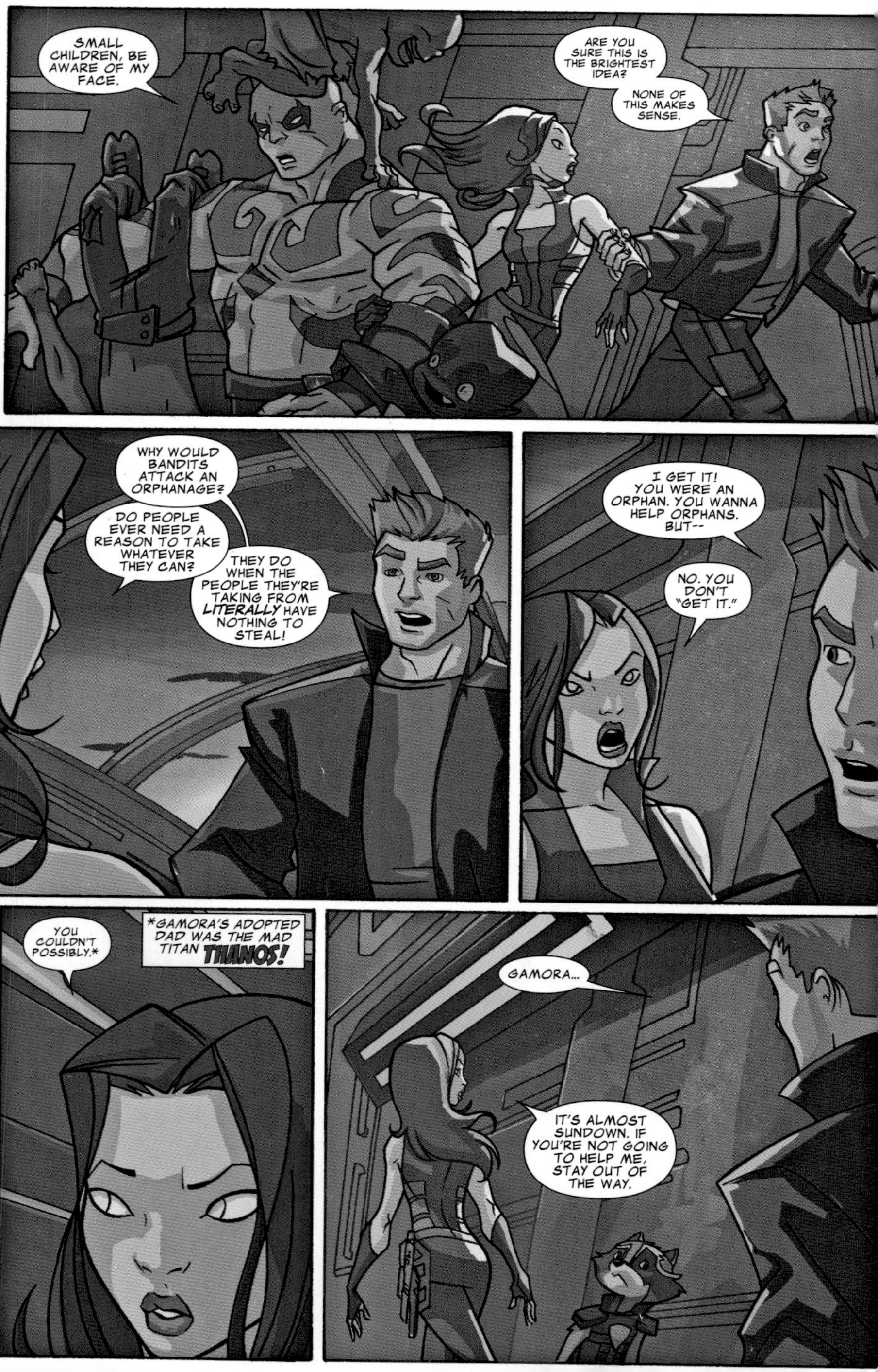
SMALL CHILDREN, BE AWARE OF MY FACE.
ARE YOU SURE THIS IS THE BRIGHTEST IDEA?
NONE OF THIS MAKES SENSE.
WHY WOULD BANDITS ATTACK AN ORPHANAGE?
DO PEOPLE EVER NEED A REASON TO TAKE WHATEVER THEY CAN?
THEY DO WHEN THE PEOPLE THEY'RE TAKING FROM LITERALLY HAVE NOTHING TO STEAL!
I GET IT! YOU WERE AN ORPHAN. YOU WANNA HELP ORPHANS. BUT--
NO. YOU DON'T "GET IT."
YOU COULDN'T POSSIBLY.*
*GAMORA'S ADOPTED DAD WAS THE MAD TITAN THANOS!
GAMORA...
IT'S ALMOST SUNDOWN. IF YOU'RE NOT GOING TO HELP ME, STAY OUT OF THE WAY.

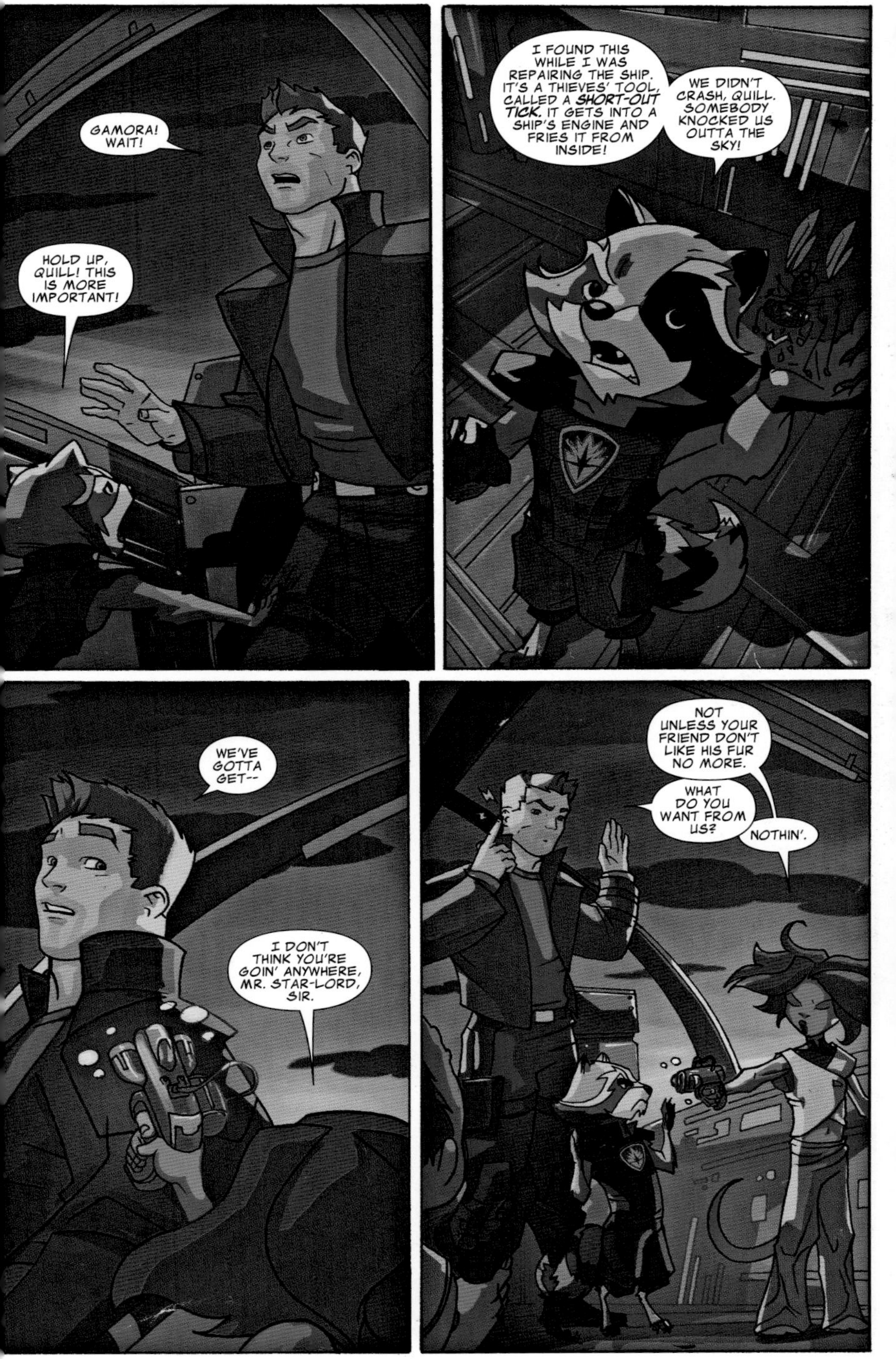
GAMORA! WAIT!
HOLD UP, QUILL! THIS IS MORE IMPORTANT!
I FOUND THIS WHILE I WAS REPAIRING THE SHIP. IT'S A THIEVES' TOOL, CALLED A **SHORT-OUT TICK.** IT GETS INTO A SHIP'S ENGINE AND FRIES IT FROM INSIDE!
WE DIDN'T CRASH, QUILL. SOMEBODY KNOCKED US OUTTA THE SKY!
WE'VE GOTTA GET--
I DON'T THINK YOU'RE GOIN' ANYWHERE, MR. STAR-LORD, SIR.
WHAT DO YOU WANT FROM US?
NOTHIN'.
NOT UNLESS YOUR FRIEND DON'T LIKE HIS FUR NO MORE.

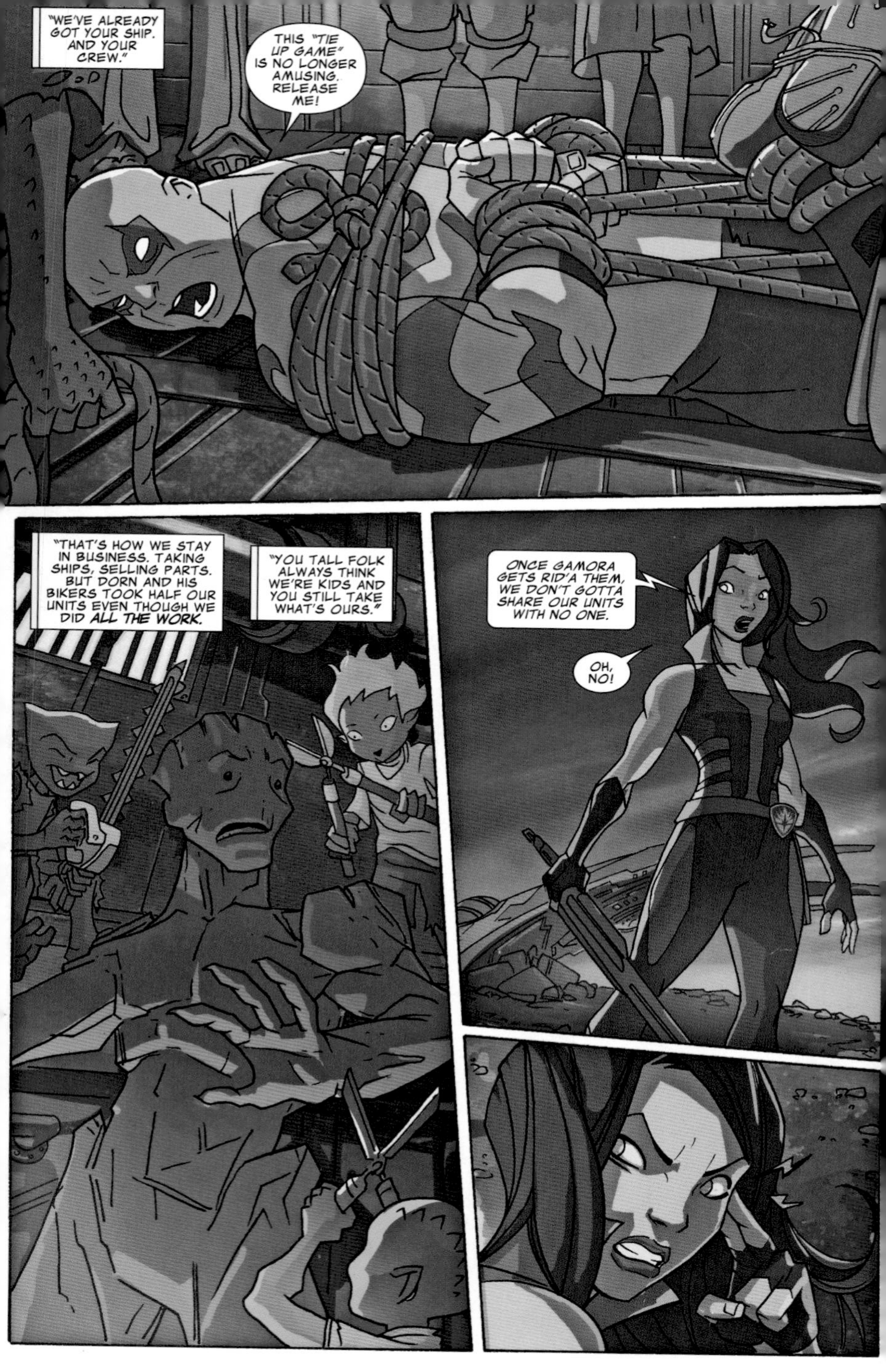
"WE'VE ALREADY GOT YOUR SHIP. AND YOUR CREW."
THIS "TIE UP GAME" IS NO LONGER AMUSING. RELEASE ME!
"THAT'S HOW WE STAY IN BUSINESS. TAKING SHIPS, SELLING PARTS. BUT DORN AND HIS BIKERS TOOK HALF OUR UNITS EVEN THOUGH WE DID ALL THE WORK.
"YOU TALL FOLK ALWAYS THINK WE'RE KIDS AND YOU STILL TAKE WHAT'S OURS."
ONCE GAMORA GETS RID'A THEM, WE DON'T GOTTA SHARE OUR UNITS WITH NO ONE.
OH, NO!

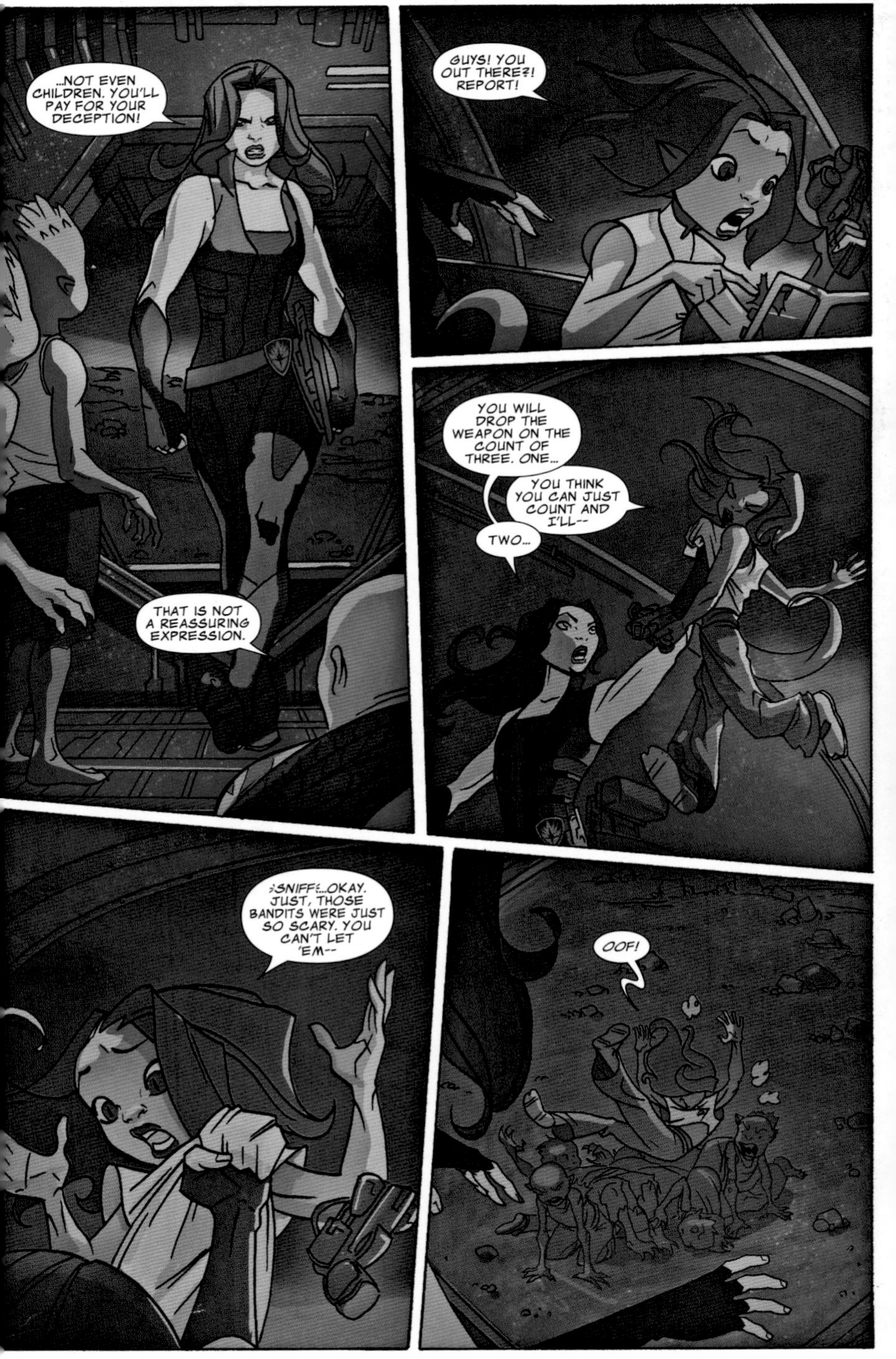
...NOT EVEN CHILDREN. YOU'LL PAY FOR YOUR DECEPTION!
THAT IS NOT A REASSURING EXPRESSION.
GUYS! YOU OUT THERE?! REPORT!
YOU WILL DROP THE WEAPON ON THE COUNT OF THREE. ONE...
YOU THINK YOU CAN JUST COUNT AND I'LL--
TWO...
SNIFF...OKAY. JUST, THOSE BANDITS WERE JUST SO SCARY. YOU CAN'T LET 'EM--
OOF!

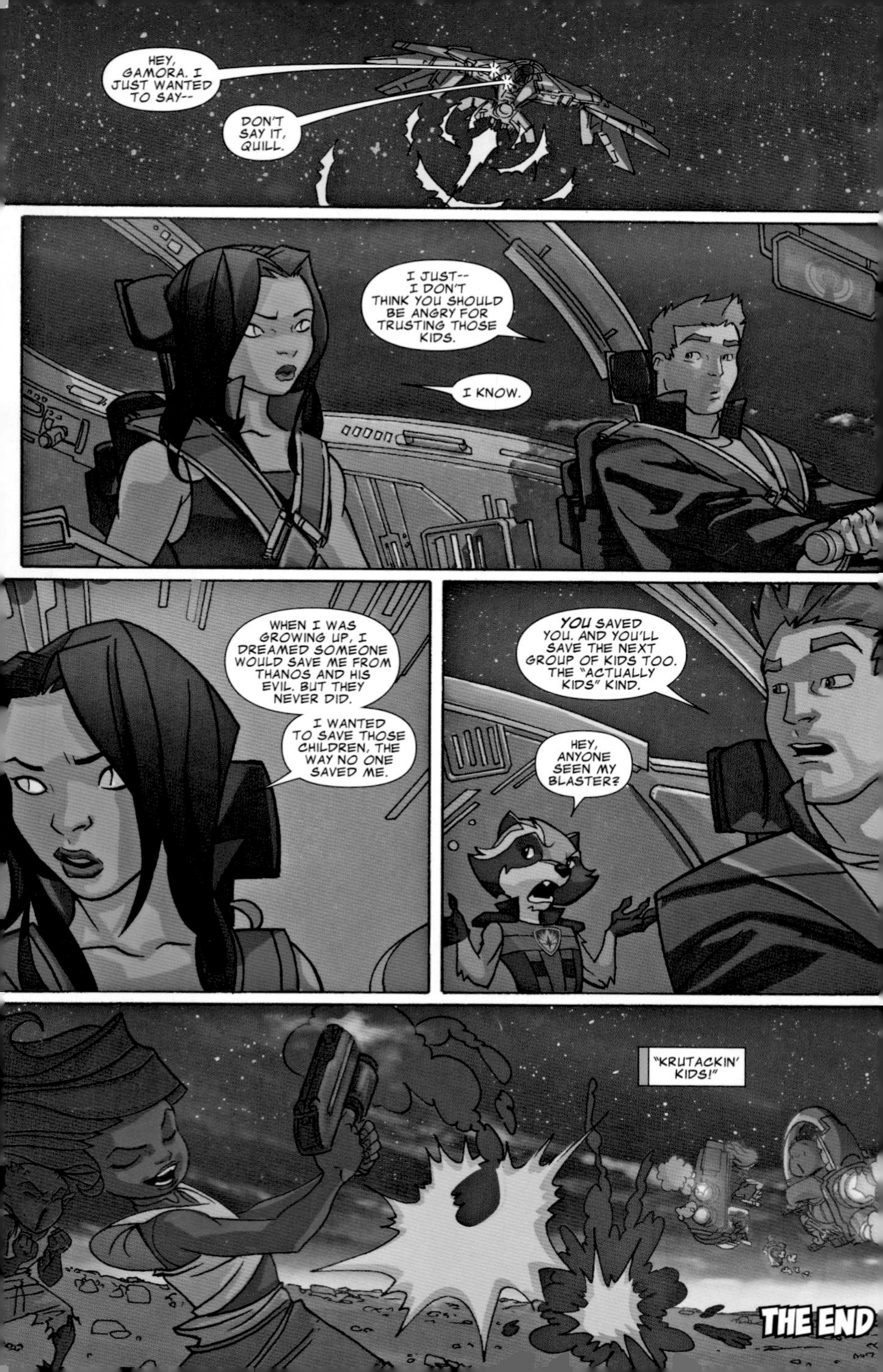
HEY, GAMORA. I JUST WANTED TO SAY--
DON'T SAY IT, QUILL.
I JUST-- I DON'T THINK YOU SHOULD BE ANGRY FOR TRUSTING THOSE KIDS.
I KNOW.
WHEN I WAS GROWING UP, I DREAMED SOMEONE WOULD SAVE ME FROM THANOS AND HIS EVIL. BUT THEY NEVER DID.
I WANTED TO SAVE THOSE CHILDREN, THE WAY NO ONE SAVED ME.
YOU SAVED YOU. AND YOU'LL SAVE THE NEXT GROUP OF KIDS TOO. THE "ACTUALLY KIDS" KIND.
HEY, ANYONE SEEN MY BLASTER?
"KRUTACKIN' KIDS!"
THE END

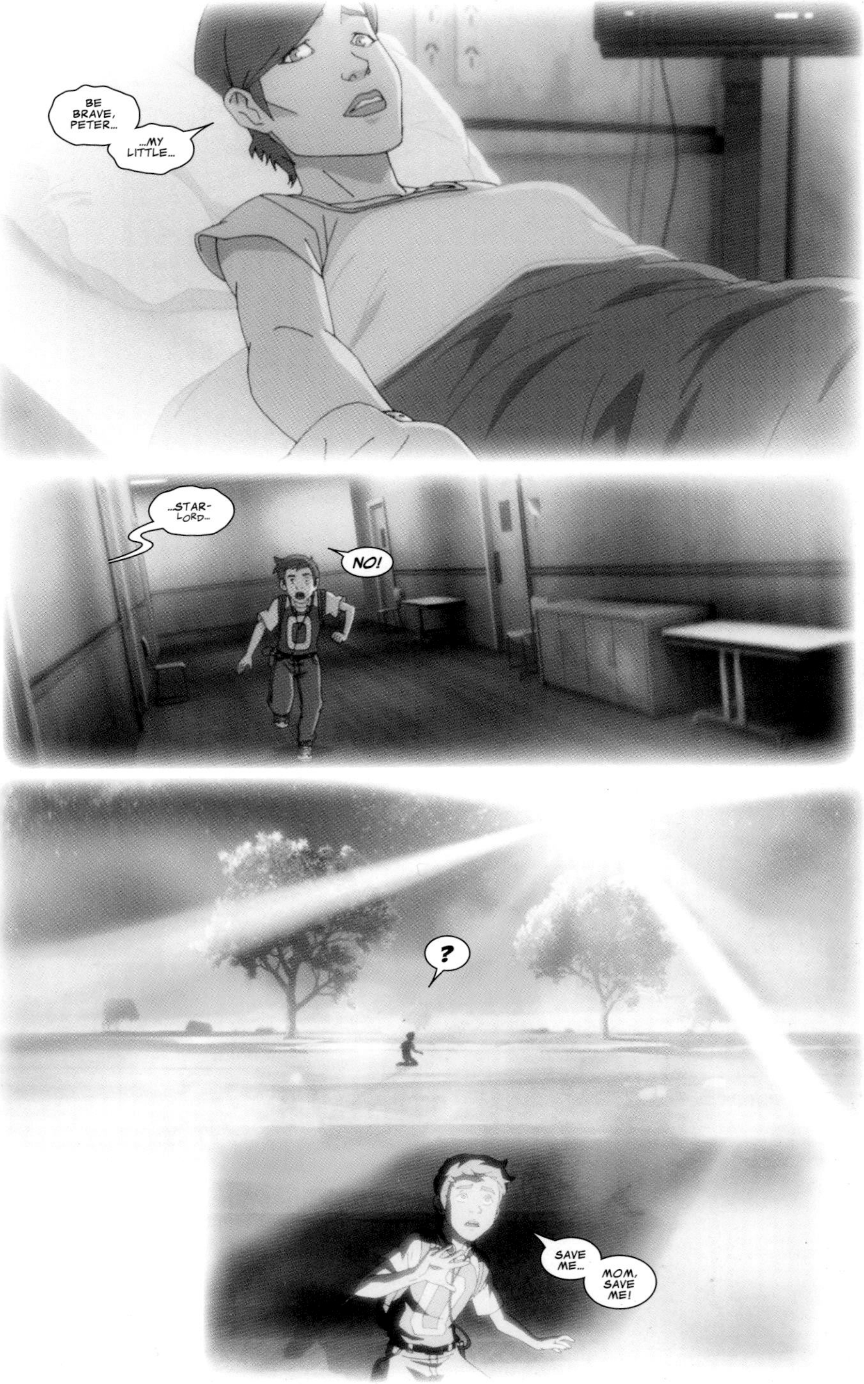
BE BRAVE, PETER...
...MY LITTLE...
...STAR-LORD...
NO!
?
SAVE ME...
MOM, SAVE ME!

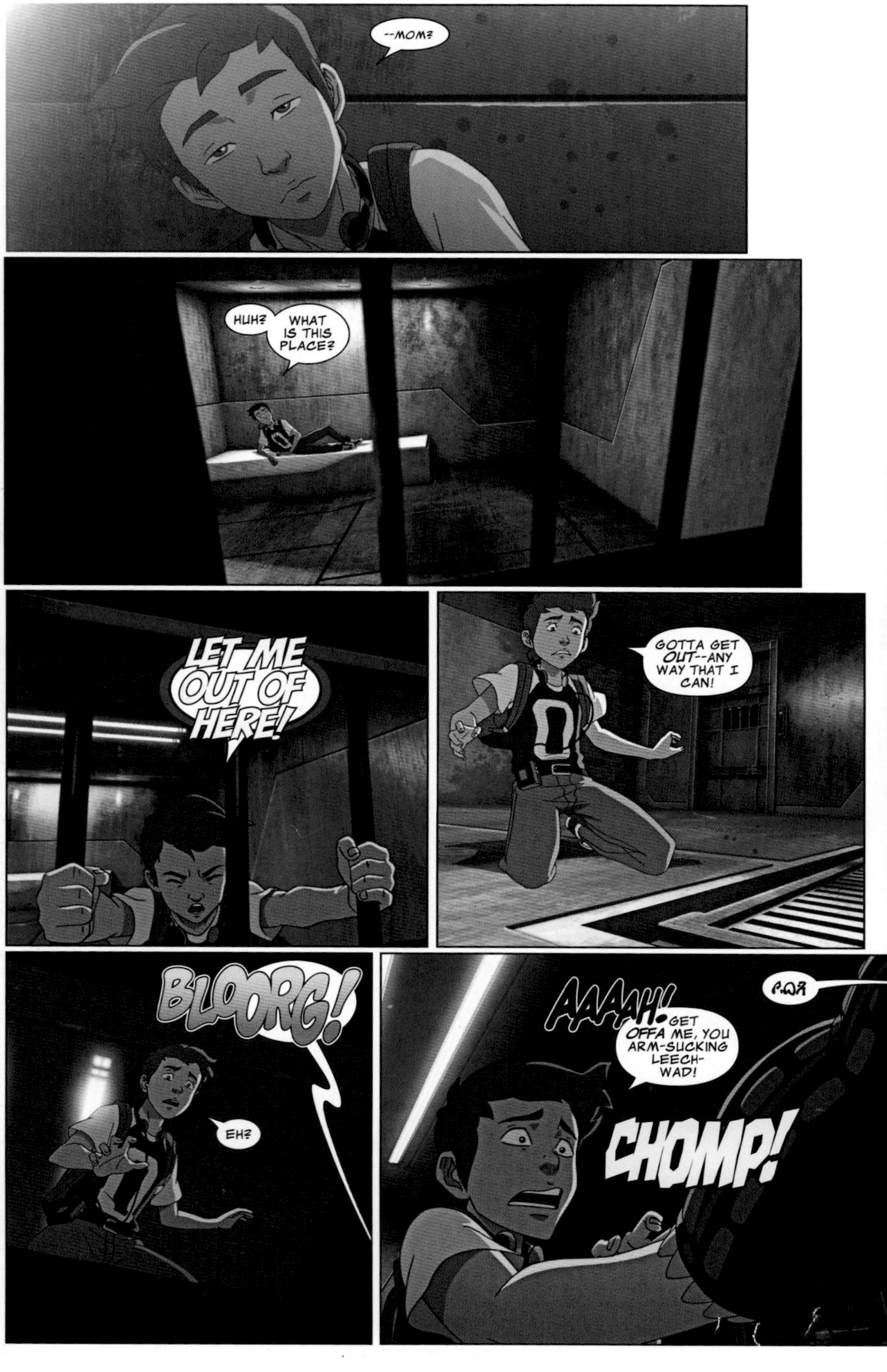
--MOM?
HUH?
WHAT IS THIS PLACE?
LET ME OUT OF HERE!
GOTTA GET OUT--ANY WAY THAT I CAN!
BLOORG!
EH?
AAAAH!
GET OFFA ME, YOU ARM-SUCKING LEECH-WAD!
CHOMP!

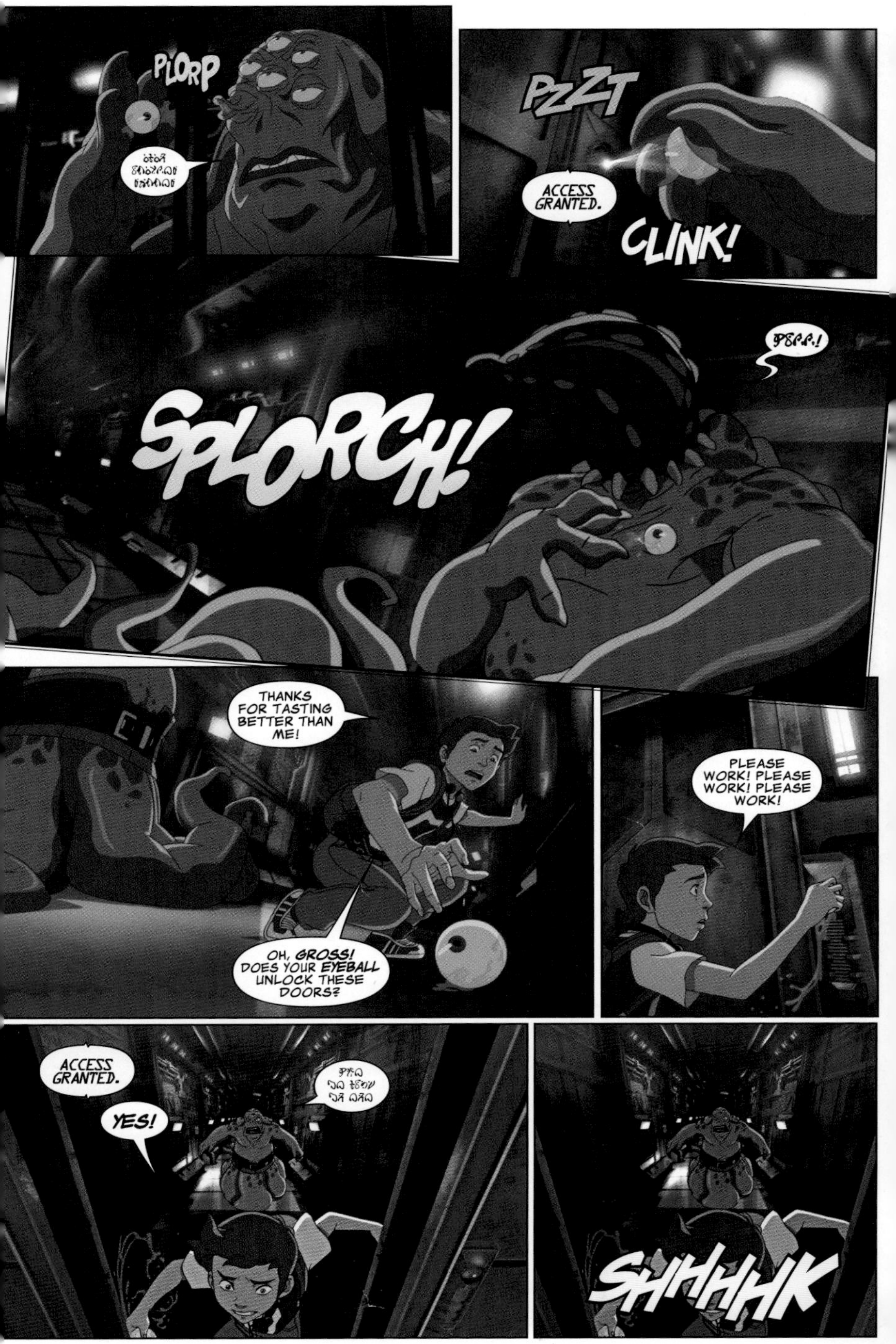
PLORP
PZZT
ACCESS GRANTED.
CLINK!
SPLORCH!
THANKS FOR TASTING BETTER THAN ME!
OH, GROSS! DOES YOUR EYEBALL UNLOCK THESE DOORS?
PLEASE WORK! PLEASE WORK! PLEASE WORK!
ACCESS GRANTED.
YES!
SHHHHK

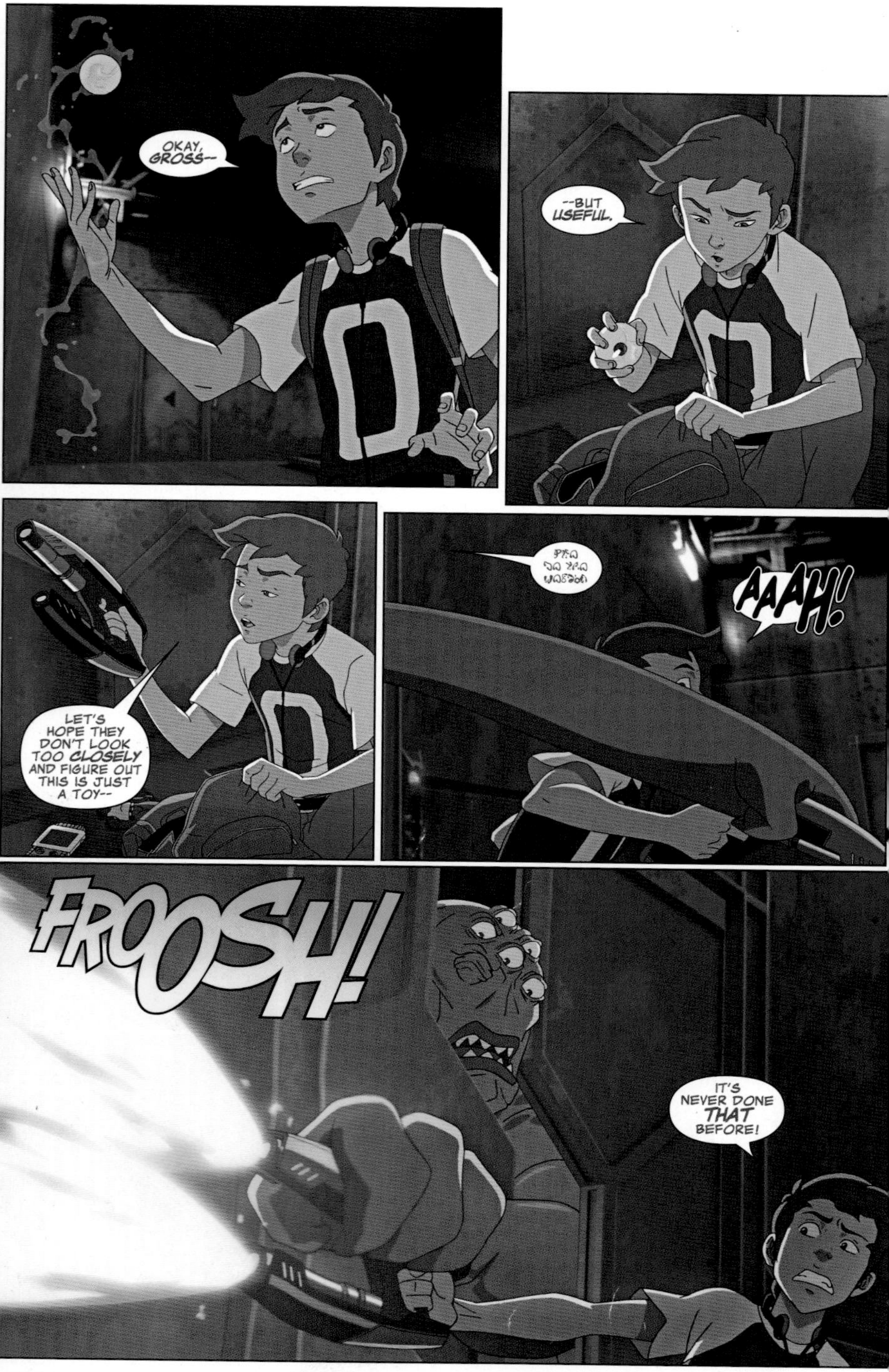
OKAY, GROSS--
--BUT USEFUL.
LET'S HOPE THEY DON'T LOOK TOO CLOSELY AND FIGURE OUT THIS IS JUST A TOY--
AAAH!
FROOSH!
IT'S NEVER DONE THAT BEFORE!

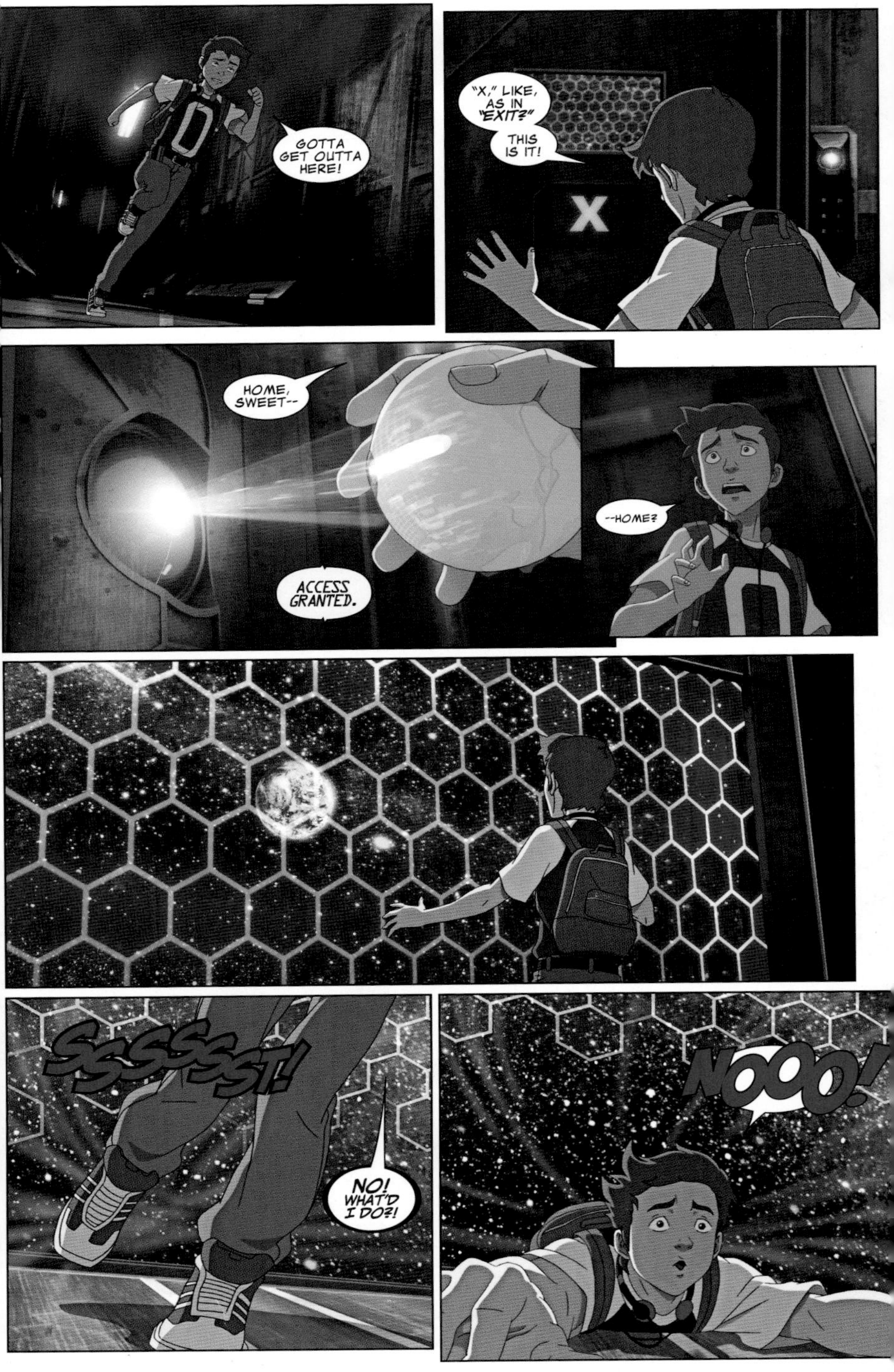
GOTTA GET OUTTA HERE!
"X," LIKE, AS IN "EXIT?"
THIS IS IT!
HOME, SWEET--
ACCESS GRANTED.
--HOME?
SSSSSST!
NO! WHAT'D I DO?!
NOOO!

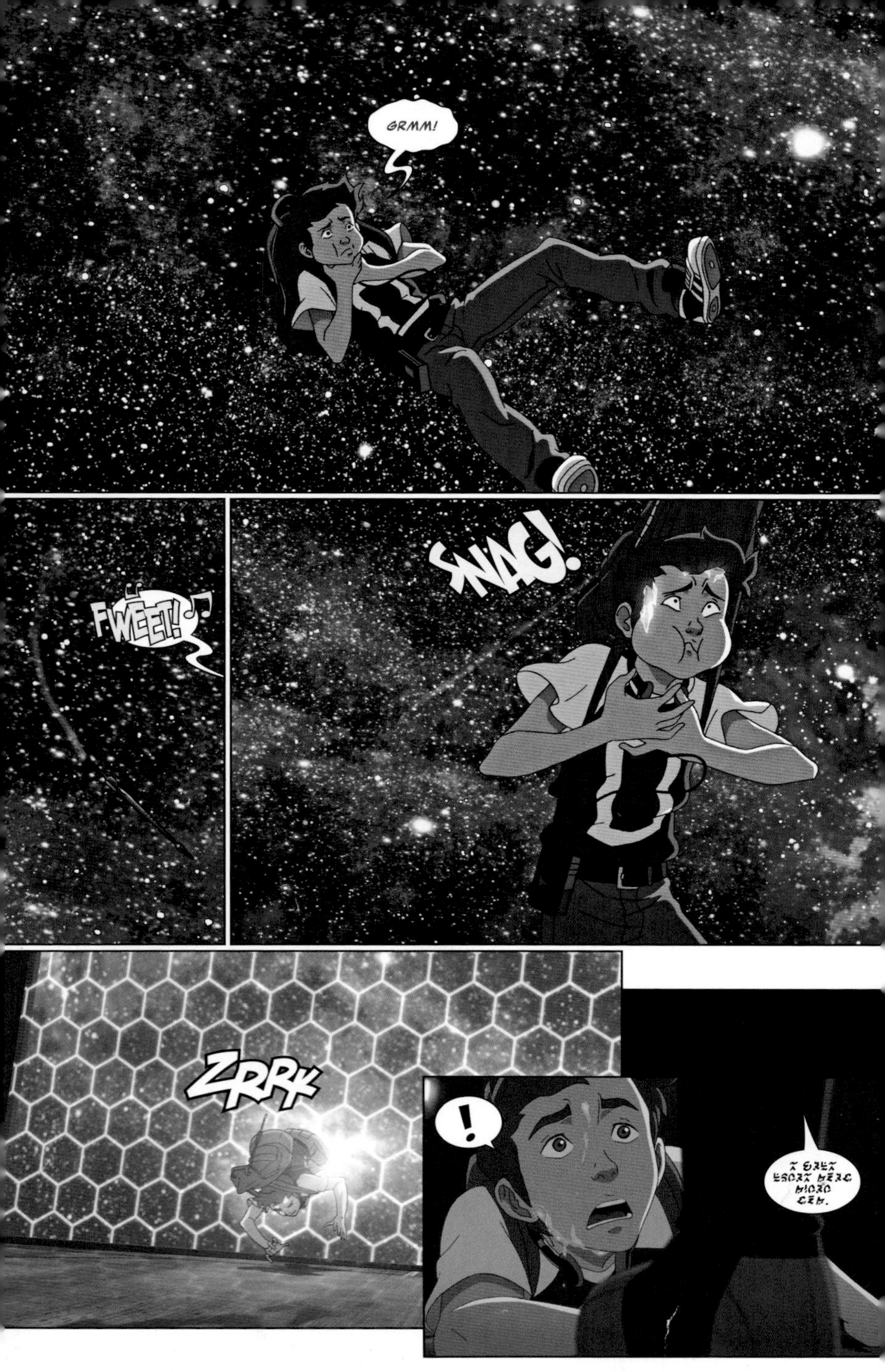
GRMM!
FWEET!
SNAG!
ZRRK
!

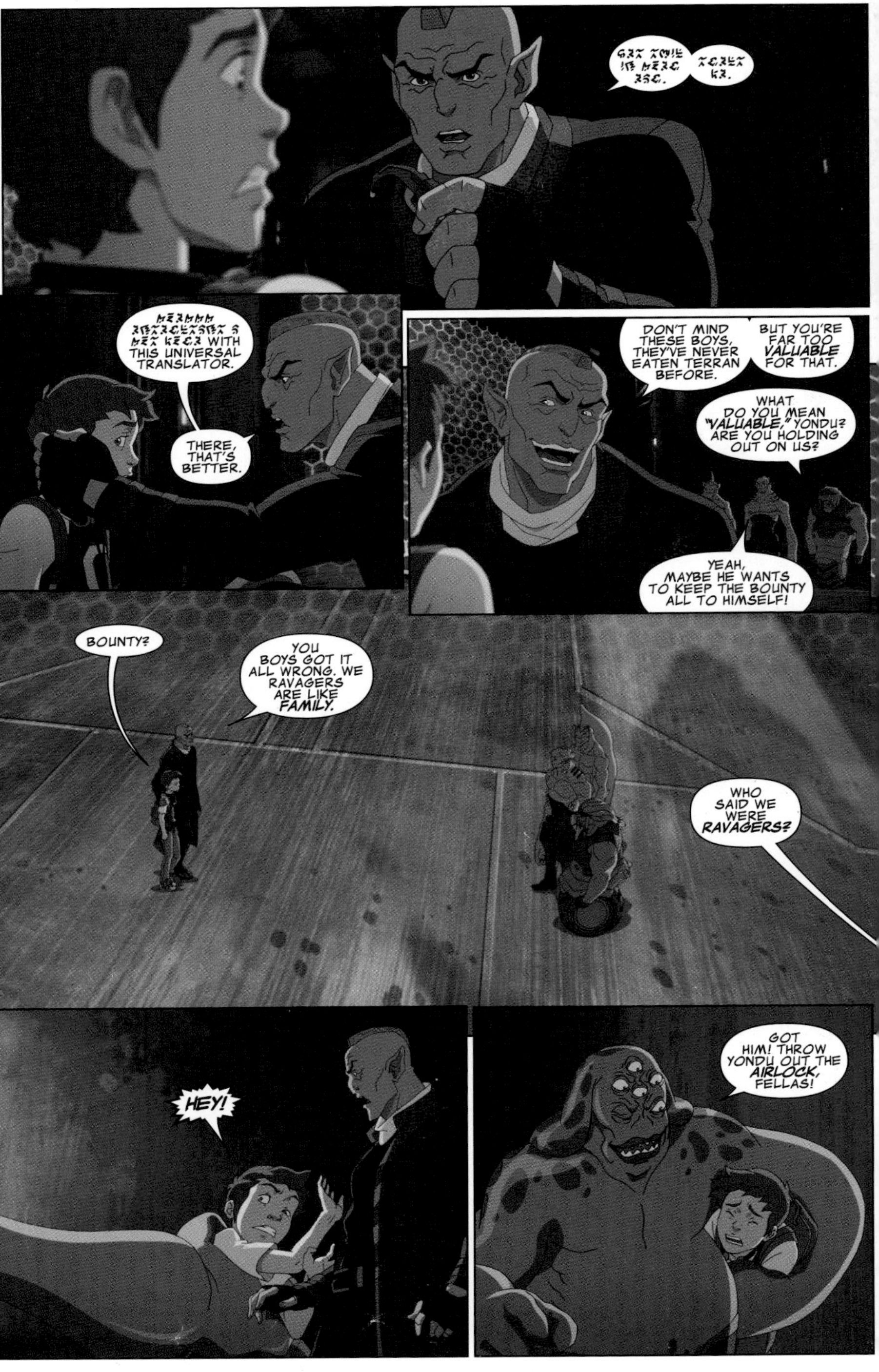
WITH THIS UNIVERSAL TRANSLATOR.
THERE, THAT'S BETTER.
DON'T MIND THESE BOYS, THEY'VE NEVER EATEN TERRAN BEFORE.
BUT YOU'RE FAR TOO VALUABLE FOR THAT.
WHAT DO YOU MEAN "VALUABLE," YONDU? ARE YOU HOLDING OUT ON US?
YEAH, MAYBE HE WANTS TO KEEP THE BOUNTY ALL TO HIMSELF!
BOUNTY?
YOU BOYS GOT IT ALL WRONG. WE RAVAGERS ARE LIKE FAMILY.
WHO SAID WE WERE RAVAGERS?
HEY!
GOT HIM! THROW YONDU OUT THE AIRLOCK, FELLAS!

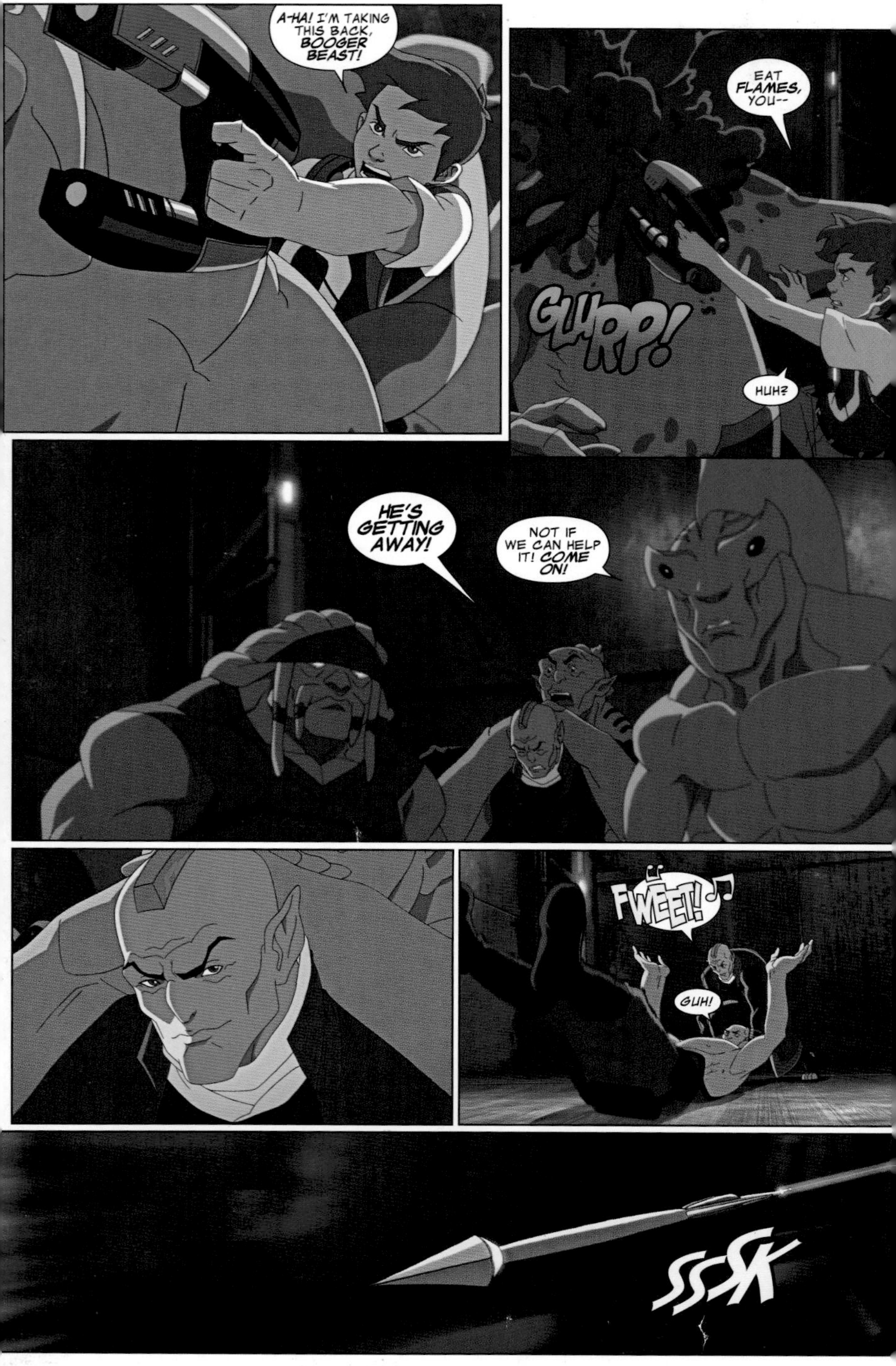
A-HA! I'M TAKING THIS BACK, BOOGER BEAST!
EAT FLAMES, YOU--
GLURP!
HUH?
HE'S GETTING AWAY!
NOT IF WE CAN HELP IT! COME ON!
FWEET!
GUH!
SSSK

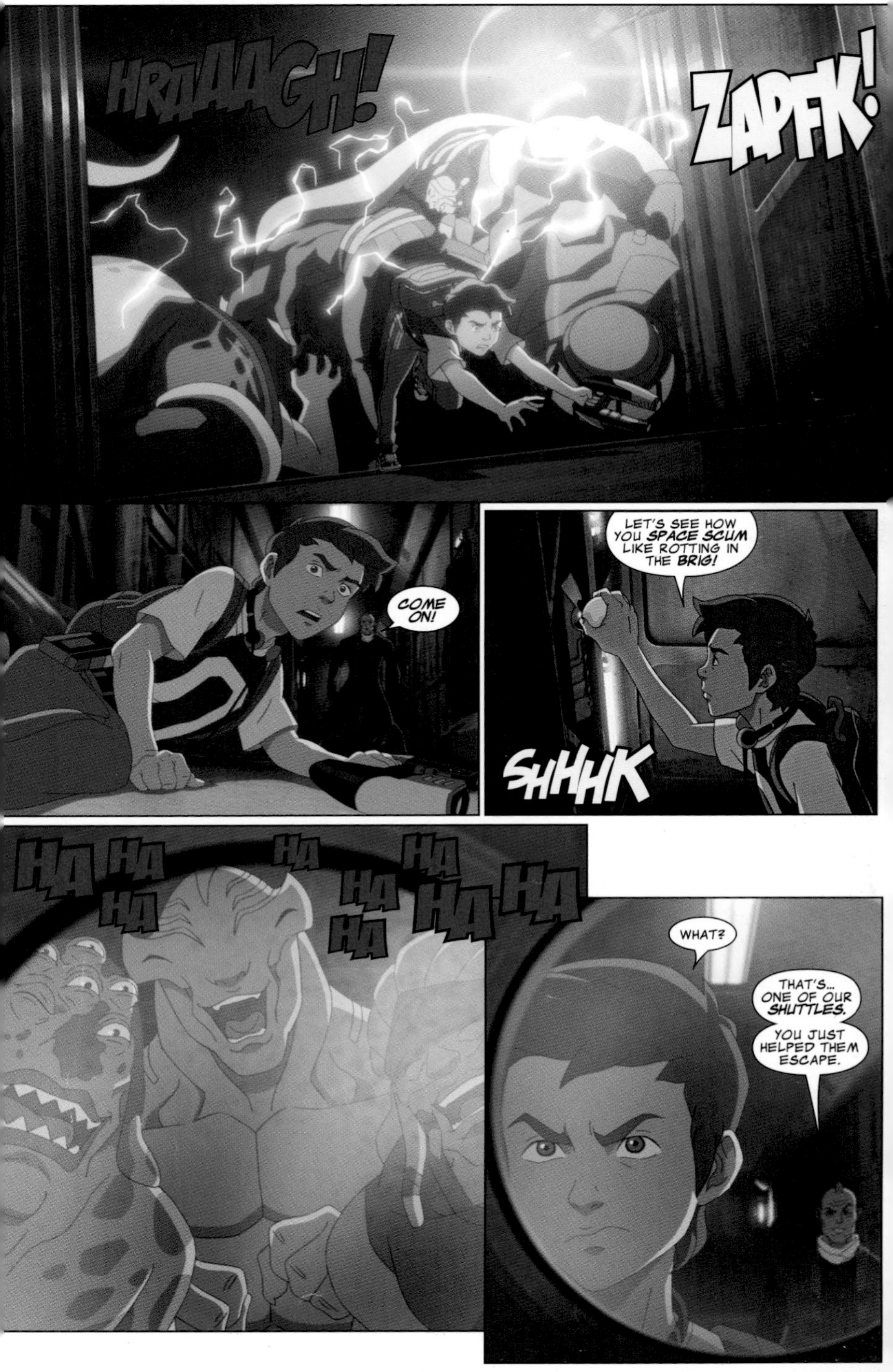
HRAAAGH!
ZAPFK!
COME ON!
LET'S SEE HOW YOU SPACE SCUM LIKE ROTTING IN THE BRIG!
SHHHK
HA HA HA HA HA HA HA HA HA HA
WHAT?
THAT'S... ONE OF OUR SHUTTLES.
YOU JUST HELPED THEM ESCAPE.

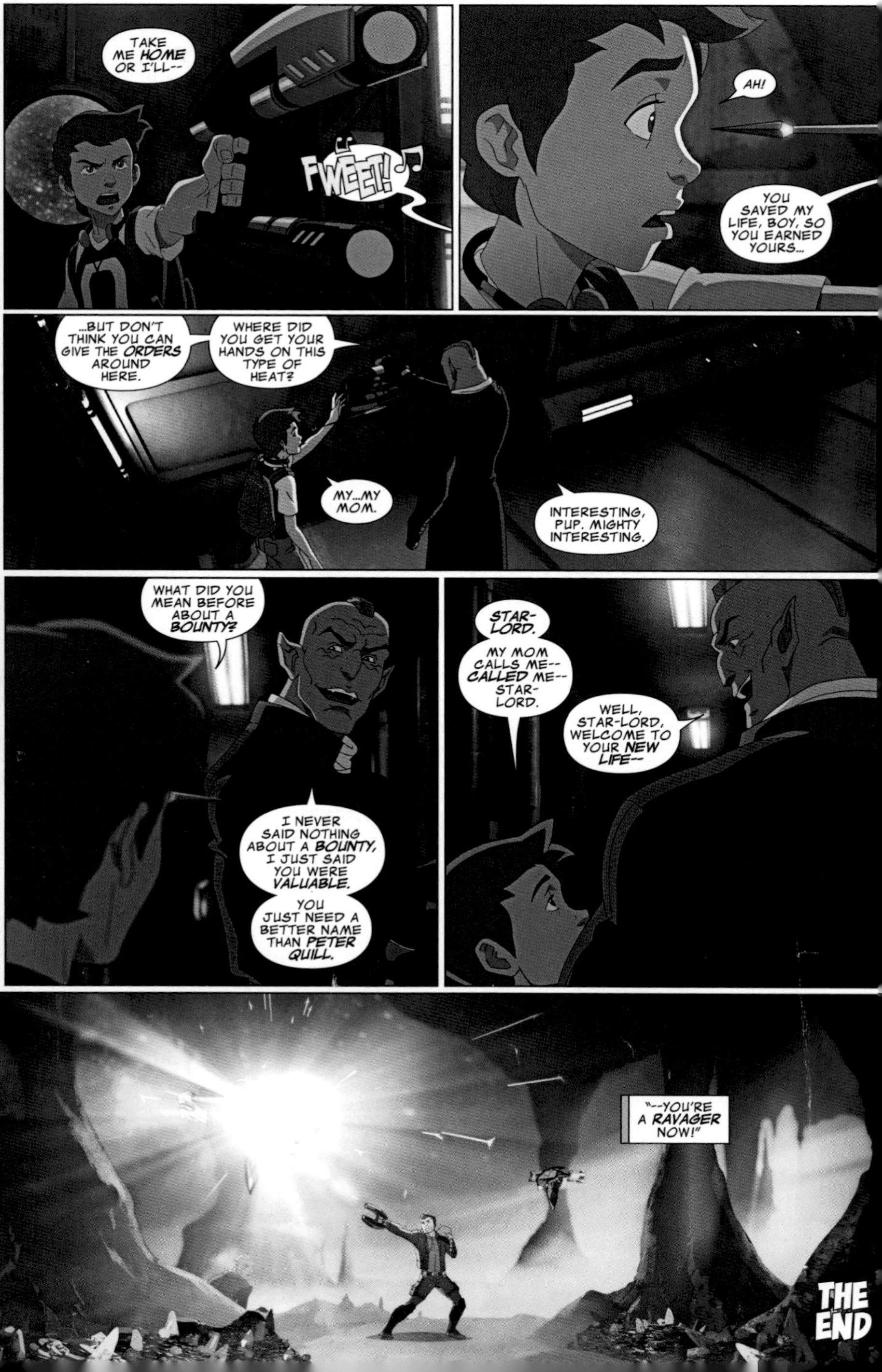
TAKE ME HOME OR I'LL--
FWEET!
AH!
YOU SAVED MY LIFE, BOY, SO YOU EARNED YOURS...
...BUT DON'T THINK YOU CAN GIVE THE ORDERS AROUND HERE.
WHERE DID YOU GET YOUR HANDS ON THIS TYPE OF HEAT?
MY...MY MOM.
INTERESTING, PUP. MIGHTY INTERESTING.
WHAT DID YOU MEAN BEFORE ABOUT A BOUNTY?
I NEVER SAID NOTHING ABOUT A BOUNTY, I JUST SAID YOU WERE VALUABLE.
YOU JUST NEED A BETTER NAME THAN PETER QUILL.
STAR-LORD.
MY MOM CALLS ME--CALLED ME--STAR-LORD.
WELL, STAR-LORD, WELCOME TO YOUR NEW LIFE--
"--YOU'RE A RAVAGER NOW!"
THE END

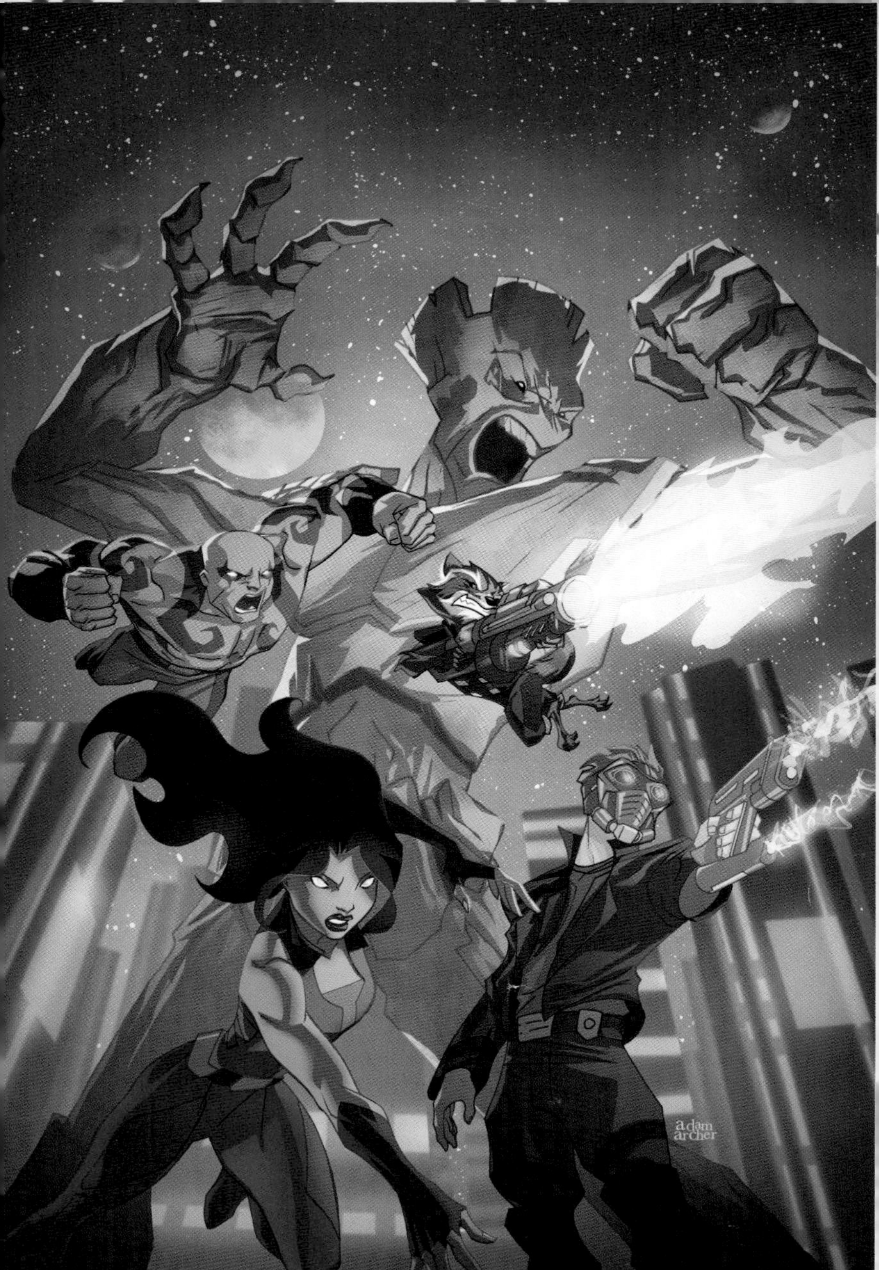
adam archer

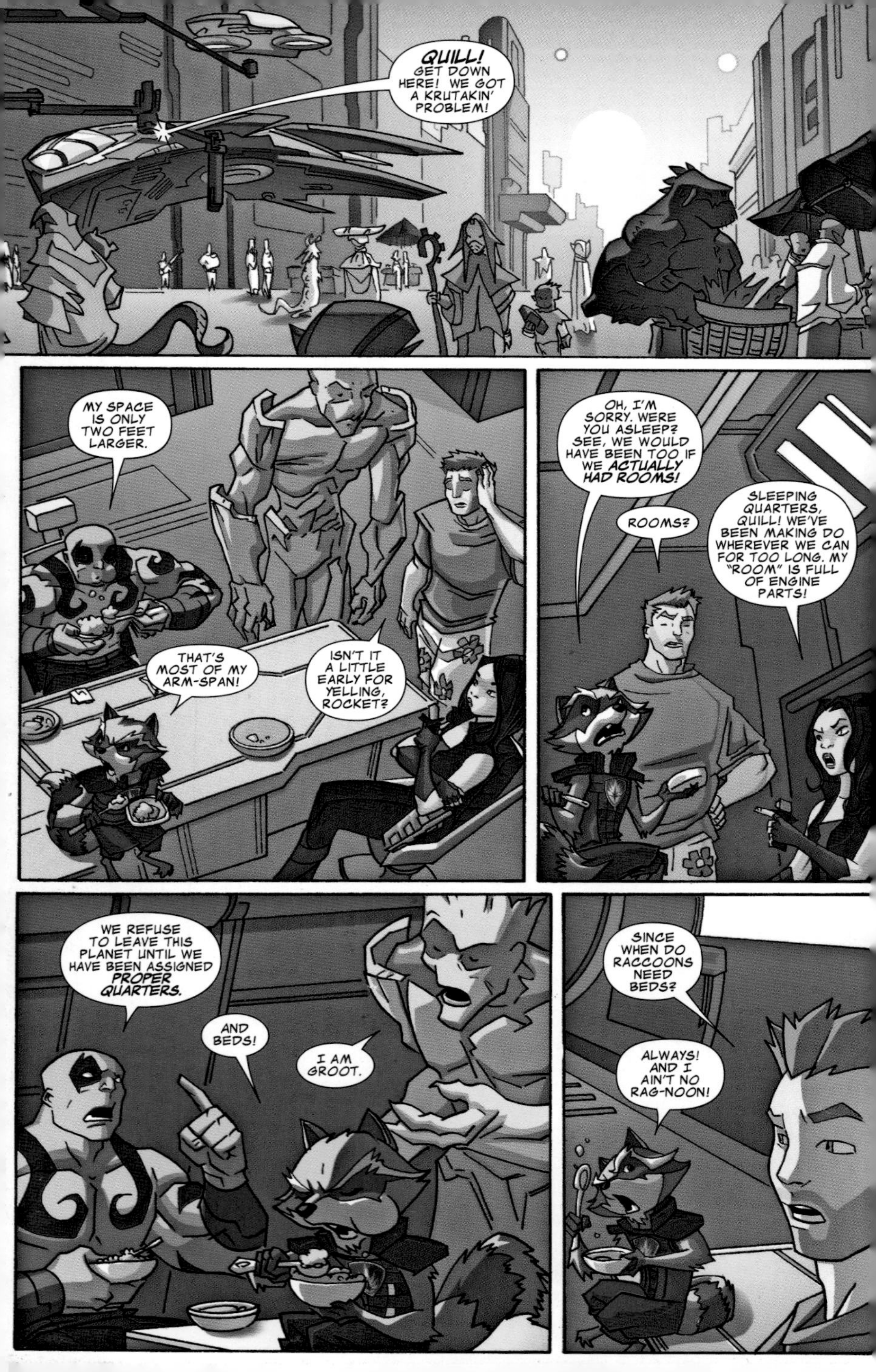
QUILL! GET DOWN HERE! WE GOT A KRUTAKIN' PROBLEM!
MY SPACE IS ONLY TWO FEET LARGER.
THAT'S MOST OF MY ARM-SPAN!
ISN'T IT A LITTLE EARLY FOR YELLING, ROCKET?
OH, I'M SORRY. WERE YOU ASLEEP? SEE, WE WOULD HAVE BEEN TOO IF WE ACTUALLY HAD ROOMS!
ROOMS?
SLEEPING QUARTERS, QUILL! WE'VE BEEN MAKING DO WHEREVER WE CAN FOR TOO LONG. MY "ROOM" IS FULL OF ENGINE PARTS!
WE REFUSE TO LEAVE THIS PLANET UNTIL WE HAVE BEEN ASSIGNED PROPER QUARTERS.
AND BEDS!
I AM GROOT.
SINCE WHEN DO RACCOONS NEED BEDS?
ALWAYS! AND I AIN'T NO RAG-NOON!

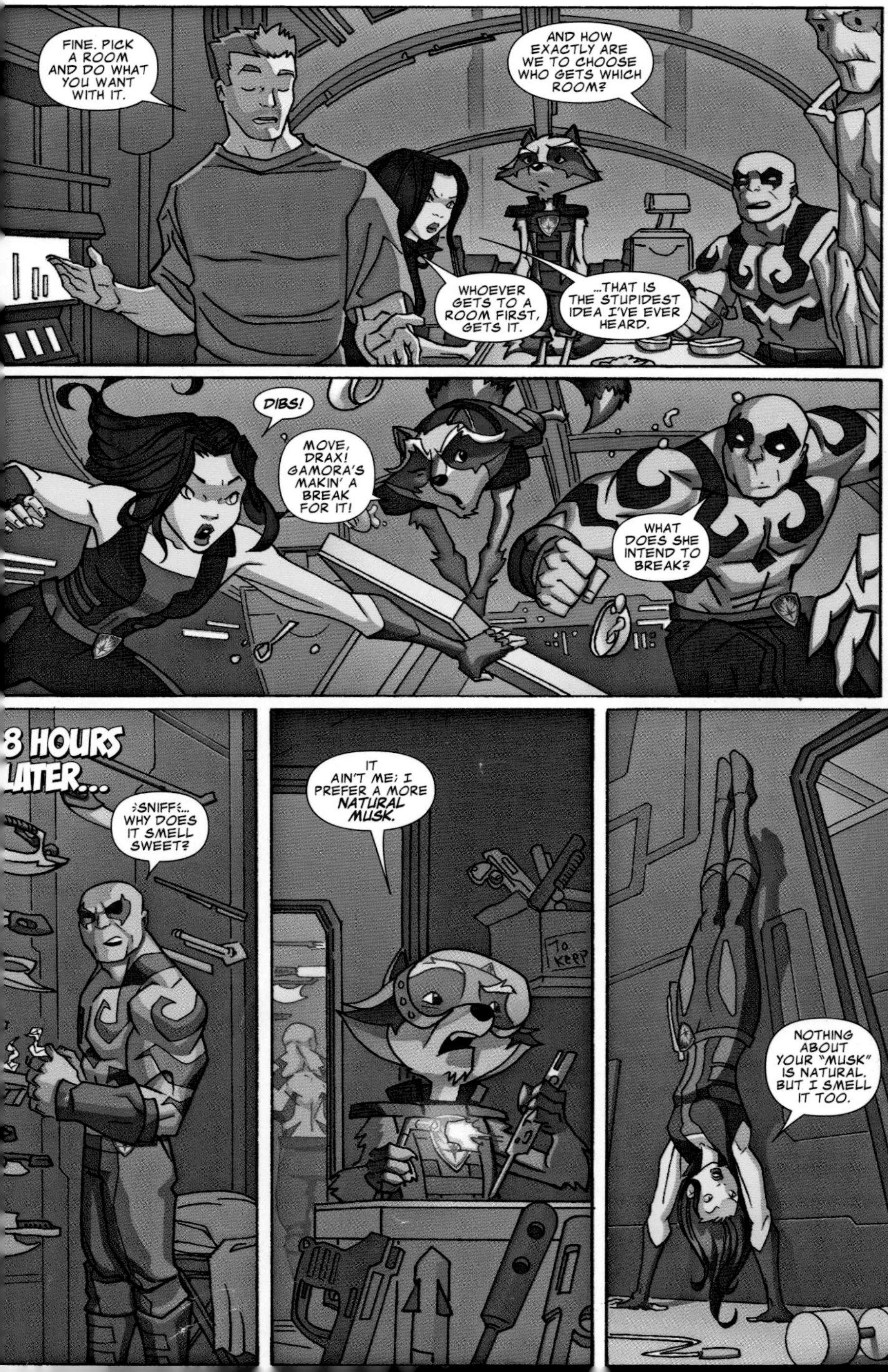
FINE. PICK A ROOM AND DO WHAT YOU WANT WITH IT.
AND HOW EXACTLY ARE WE TO CHOOSE WHO GETS WHICH ROOM?
WHOEVER GETS TO A ROOM FIRST, GETS IT.
...THAT IS THE STUPIDEST IDEA I'VE EVER HEARD.
DIBS!
MOVE, DRAX! GAMORA'S MAKIN' A BREAK FOR IT!
WHAT DOES SHE INTEND TO BREAK?
8 HOURS LATER...
SNIFF... WHY DOES IT SMELL SWEET?
IT AIN'T ME; I PREFER A MORE NATURAL MUSK.
TO KEEP
NOTHING ABOUT YOUR "MUSK" IS NATURAL. BUT I SMELL IT TOO.

SKRT!
SKRT!

I AM
GROOT?

I AM
GROOT?

NO, I
AIN'T OUT
THERE! AND
STOP TALKING
ABOUT MY
SMELL!

I AM
GROOT!

HSSS!

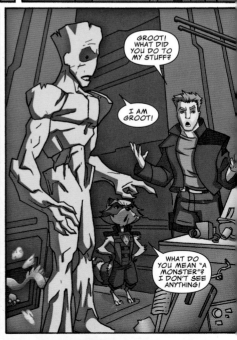

GROOT!
WHAT DID
YOU DO TO
MY STUFF?

I AM
GROOT!

WHAT DO
YOU MEAN "A
MONSTER"? I
DON'T SEE
ANYTHING!

ROCKET!

YOU DESTROYED MY QUARTERS, VERMIN!

I DID NO SUCH--

I AM GROOOT!

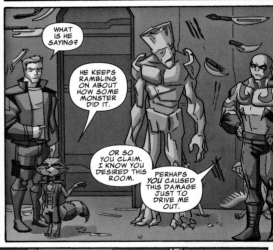

WHAT IS HE SAYING?

HE KEEPS RAMBLING ON ABOUT HOW SOME MONSTER DID IT.

OR SO YOU CLAIM. I KNOW YOU DESIRED THIS ROOM.

PERHAPS YOU CAUSED THIS DAMAGE JUST TO DRIVE ME OUT.

LOOK WE JUST HAVE TO SETTLE DOWN. LET'S GET SOME SLEEP AND FIGURE THIS OUT IN THE MORNING.

HMPH.

NEXT MORNING...

BZZT!
BZZT!

SERIOUSLY?!

THE SHIP IS WRECKED. WE GOT CIRCUITS FAILIN' ALL OVER THE PLACE.

WHAT ABOUT THE ENGINES?

THEY'RE FINE FOR NOW, BUT SOMETHING TRASHED THE SHIP'S WIRING.

AND MY ROOM.

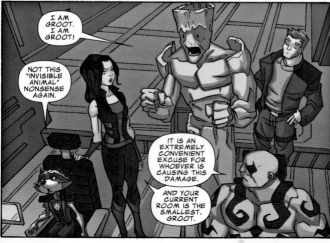

I AM GROOT. I AM GROOT!

NOT THIS "INVISIBLE ANIMAL" NONSENSE AGAIN.

IT IS AN EXTREMELY CONVENIENT EXCUSE FOR WHOEVER IS CAUSING THIS DAMAGE.

AND YOUR CURRENT ROOM IS THE SMALLEST, GROOT.

I AM GROOT!

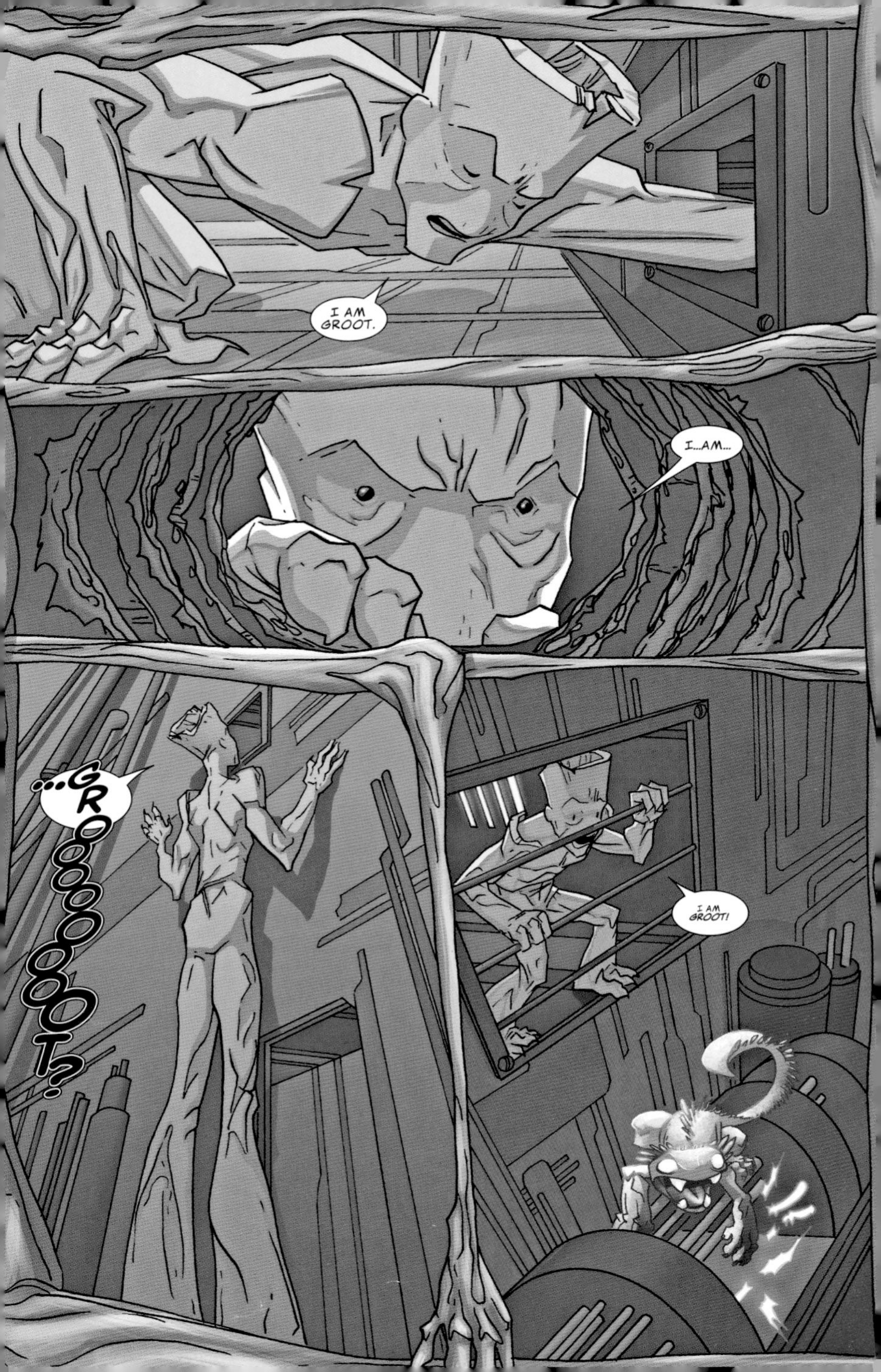
I AM GROOT.
I...AM...
...GROOOOOOOOT?
I AM GROOT!

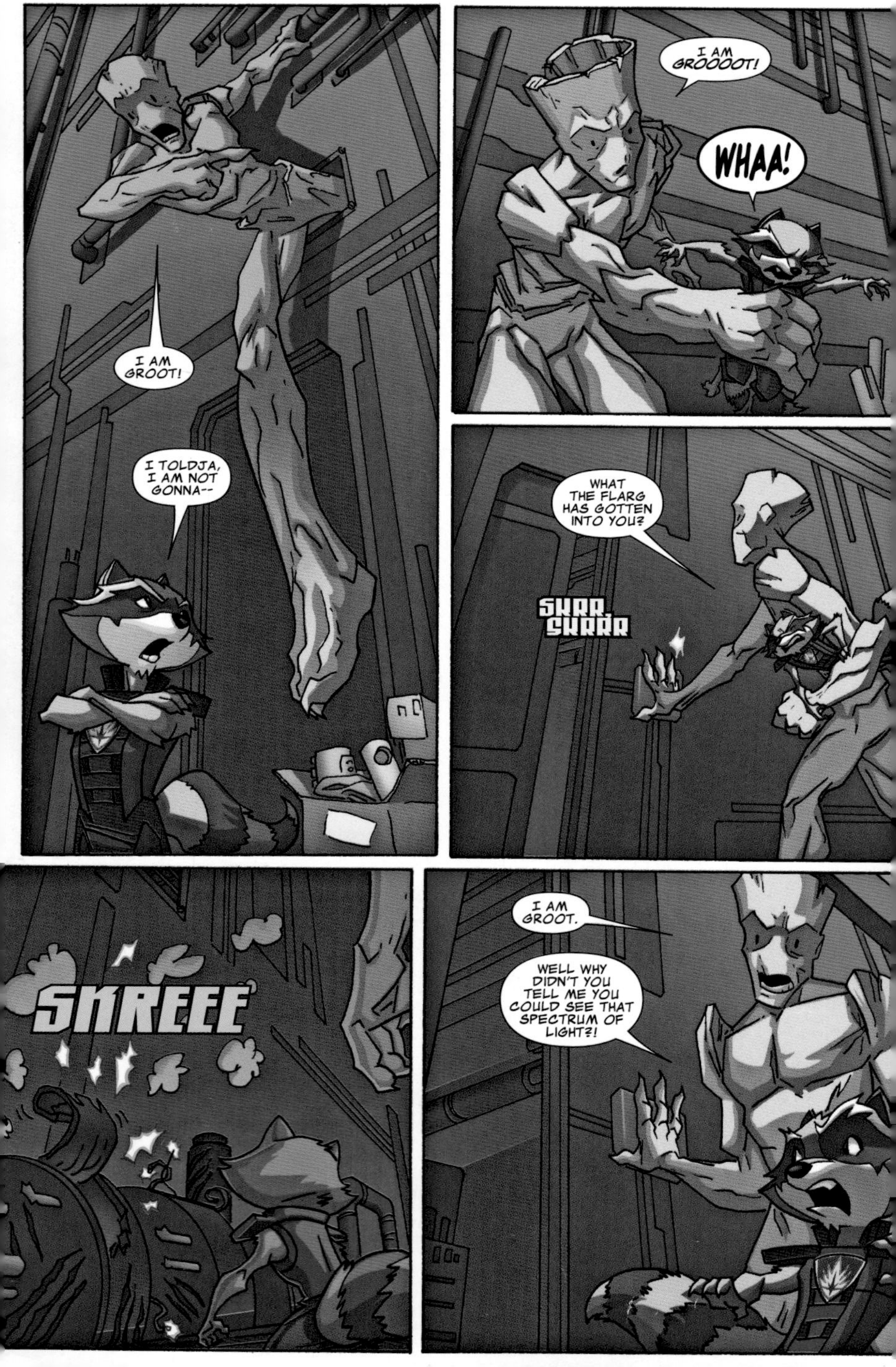
I AM GROOT!
I TOLDJA, I AM NOT GONNA--
I AM GROOOOT!
WHAA!
WHAT THE FLARG HAS GOTTEN INTO YOU?
SKRR SKRRR
SKREEE
I AM GROOT.
WELL WHY DIDN'T YOU TELL ME YOU COULD SEE THAT SPECTRUM OF LIGHT?!

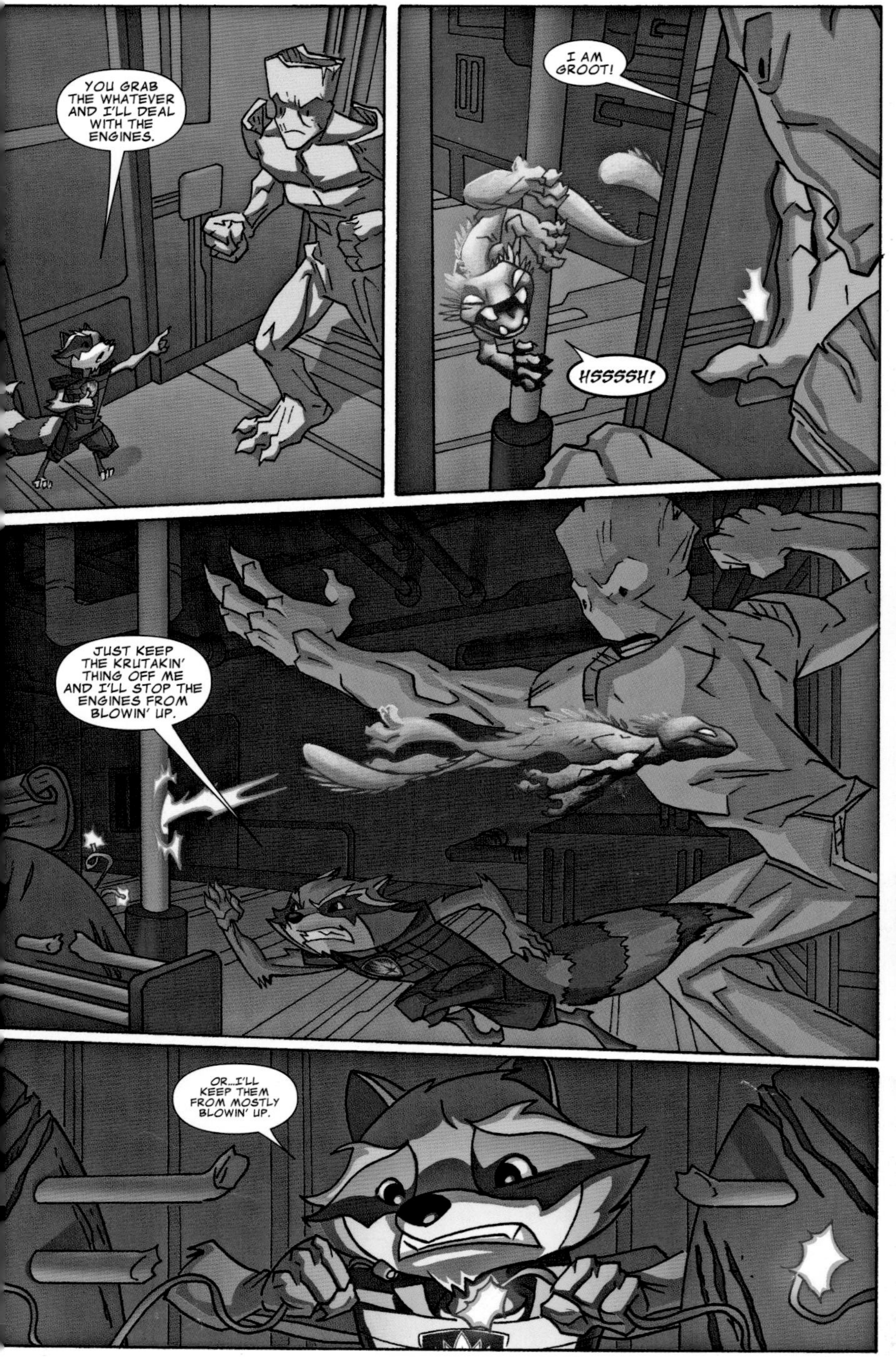
YOU GRAB THE WHATEVER AND I'LL DEAL WITH THE ENGINES.
I AM GROOT!
HSSSSH!
JUST KEEP THE KRUTAKIN' THING OFF ME AND I'LL STOP THE ENGINES FROM BLOWIN' UP.
OR...I'LL KEEP THEM FROM MOSTLY BLOWIN' UP.

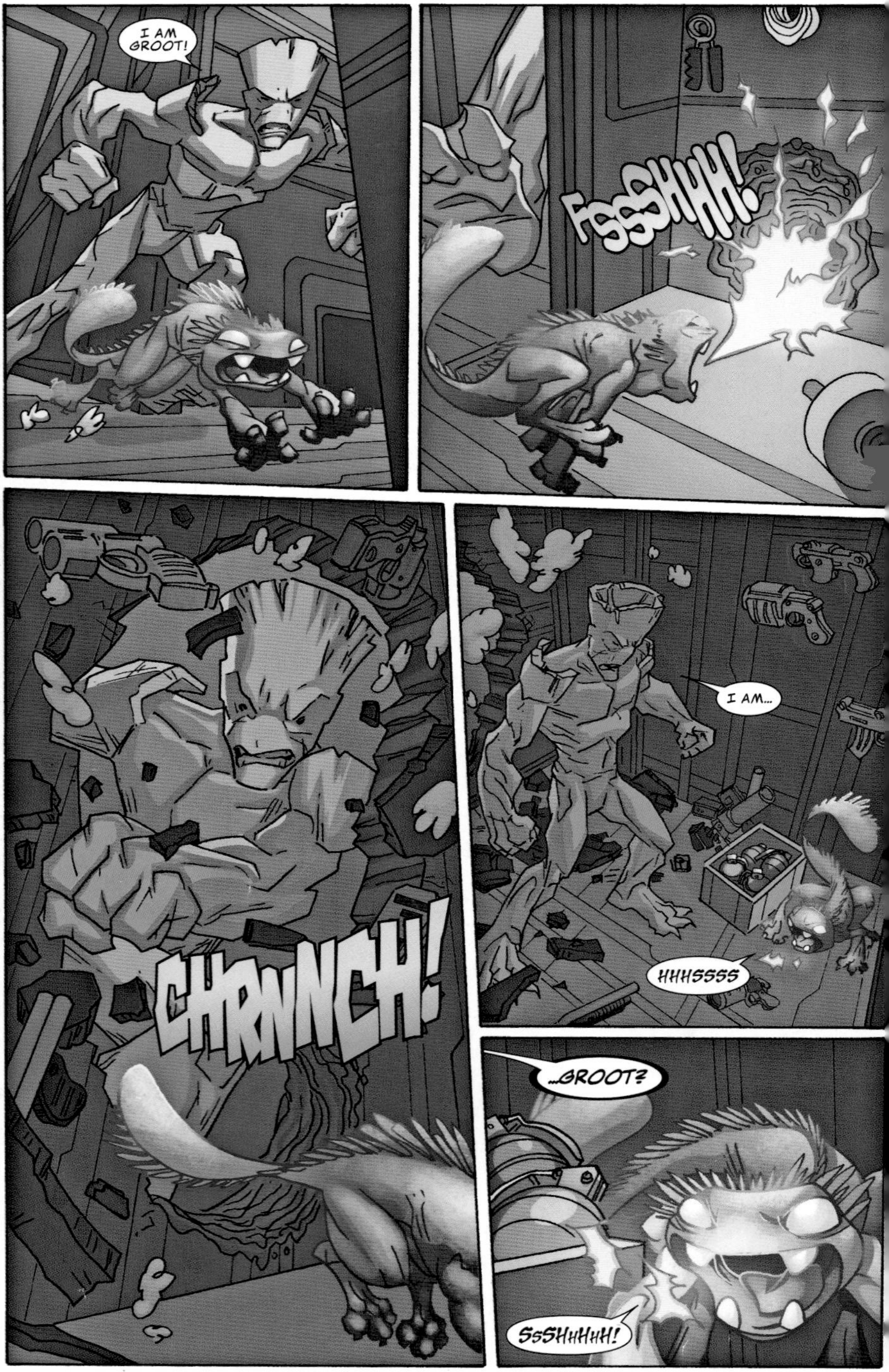
I AM GROOT!
FSSSHHH!
CHRNNCH!
I AM...
HHHSSSS
...GROOT?
SsSHHHHH!

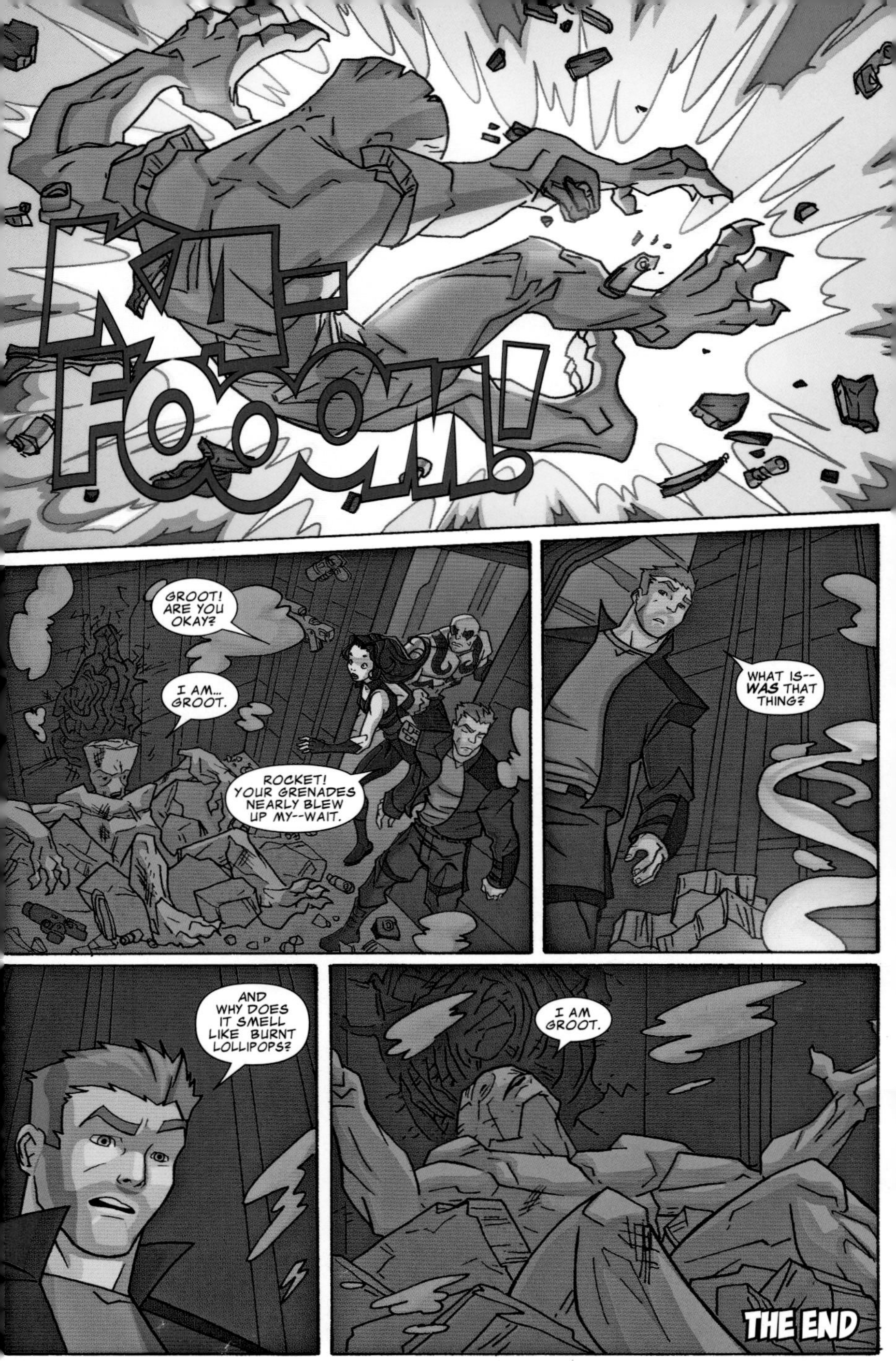
KA-FOOM!
GROOT! ARE YOU OKAY?
I AM... GROOT.
ROCKET! YOUR GRENADES NEARLY BLEW UP MY--WAIT.
WHAT IS-- WAS THAT THING?
AND WHY DOES IT SMELL LIKE BURNT LOLLIPOPS?
I AM GROOT.
THE END

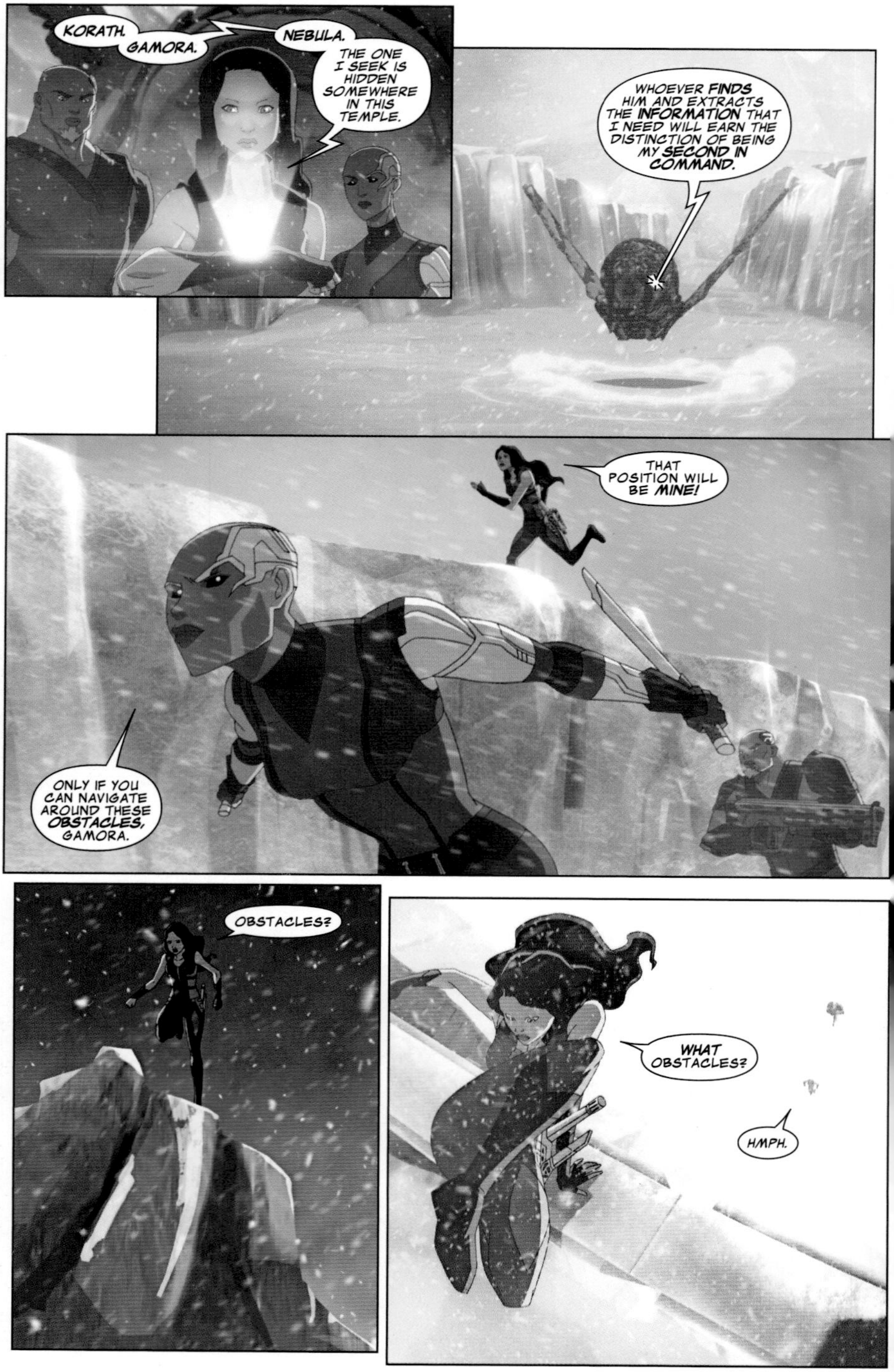
KORATH.
GAMORA.
NEBULA.
THE ONE I SEEK IS HIDDEN SOMEWHERE IN THIS TEMPLE.
WHOEVER **FINDS** HIM AND EXTRACTS THE **INFORMATION** THAT I NEED WILL EARN THE DISTINCTION OF BEING MY **SECOND IN COMMAND.**
THAT POSITION WILL BE ***MINE!***
ONLY IF YOU CAN NAVIGATE AROUND THESE ***OBSTACLES,*** GAMORA.
OBSTACLES?
WHAT OBSTACLES?
HMPH.

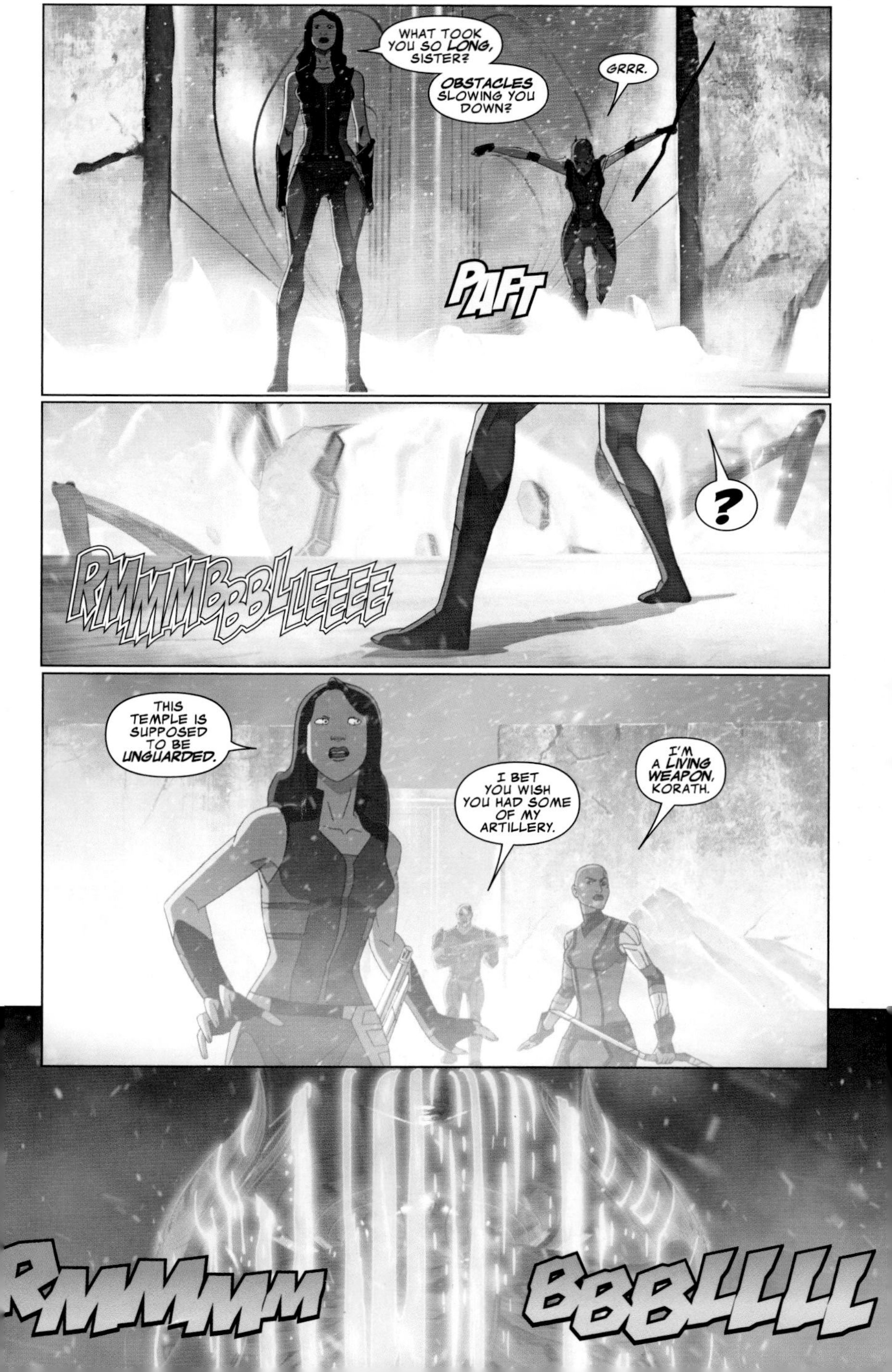
WHAT TOOK YOU SO LONG, SISTER?
OBSTACLES SLOWING YOU DOWN?
GRRR.
PAFT
?
RMMMBBBLLEEEE
THIS TEMPLE IS SUPPOSED TO BE UNGUARDED.
I BET YOU WISH YOU HAD SOME OF MY ARTILLERY.
I'M A LIVING WEAPON, KORATH.
RMMMMM
BBBLLLL

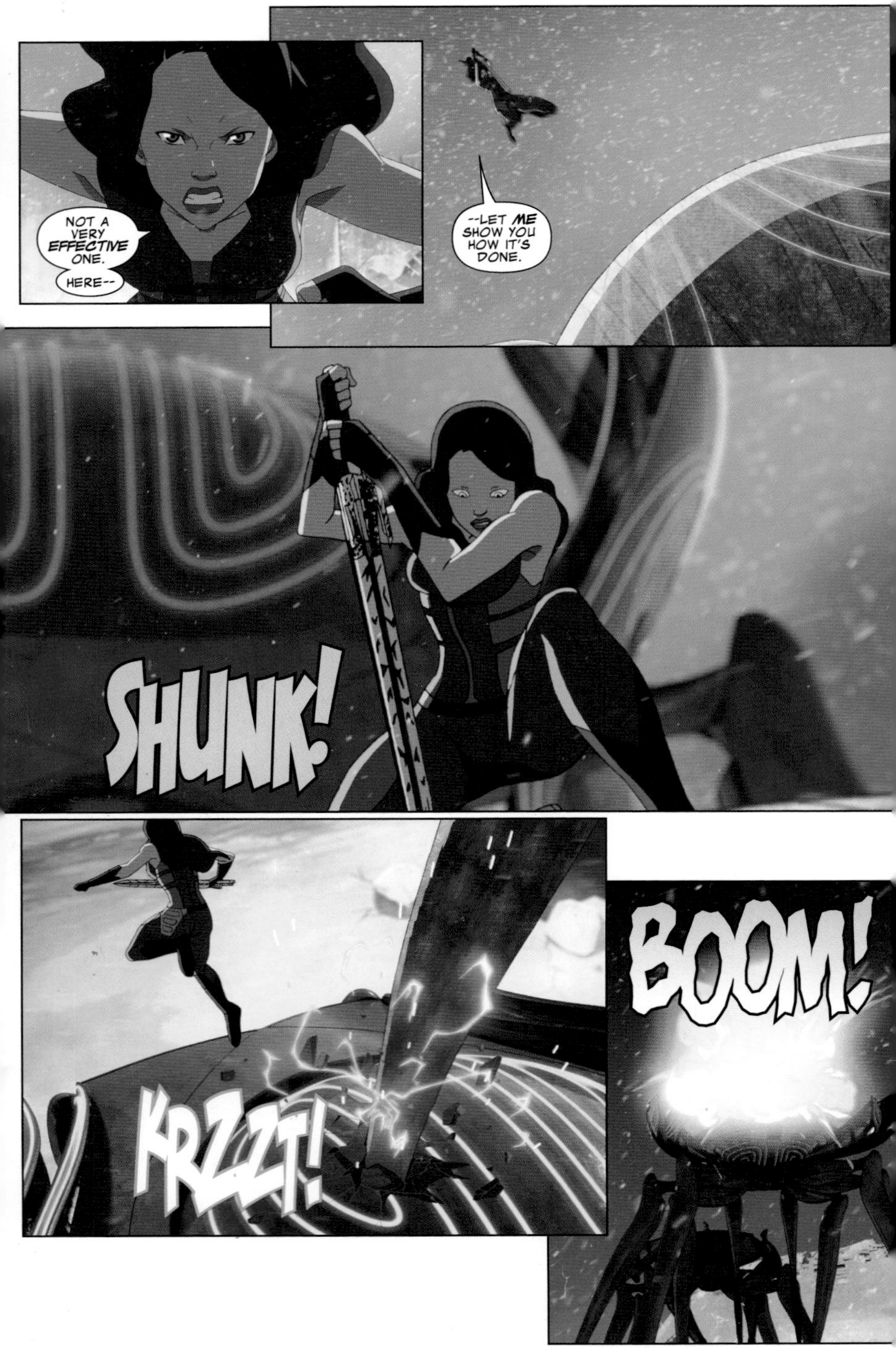
NOT A VERY EFFECTIVE ONE.
HERE--
--LET ME SHOW YOU HOW IT'S DONE.
SHUNK!
KRZZT!
BOOM!

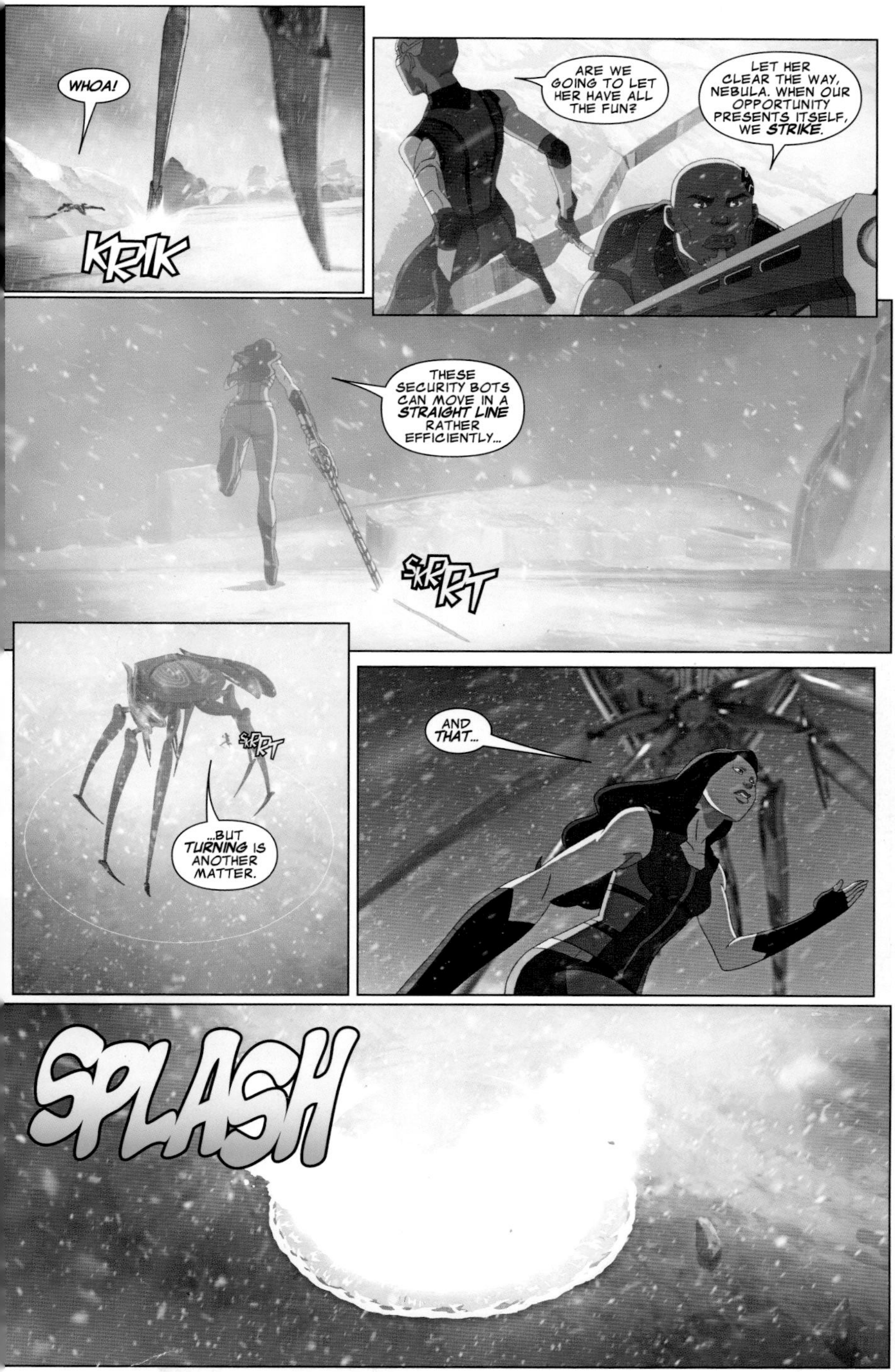
WHOA!
KRIK
ARE WE GOING TO LET HER HAVE ALL THE FUN?
LET HER CLEAR THE WAY, NEBULA. WHEN OUR OPPORTUNITY PRESENTS ITSELF, WE STRIKE.
THESE SECURITY BOTS CAN MOVE IN A STRAIGHT LINE RATHER EFFICIENTLY...
SKRRRT
SKRRRT
...BUT TURNING IS ANOTHER MATTER.
AND THAT...
SPLASH

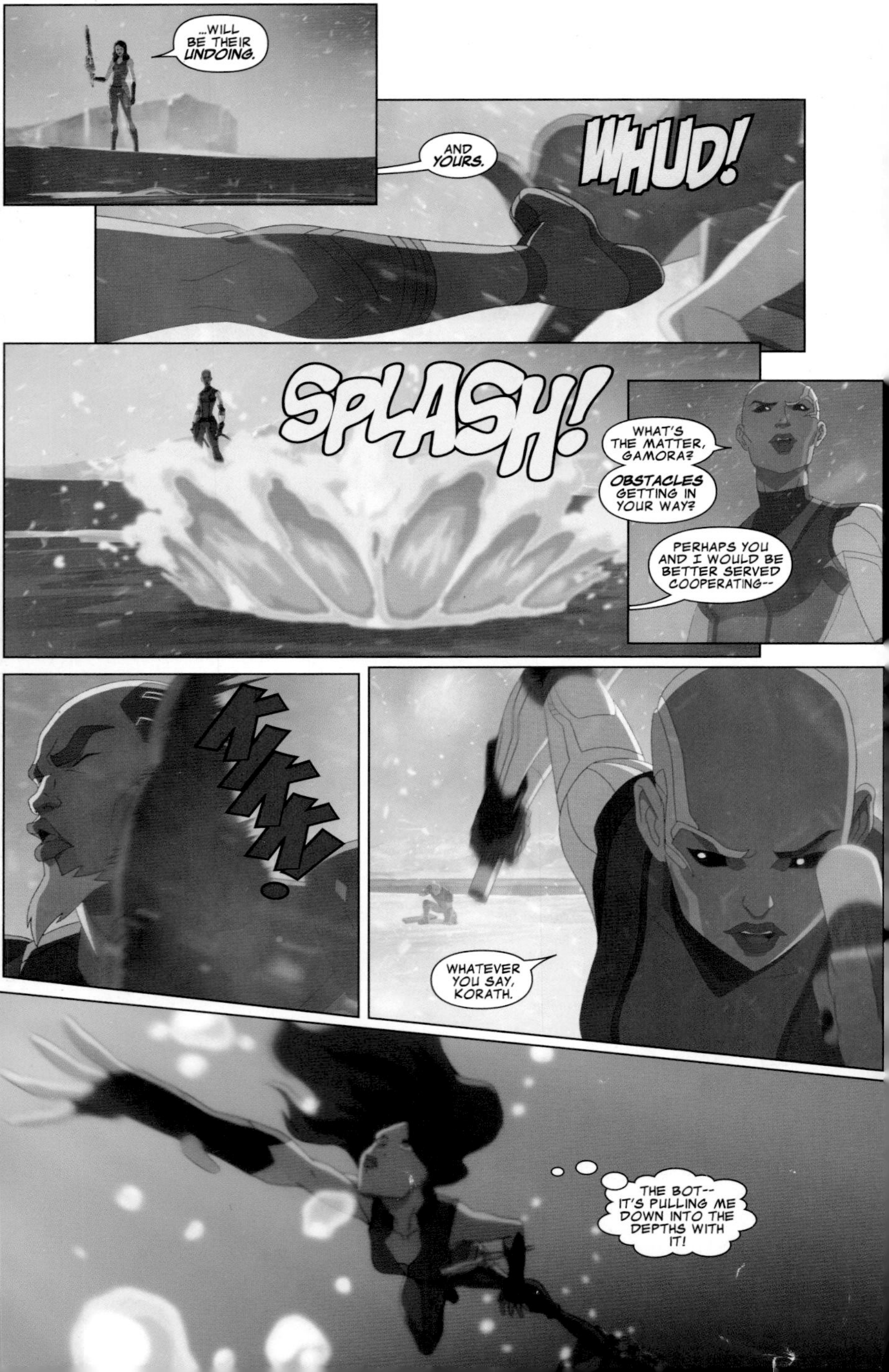
...WILL BE THEIR UNDOING.
AND YOURS.
WHUD!
SPLASH!
WHAT'S THE MATTER, GAMORA?
OBSTACLES GETTING IN YOUR WAY?
PERHAPS YOU AND I WOULD BE BETTER SERVED COOPERATING--
KIKK!
WHATEVER YOU SAY, KORATH.
THE BOT-- IT'S PULLING ME DOWN INTO THE DEPTHS WITH IT!

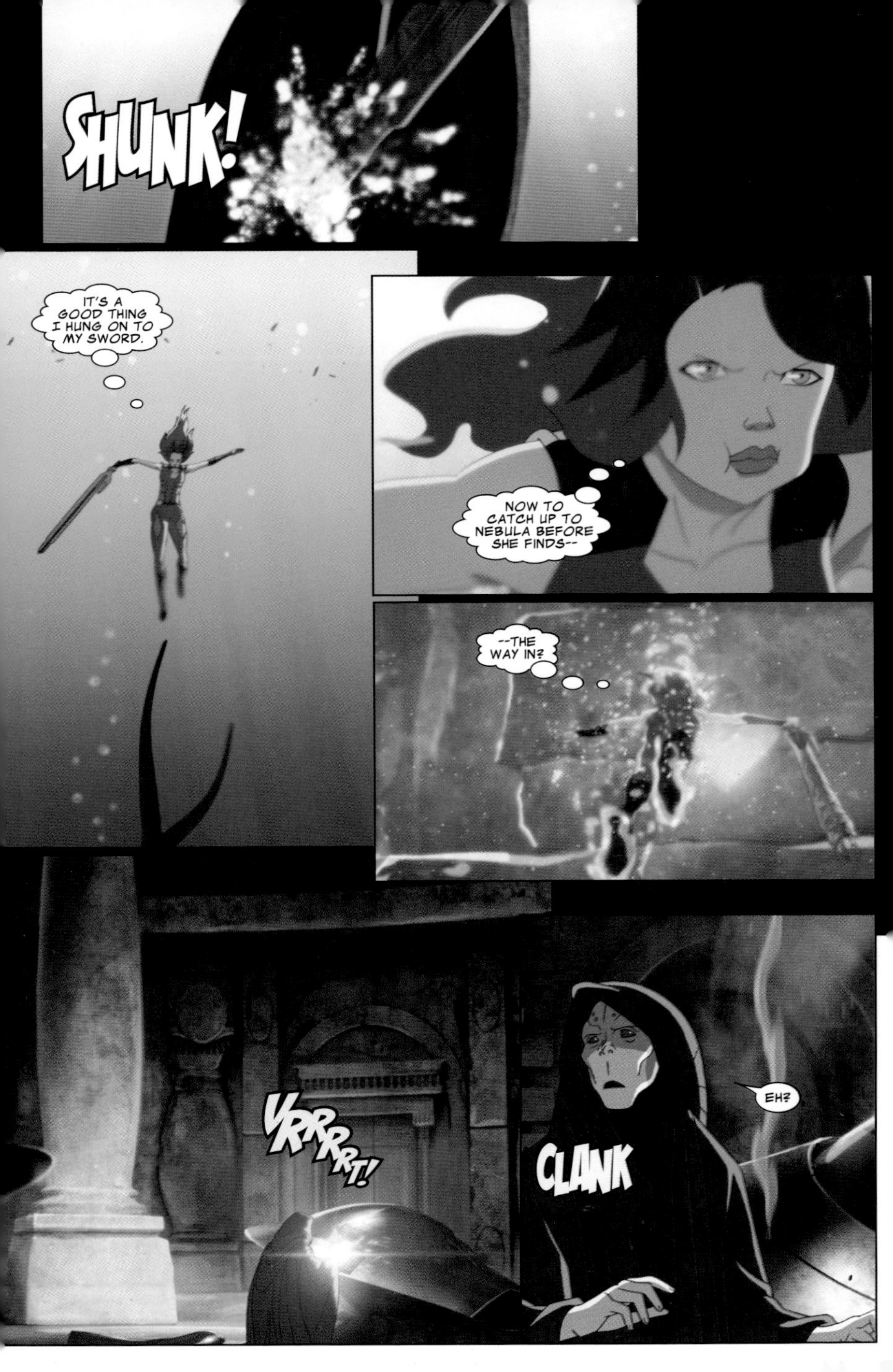
SHUNK!
IT'S A GOOD THING I HUNG ON TO MY SWORD.
NOW TO CATCH UP TO NEBULA BEFORE SHE FINDS--
--THE WAY IN?
VRRRRT!
CLANK
EH?

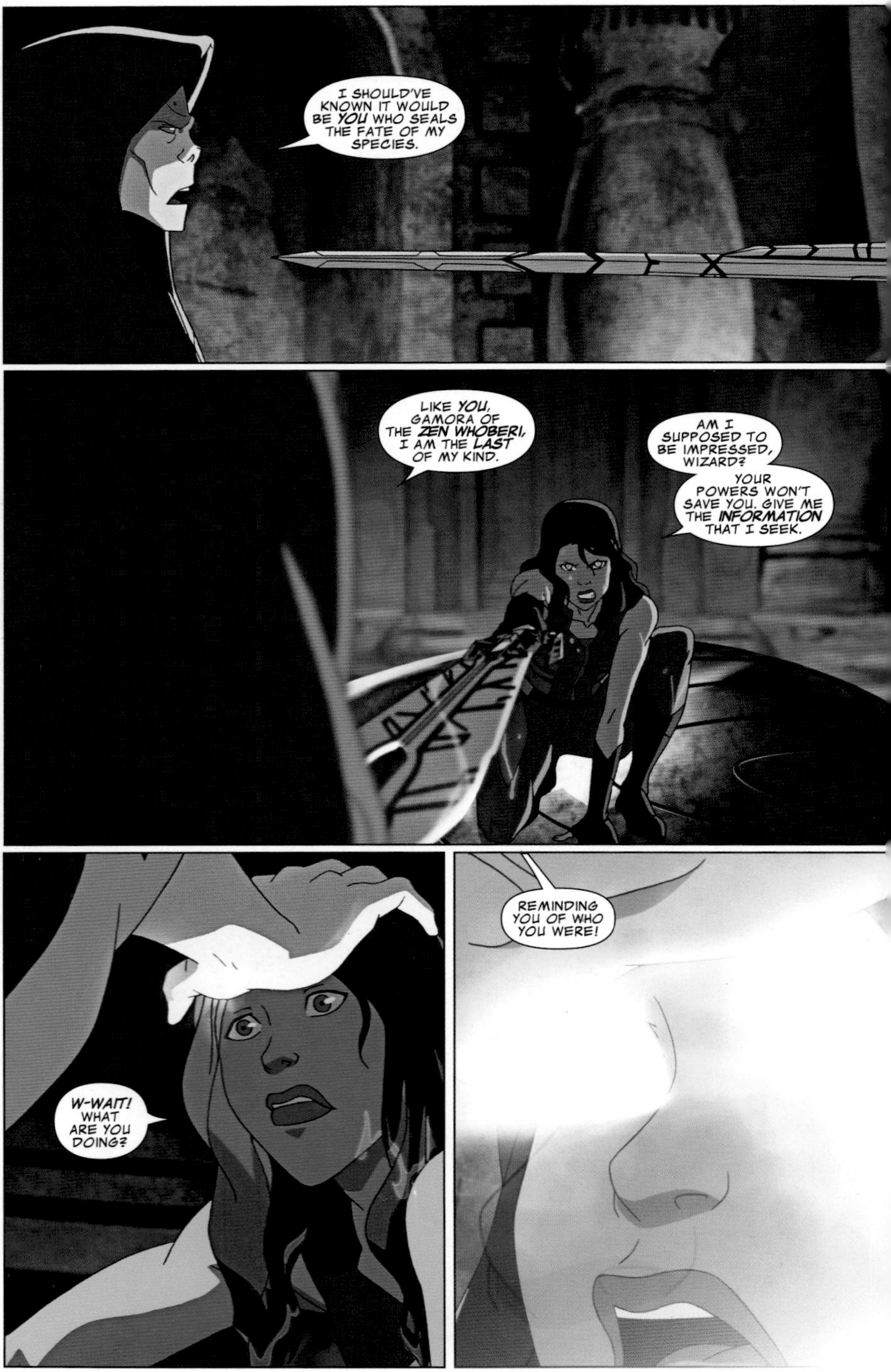
I SHOULD'VE KNOWN IT WOULD BE *YOU* WHO SEALS THE FATE OF MY SPECIES.
LIKE *YOU*, GAMORA OF THE *ZEN WHOBERI*, I AM THE *LAST* OF MY KIND.
AM I SUPPOSED TO BE IMPRESSED, WIZARD?
YOUR POWERS WON'T SAVE YOU. GIVE ME THE *INFORMATION* THAT I SEEK.
W-WAIT! WHAT ARE YOU DOING?
REMINDING YOU OF WHO YOU WERE!

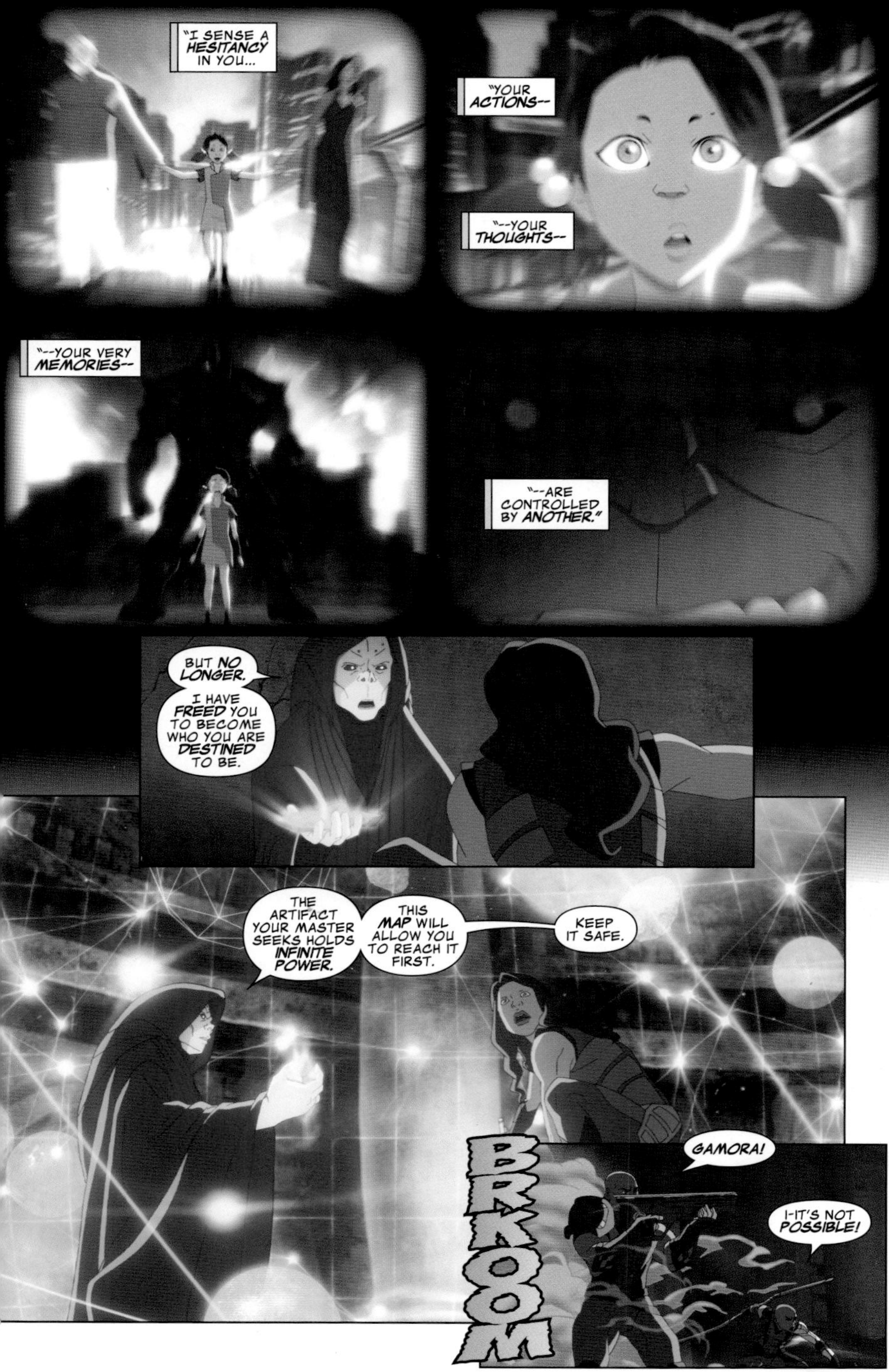
"I SENSE A HESITANCY IN YOU...
"YOUR ACTIONS--
"--YOUR THOUGHTS--
"--YOUR VERY MEMORIES--
"--ARE CONTROLLED BY ANOTHER."
BUT NO LONGER.
I HAVE FREED YOU TO BECOME WHO YOU ARE DESTINED TO BE.
THE ARTIFACT YOUR MASTER SEEKS HOLDS INFINITE POWER.
THIS MAP WILL ALLOW YOU TO REACH IT FIRST.
KEEP IT SAFE.
BRKOOM
GAMORA!
I-IT'S NOT POSSIBLE!

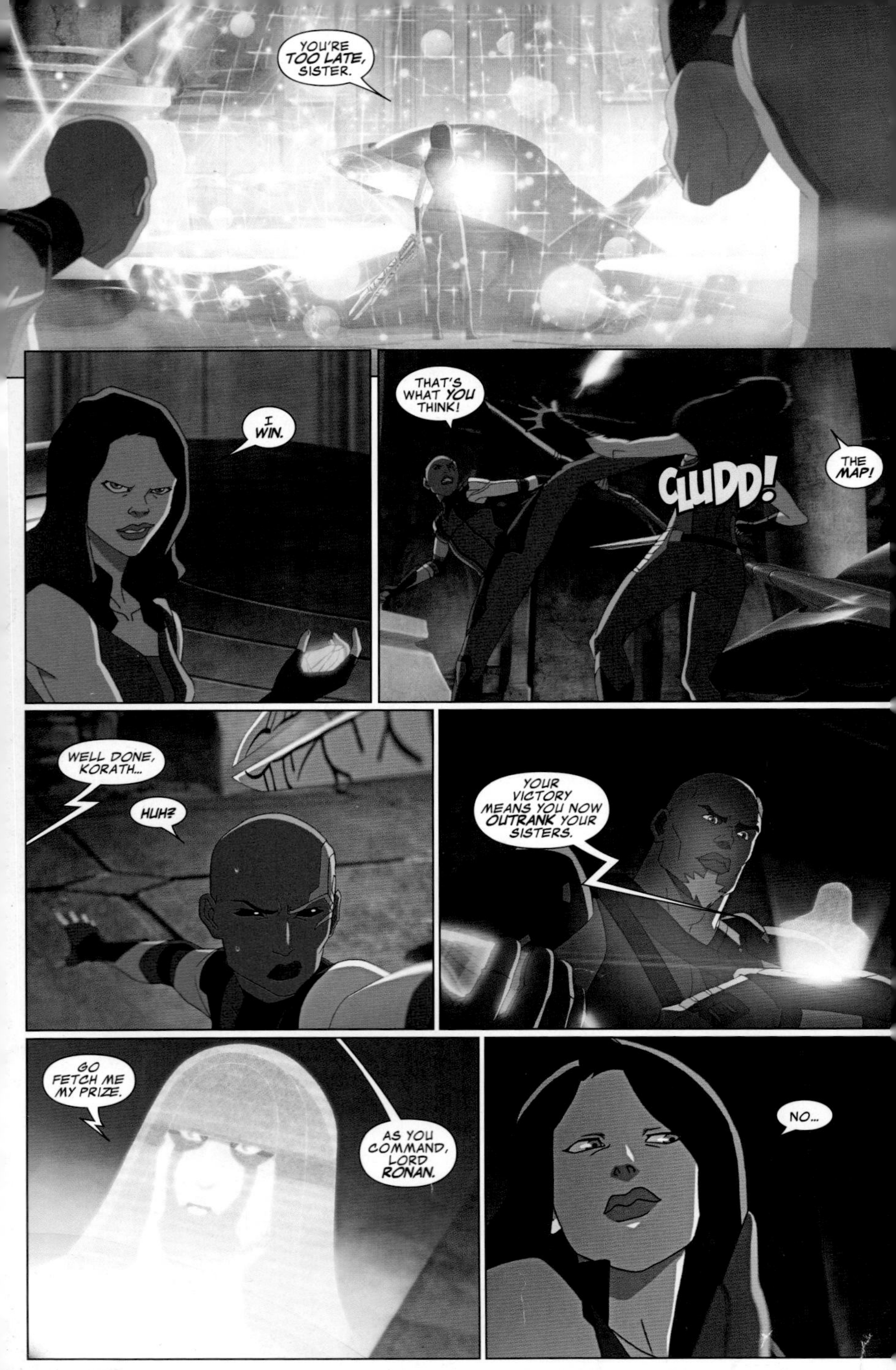

YOU'RE TOO LATE, SISTER.
I WIN.
THAT'S WHAT YOU THINK!
CLUDD!
THE MAP!
WELL DONE, KORATH...
HUH?
YOUR VICTORY MEANS YOU NOW OUTRANK YOUR SISTERS.
GO FETCH ME MY PRIZE.
AS YOU COMMAND, LORD RONAN.
NO...

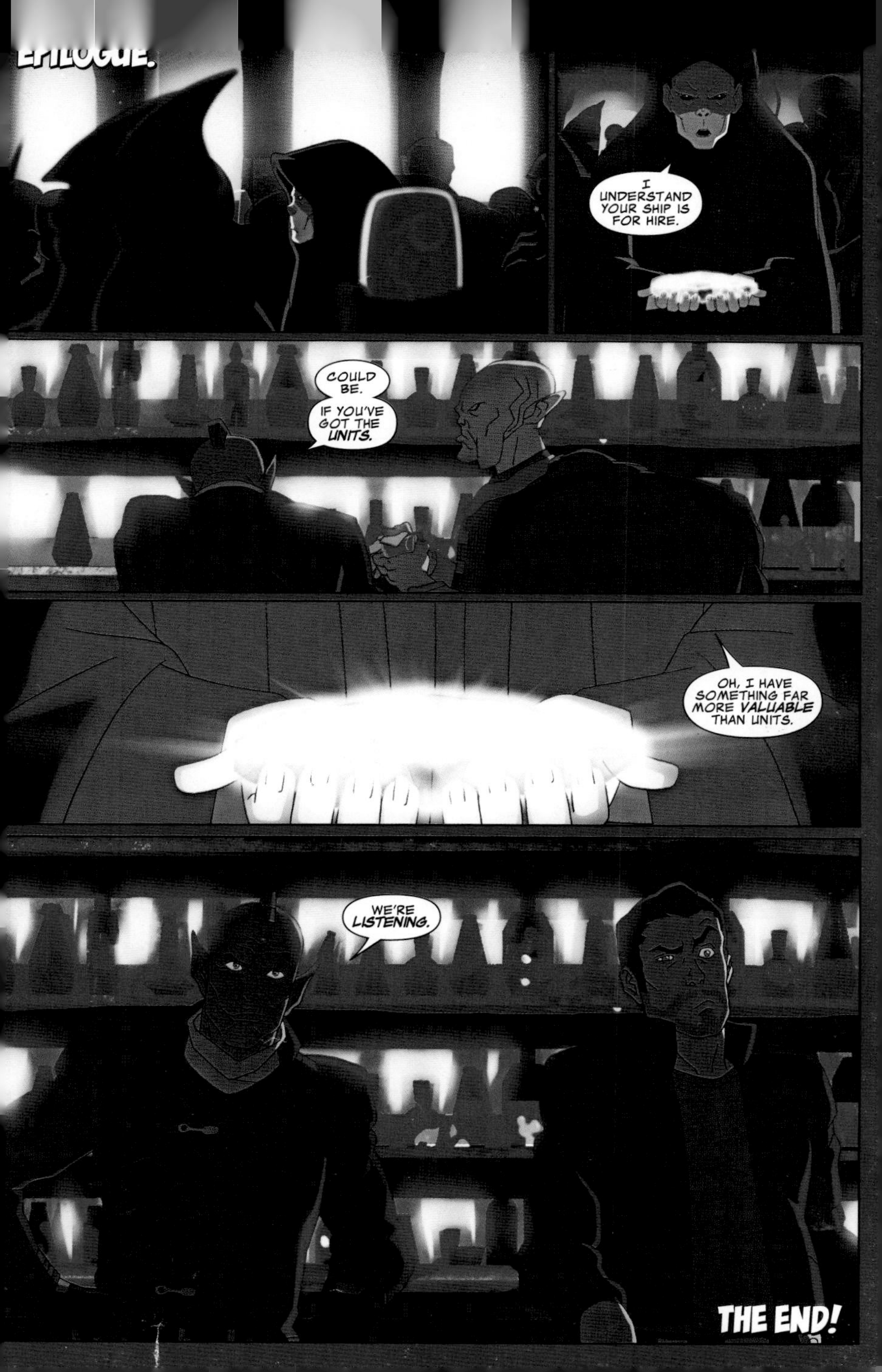
EPILOGUE.
I UNDERSTAND YOUR SHIP IS FOR HIRE.
COULD BE.
IF YOU'VE GOT THE UNITS.
OH, I HAVE SOMETHING FAR MORE VALUABLE THAN UNITS.
WE'RE LISTENING.
THE END!

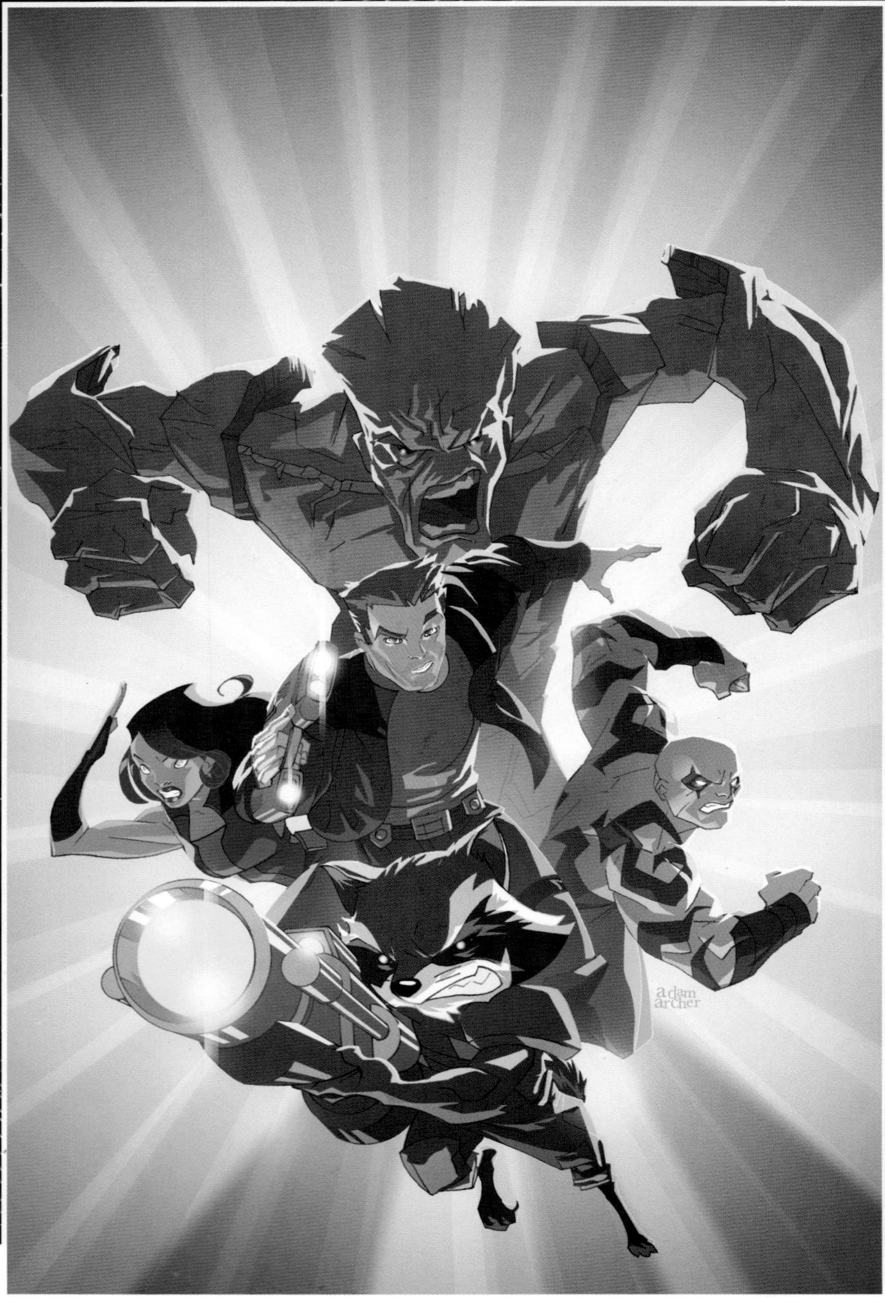
adam
archer

3

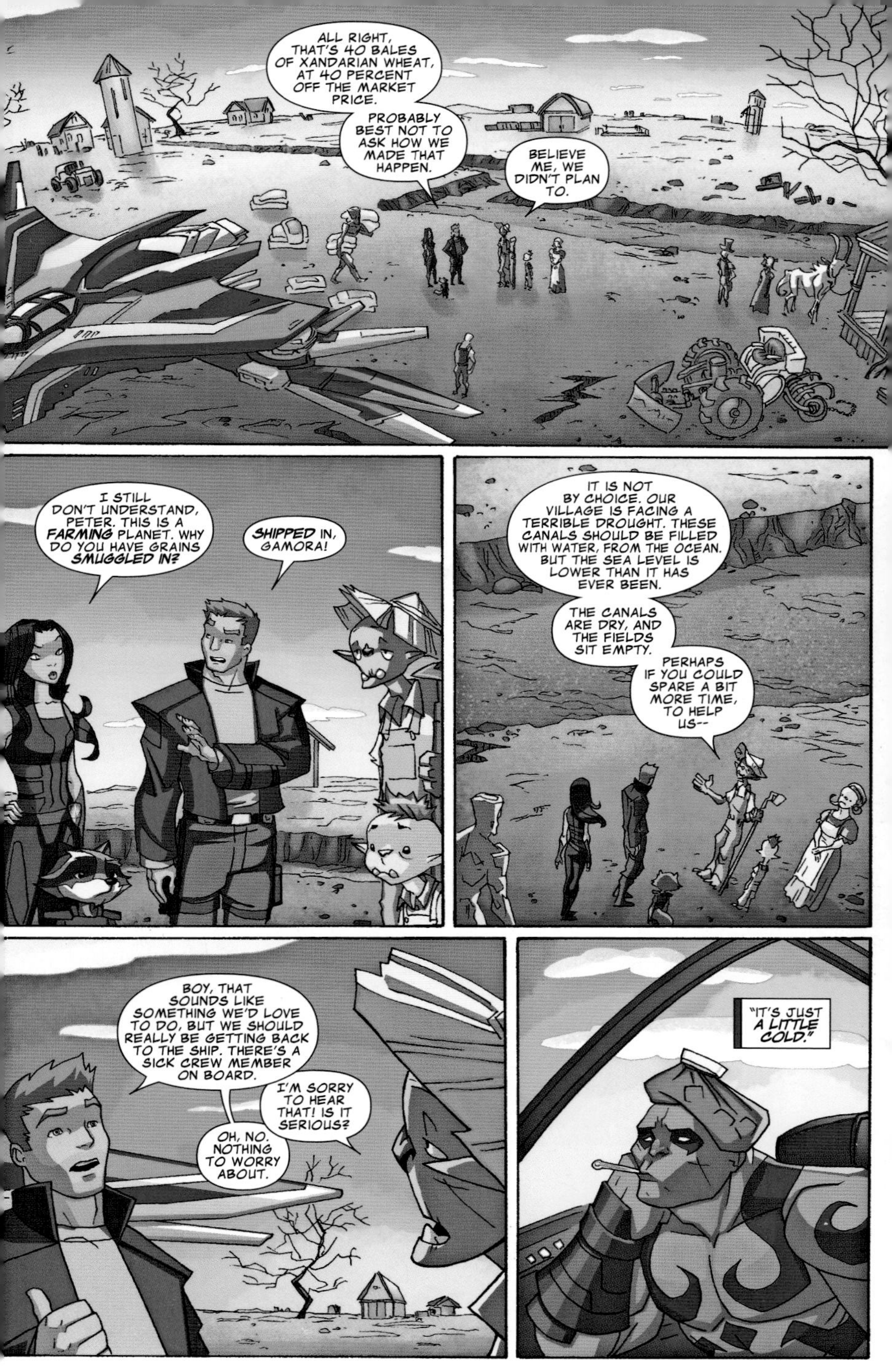
ALL RIGHT, THAT'S 40 BALES OF XANDARIAN WHEAT, AT 40 PERCENT OFF THE MARKET PRICE.
PROBABLY BEST NOT TO ASK HOW WE MADE THAT HAPPEN.
BELIEVE ME, WE DIDN'T PLAN TO.
I STILL DON'T UNDERSTAND, PETER. THIS IS A FARMING PLANET. WHY DO YOU HAVE GRAINS SMUGGLED IN?
SHIPPED IN, GAMORA!
IT IS NOT BY CHOICE. OUR VILLAGE IS FACING A TERRIBLE DROUGHT. THESE CANALS SHOULD BE FILLED WITH WATER, FROM THE OCEAN. BUT THE SEA LEVEL IS LOWER THAN IT HAS EVER BEEN.
THE CANALS ARE DRY, AND THE FIELDS SIT EMPTY.
PERHAPS IF YOU COULD SPARE A BIT MORE TIME, TO HELP US--
BOY, THAT SOUNDS LIKE SOMETHING WE'D LOVE TO DO, BUT WE SHOULD REALLY BE GETTING BACK TO THE SHIP. THERE'S A SICK CREW MEMBER ON BOARD.
I'M SORRY TO HEAR THAT! IS IT SERIOUS?
OH, NO. NOTHING TO WORRY ABOUT.
"IT'S JUST A LITTLE COLD."

HEY THERE, DRAX. YOU STILL UNDER THE WEATHER?

WHAT? NO. THE WEATHER SURROUNDS US ON *ALL SIDES*. THAT IS ITS NATURE.

RIGHT. SILLY ME. WELL, JUST TRY TO TAKE IT EASY. I THINK WE HAVE SOME CANS OF CHICKEN SOUP. THAT'LL FIX YOU RIGHT UP.

DRAX'S *DIET* IS WHAT MADE HIM ILL IN THE FIRST PLACE. HE WILL EAT ANYTHING IN THE MESS HALL. GRUBS. VERMIN. POND SCUM. WHY DO WE EVEN *HAVE* POND SCUM?

HEY, I'VE HAD A LOT OF VISITORS ON THIS SHIP, INCLUDING A COUPLE WITH SOME PRETTY ODD EATING HABITS. I DON'T JUDGE.

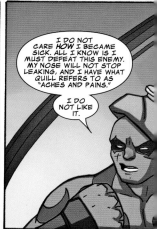

I DO NOT CARE *HOW* I BECAME SICK. ALL I KNOW IS I MUST DEFEAT THIS ENEMY. MY NOSE WILL NOT STOP LEAKING, AND I HAVE WHAT QUILL REFERS TO AS "ACHES AND PAINS."

I DO NOT LIKE IT.

WELL, IT COULD BE WORSE. AT LEAST YOU HAVEN'T STARTED TO--

ACHOOOOO!

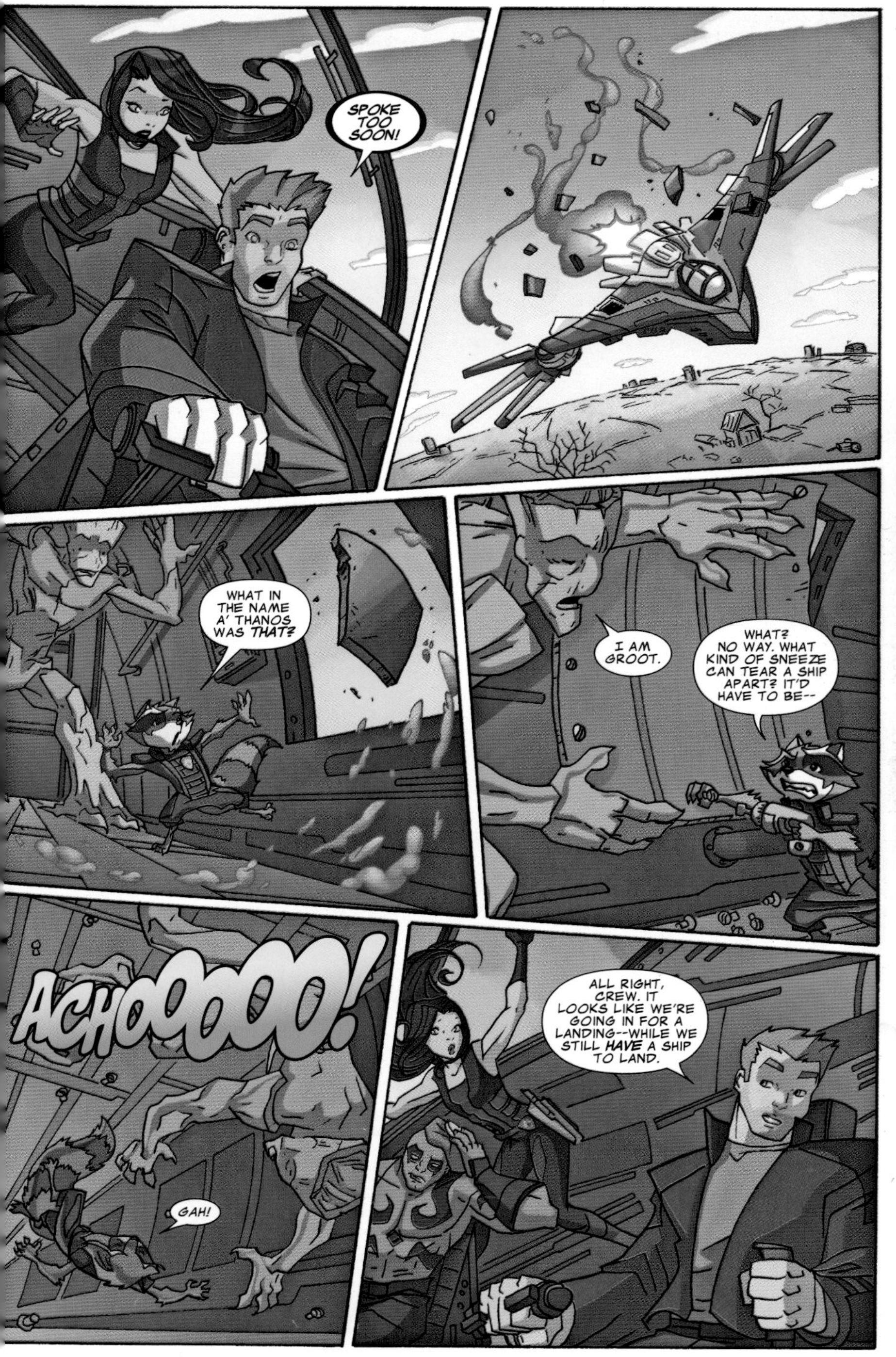
SPOKE TOO SOON!
WHAT IN THE NAME A' THANOS WAS THAT?
I AM GROOT.
WHAT? NO WAY. WHAT KIND OF SNEEZE CAN TEAR A SHIP APART? IT'D HAVE TO BE--
ACHOOOOO!
GAH!
ALL RIGHT, CREW. IT LOOKS LIKE WE'RE GOING IN FOR A LANDING--WHILE WE STILL HAVE A SHIP TO LAND.

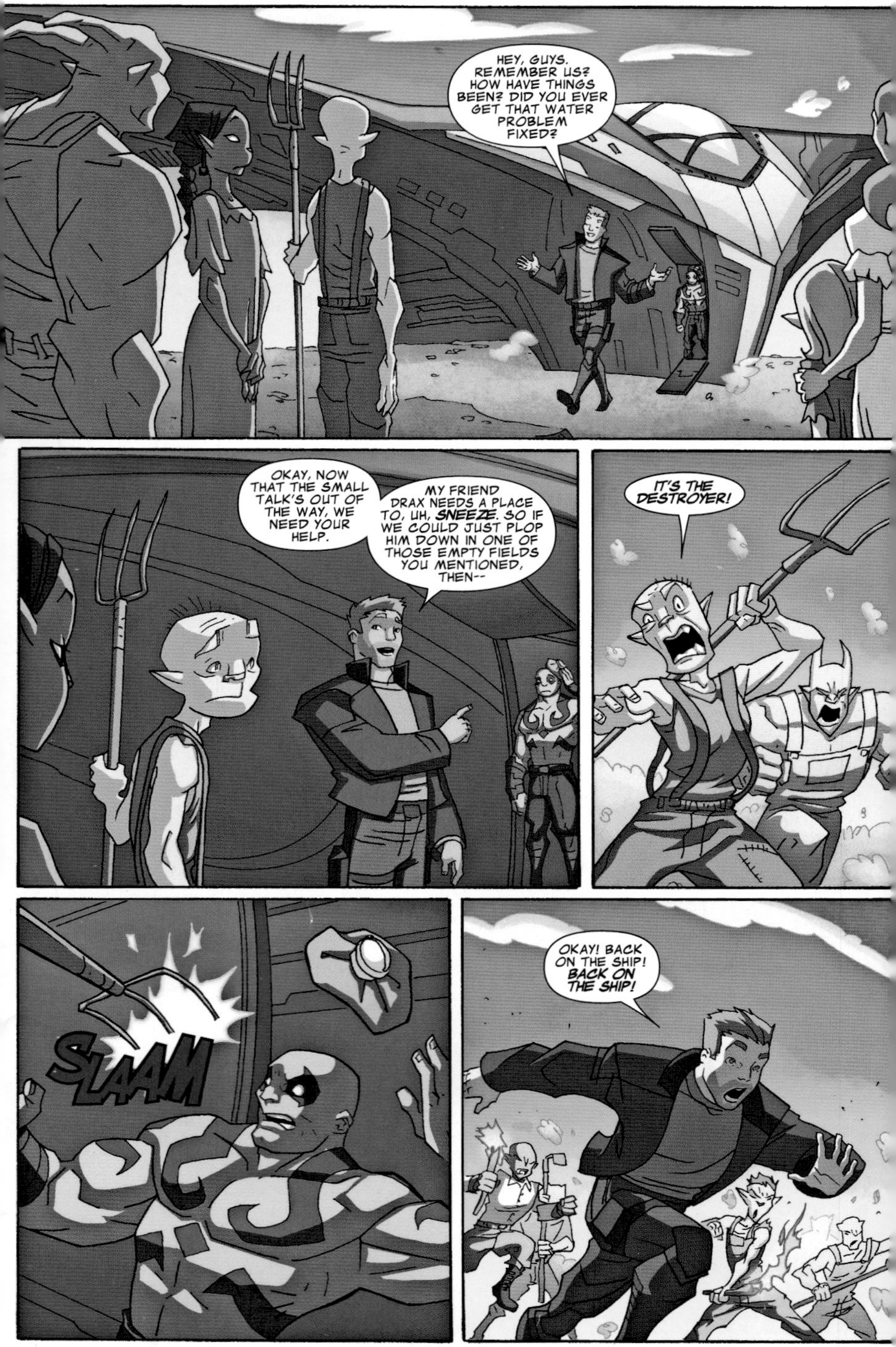
HEY, GUYS. REMEMBER US? HOW HAVE THINGS BEEN? DID YOU EVER GET THAT WATER PROBLEM FIXED?
OKAY, NOW THAT THE SMALL TALK'S OUT OF THE WAY, WE NEED YOUR HELP.
MY FRIEND DRAX NEEDS A PLACE TO, UH, **SNEEZE**. SO IF WE COULD JUST PLOP HIM DOWN IN ONE OF THOSE EMPTY FIELDS YOU MENTIONED, THEN--
IT'S THE DESTROYER!
SLAAM
OKAY! BACK ON THE SHIP! ***BACK ON THE SHIP!***

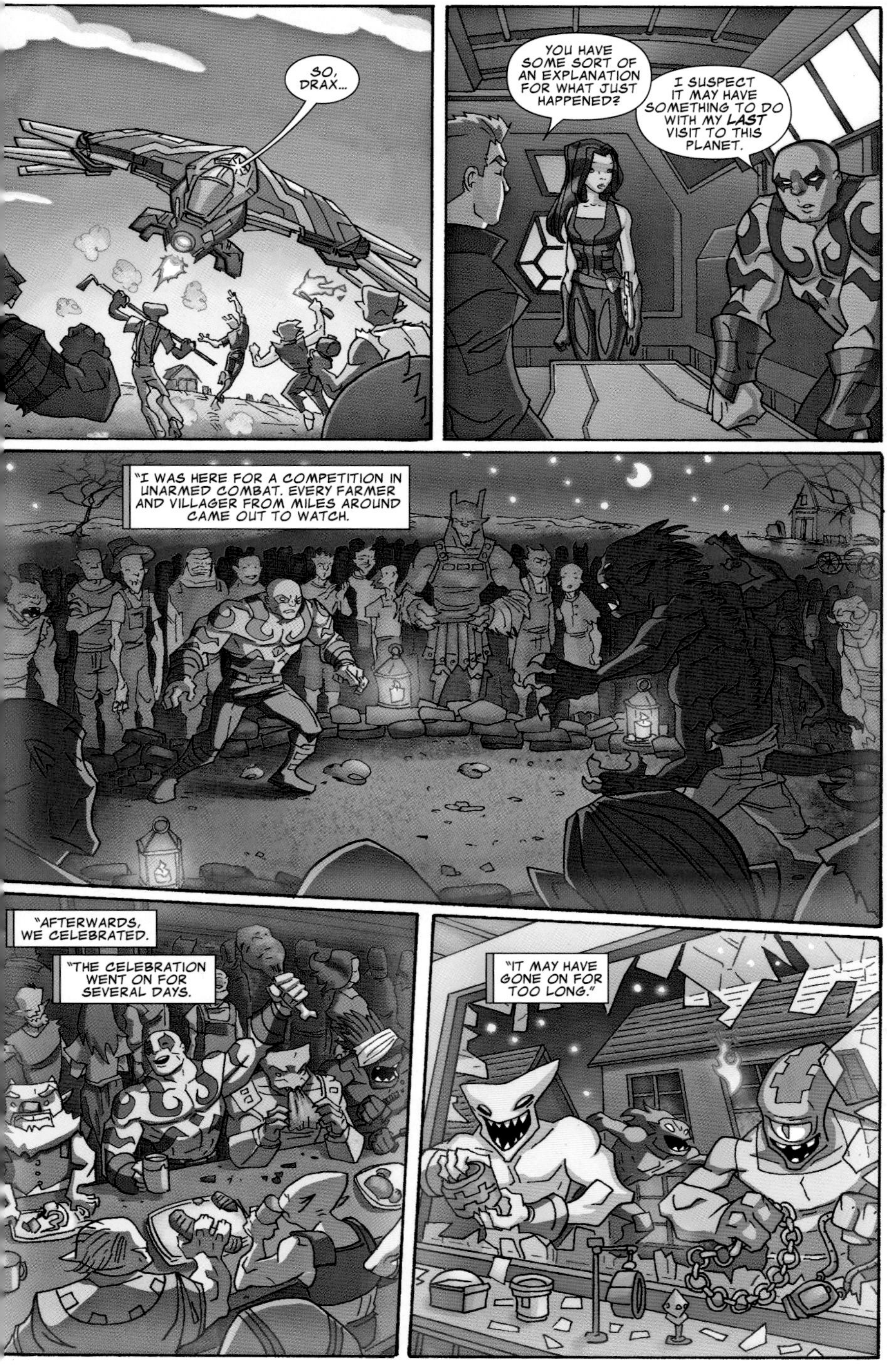
SO, DRAX...
YOU HAVE SOME SORT OF AN EXPLANATION FOR WHAT JUST HAPPENED?
I SUSPECT IT MAY HAVE SOMETHING TO DO WITH MY LAST VISIT TO THIS PLANET.
"I WAS HERE FOR A COMPETITION IN UNARMED COMBAT. EVERY FARMER AND VILLAGER FROM MILES AROUND CAME OUT TO WATCH.
"AFTERWARDS, WE CELEBRATED.
"THE CELEBRATION WENT ON FOR SEVERAL DAYS.
"IT MAY HAVE GONE ON FOR TOO LONG."

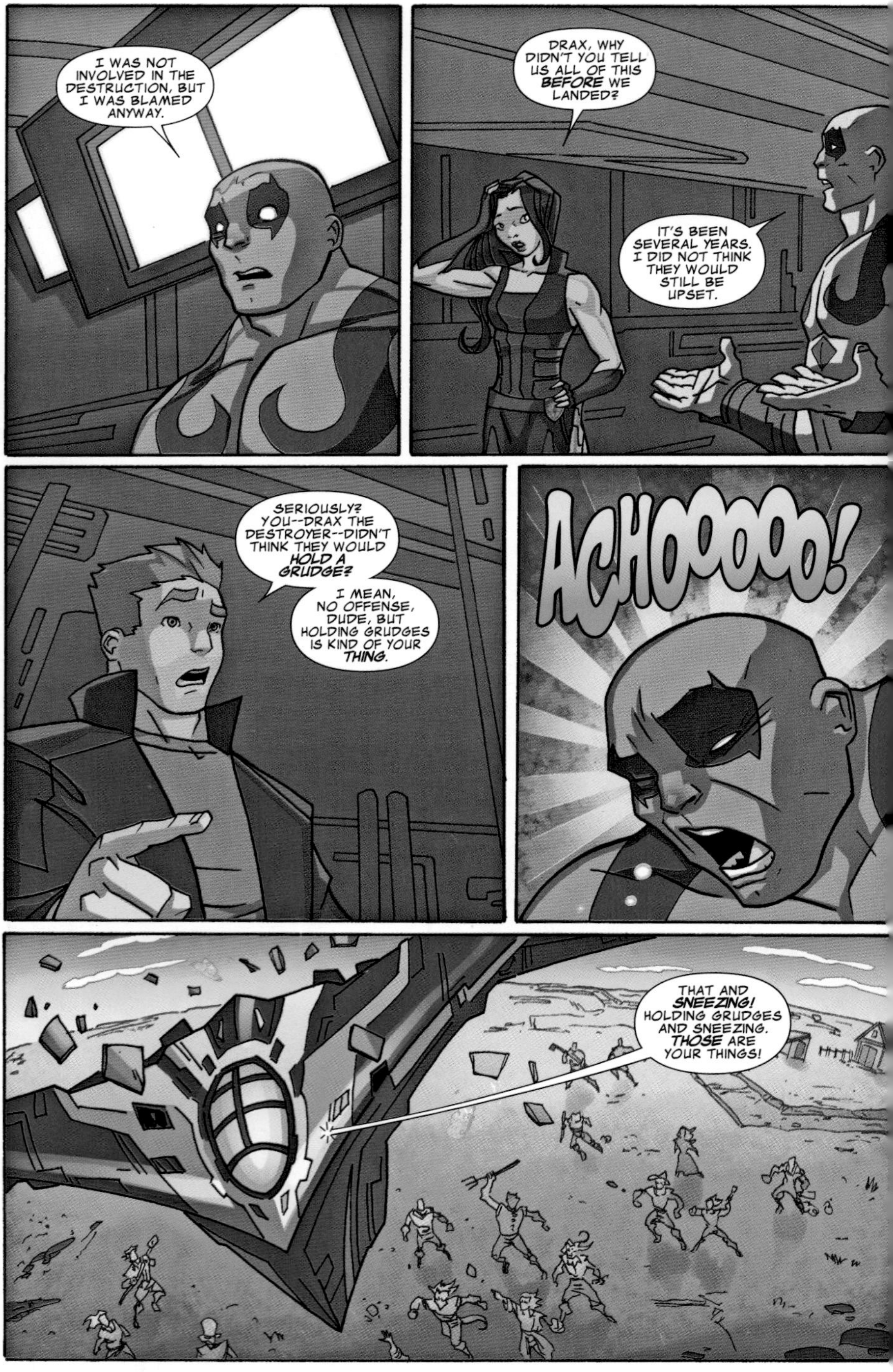
I WAS NOT INVOLVED IN THE DESTRUCTION, BUT I WAS BLAMED ANYWAY.
DRAX, WHY DIDN'T YOU TELL US ALL OF THIS BEFORE WE LANDED?
IT'S BEEN SEVERAL YEARS. I DID NOT THINK THEY WOULD STILL BE UPSET.
SERIOUSLY? YOU--DRAX THE DESTROYER--DIDN'T THINK THEY WOULD HOLD A GRUDGE?
I MEAN, NO OFFENSE, DUDE, BUT HOLDING GRUDGES IS KIND OF YOUR THING.
ACHOOOOO!
THAT AND SNEEZING! HOLDING GRUDGES AND SNEEZING. THOSE ARE YOUR THINGS!

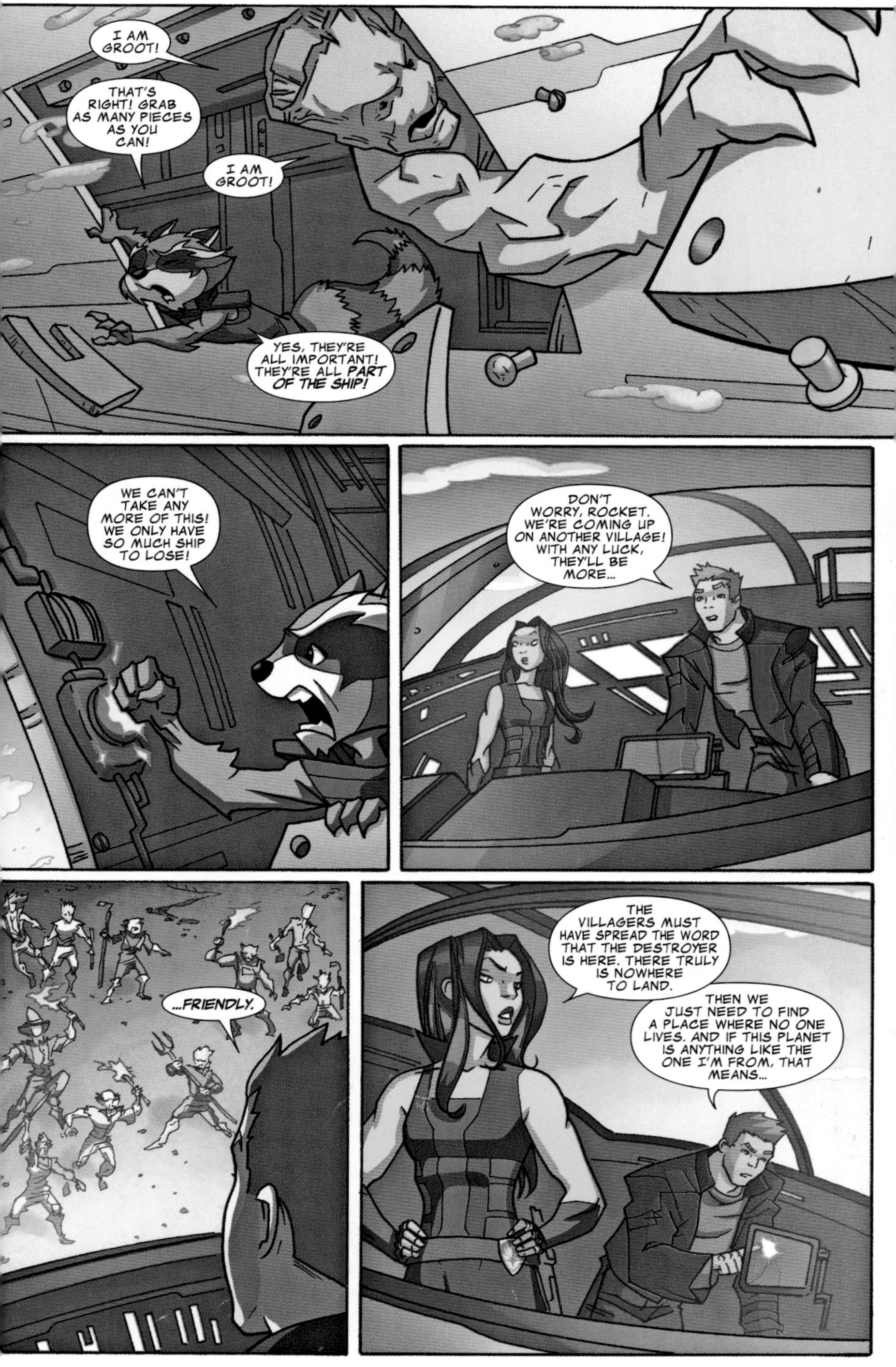
I AM GROOT!
THAT'S RIGHT! GRAB AS MANY PIECES AS YOU CAN!
I AM GROOT!
YES, THEY'RE ALL IMPORTANT! THEY'RE ALL PART OF THE SHIP!
WE CAN'T TAKE ANY MORE OF THIS! WE ONLY HAVE SO MUCH SHIP TO LOSE!
DON'T WORRY, ROCKET. WE'RE COMING UP ON ANOTHER VILLAGE! WITH ANY LUCK, THEY'LL BE MORE...
...FRIENDLY.
THE VILLAGERS MUST HAVE SPREAD THE WORD THAT THE DESTROYER IS HERE. THERE TRULY IS NOWHERE TO LAND.
THEN WE JUST NEED TO FIND A PLACE WHERE NO ONE LIVES. AND IF THIS PLANET IS ANYTHING LIKE THE ONE I'M FROM, THAT MEANS...

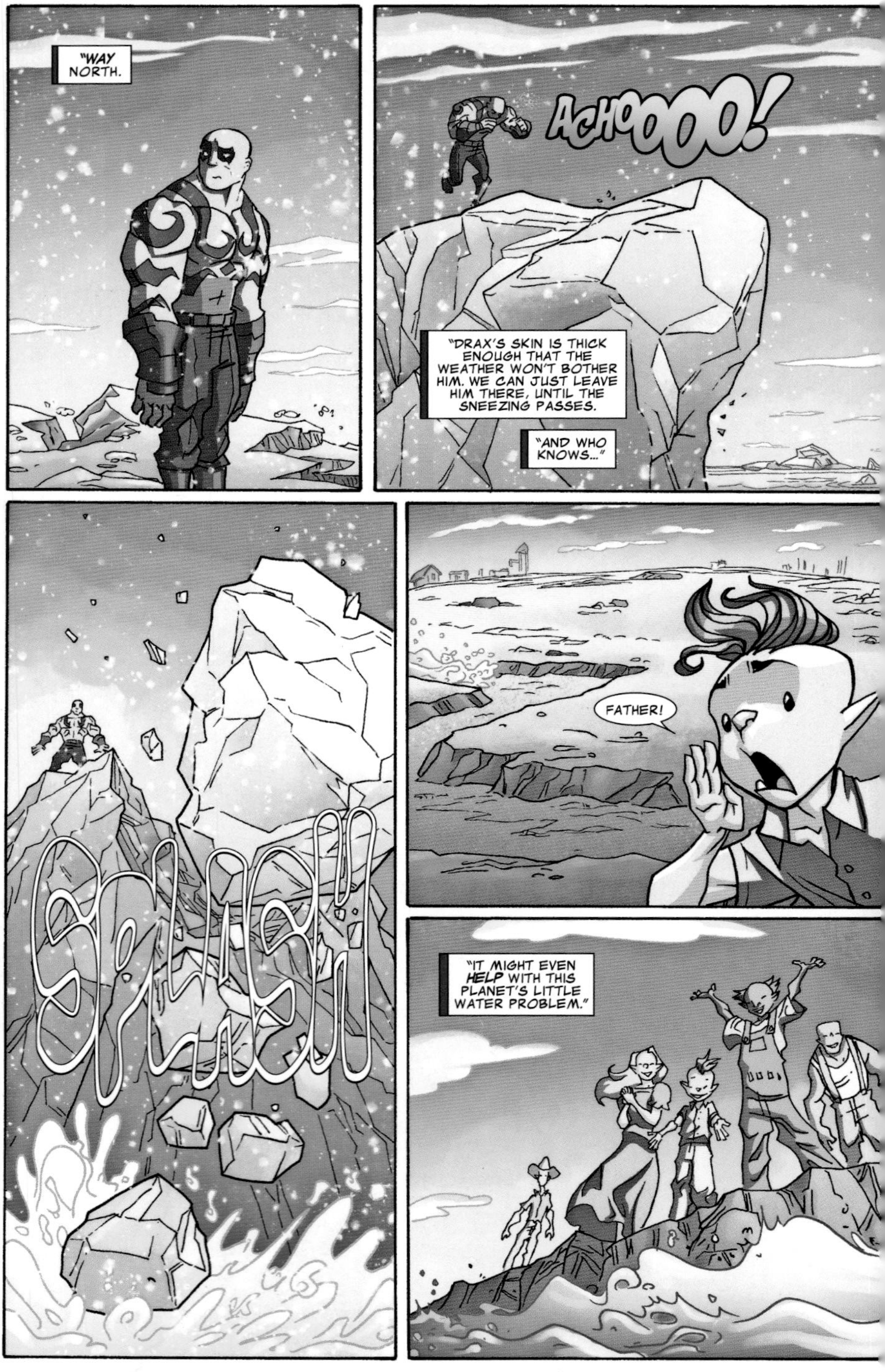
"WAY NORTH.
ACHOOOOO!
"DRAX'S SKIN IS THICK ENOUGH THAT THE WEATHER WON'T BOTHER HIM. WE CAN JUST LEAVE HIM THERE, UNTIL THE SNEEZING PASSES.
"AND WHO KNOWS..."
SPLASH!
FATHER!
"IT MIGHT EVEN HELP WITH THIS PLANET'S LITTLE WATER PROBLEM."

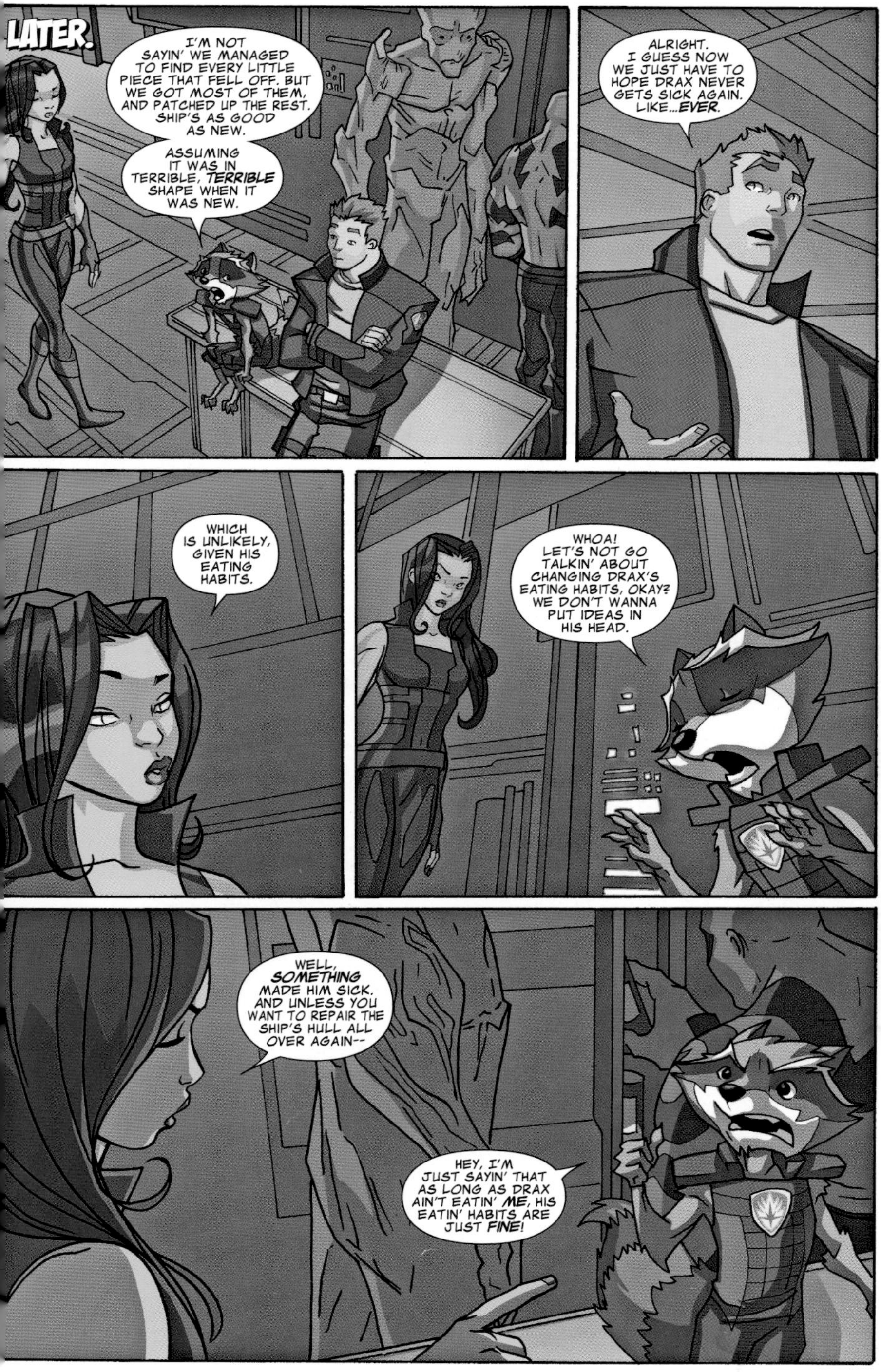
LATER.
I'M NOT SAYIN' WE MANAGED TO FIND EVERY LITTLE PIECE THAT FELL OFF. BUT WE GOT MOST OF THEM, AND PATCHED UP THE REST. SHIP'S AS GOOD AS NEW.
ASSUMING IT WAS IN TERRIBLE, *TERRIBLE* SHAPE WHEN IT WAS NEW.
ALRIGHT. I GUESS NOW WE JUST HAVE TO HOPE DRAX NEVER GETS SICK AGAIN. LIKE...*EVER*.
WHICH IS UNLIKELY, GIVEN HIS EATING HABITS.
WHOA! LET'S NOT GO TALKIN' ABOUT CHANGING DRAX'S EATING HABITS, OKAY? WE DON'T WANNA PUT IDEAS IN HIS HEAD.
WELL, *SOMETHING* MADE HIM SICK. AND UNLESS YOU WANT TO REPAIR THE SHIP'S HULL ALL OVER AGAIN--
HEY, I'M JUST SAYIN' THAT AS LONG AS DRAX AIN'T EATIN' *ME*, HIS EATIN' HABITS ARE JUST *FINE*!

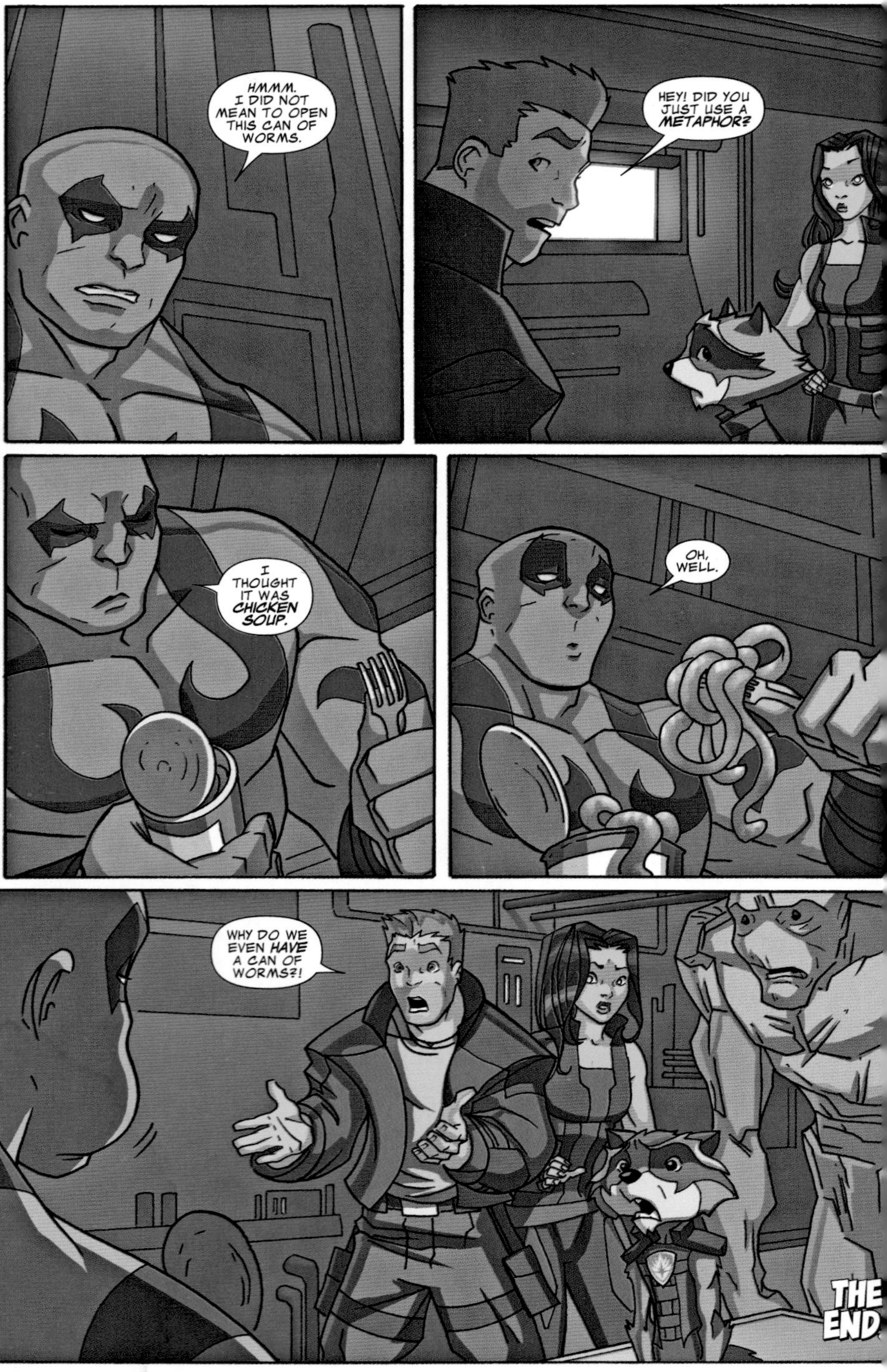
HMMM. I DID NOT MEAN TO OPEN THIS CAN OF WORMS.
HEY! DID YOU JUST USE A *METAPHOR?*
I THOUGHT IT WAS *CHICKEN SOUP.*
OH, WELL.
WHY DO WE EVEN *HAVE* A CAN OF WORMS?!
THE END.

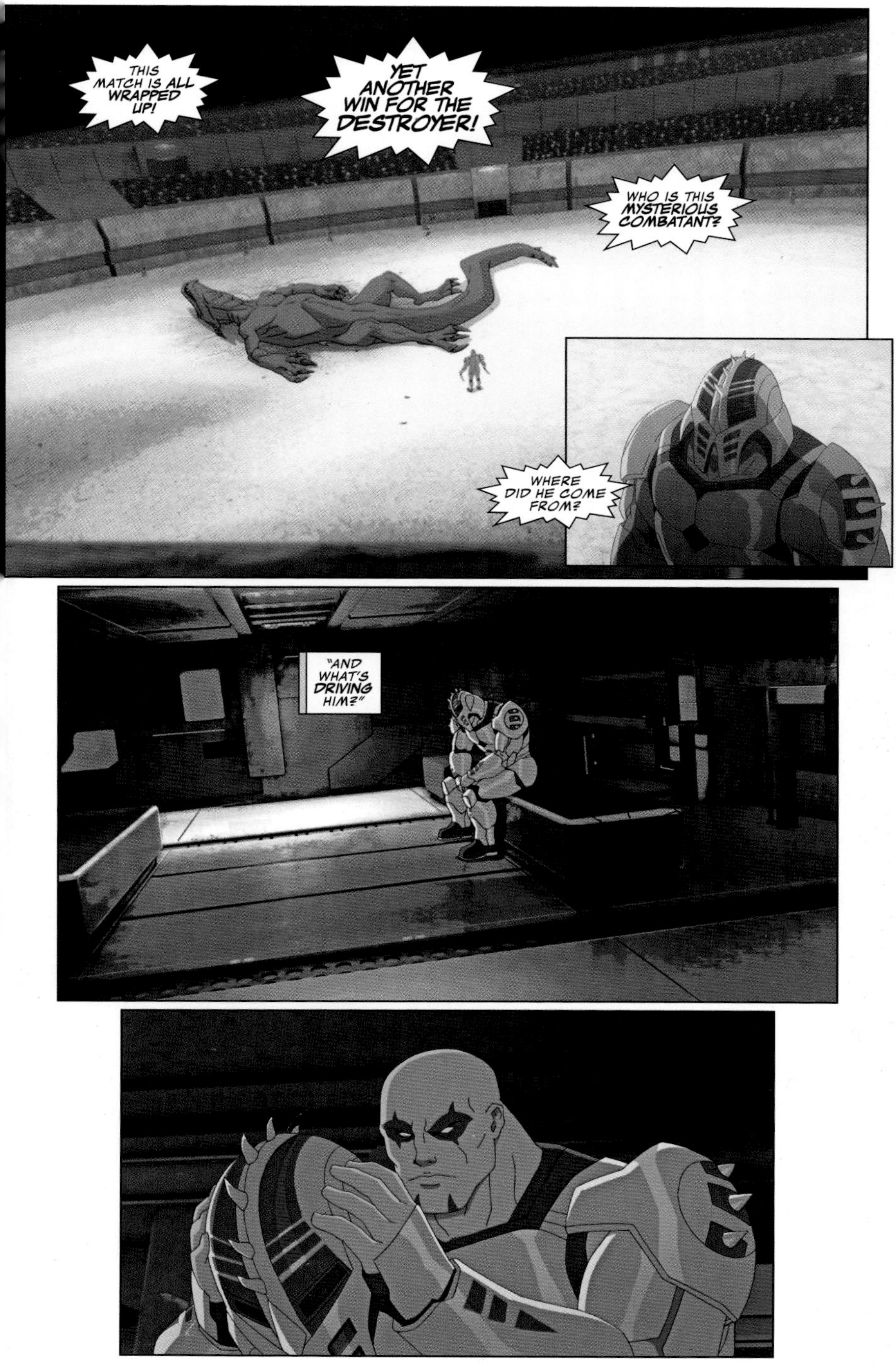
THIS MATCH IS ALL WRAPPED UP!
YET ANOTHER WIN FOR THE DESTROYER!
WHO IS THIS MYSTERIOUS COMBATANT?
WHERE DID HE COME FROM?
"AND WHAT'S DRIVING HIM?"

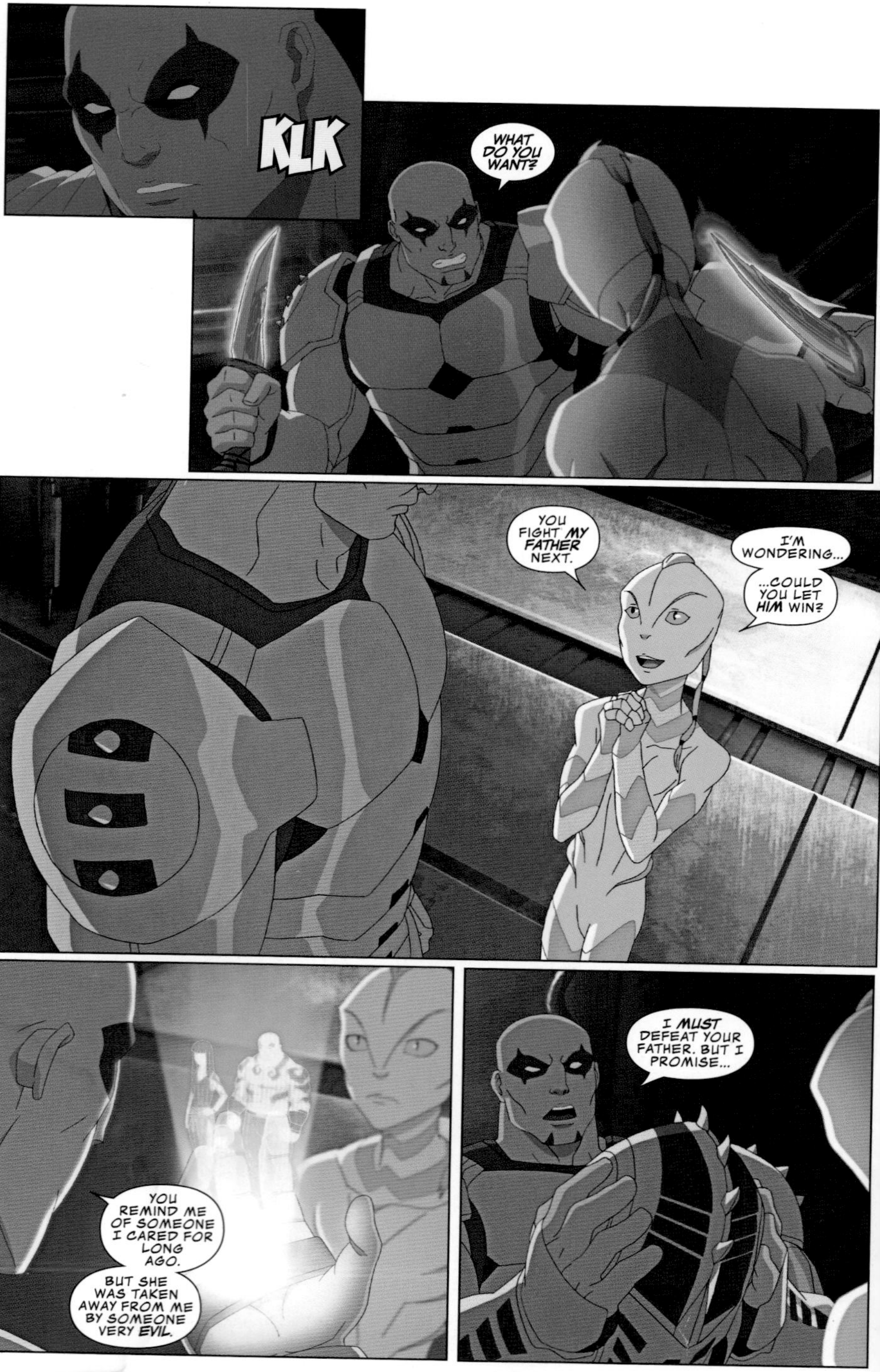
KLK
WHAT DO YOU WANT?
YOU FIGHT MY FATHER NEXT.
I'M WONDERING...
...COULD YOU LET HIM WIN?
YOU REMIND ME OF SOMEONE I CARED FOR LONG AGO.
BUT SHE WAS TAKEN AWAY FROM ME BY SOMEONE VERY EVIL.
I MUST DEFEAT YOUR FATHER. BUT I PROMISE...

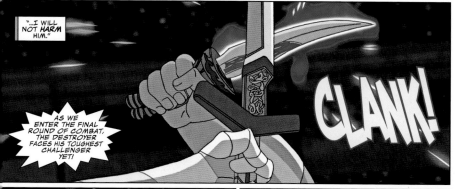

"...I WILL NOT **HARM** HIM."

AS WE ENTER THE FINAL ROUND OF COMBAT, THE DESTROYER FACES HIS TOUGHEST CHALLENGER YET!

CLANK!

WHOOSH!

WHOOSH!

NO SURPRISE SINCE THERE'S A LOT AT STAKE!

THE CHAMPION WILL EARN THE RIGHT TO SERVE AS ENFORCER AND STAND AT THE RIGHT HAND OF **RONAN THE ACCUSER!**

CLANK!

CLINK!

HNN!

WHUDD!

IT'S ALL OVER BUT THE SLAYING--

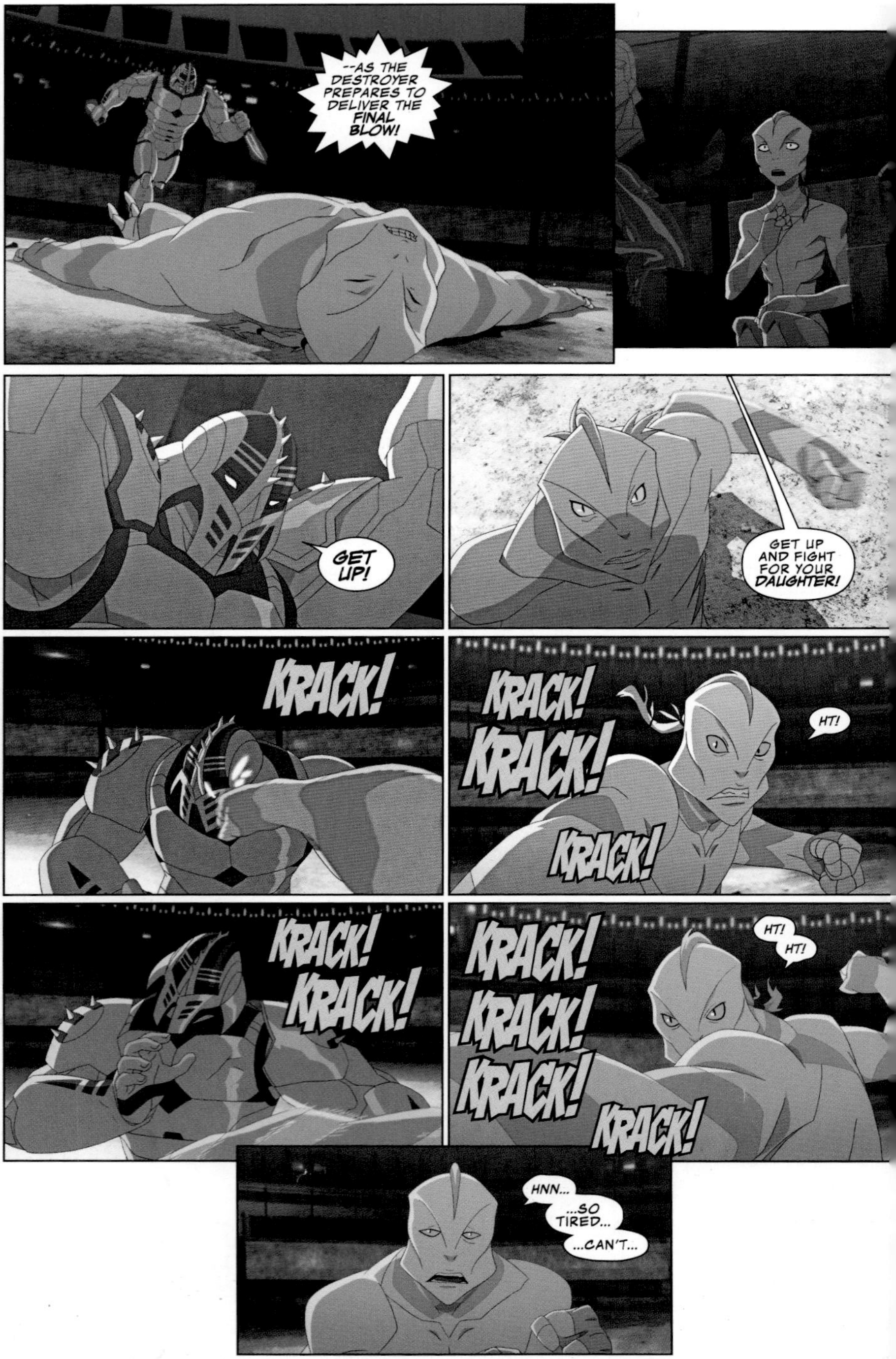
--AS THE DESTROYER PREPARES TO DELIVER THE FINAL BLOW!
GET UP!
GET UP AND FIGHT FOR YOUR DAUGHTER!
KRACK!
KRACK!
KRACK!
HT!
KRACK!
KRACK!
KRACK!
KRACK!
KRACK!
HT! HT!
KRACK!
KRACK!
HNN...
...SO TIRED...
...CAN'T...

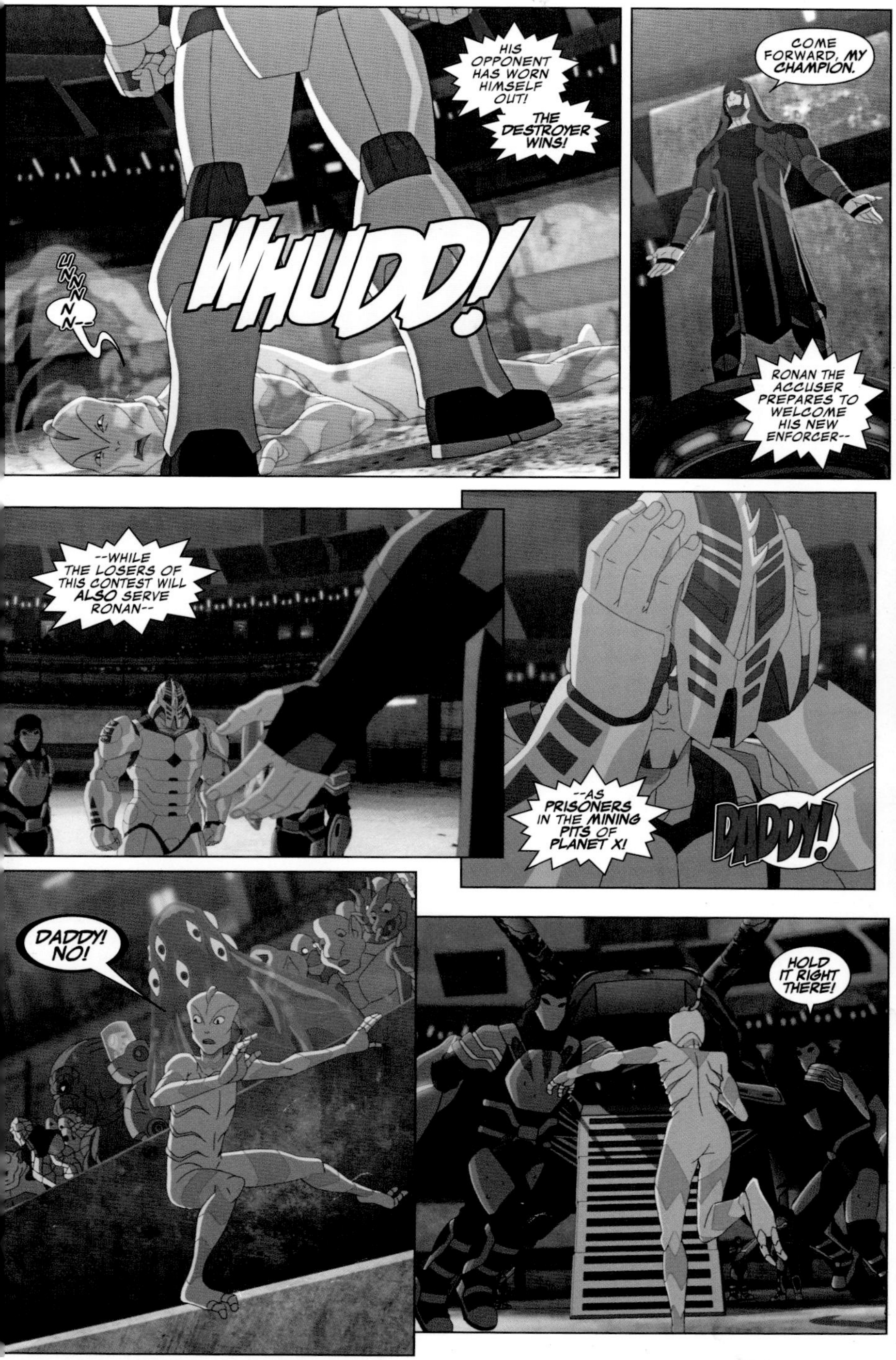
HIS OPPONENT HAS WORN HIMSELF OUT!
THE DESTROYER WINS!
WHUDD!
UNNNNN--
COME FORWARD, MY CHAMPION.
RONAN THE ACCUSER PREPARES TO WELCOME HIS NEW ENFORCER--
--WHILE THE LOSERS OF THIS CONTEST WILL ALSO SERVE RONAN--
--AS PRISONERS IN THE MINING PITS OF PLANET X!
DADDY!
DADDY! NO!
HOLD IT RIGHT THERE!

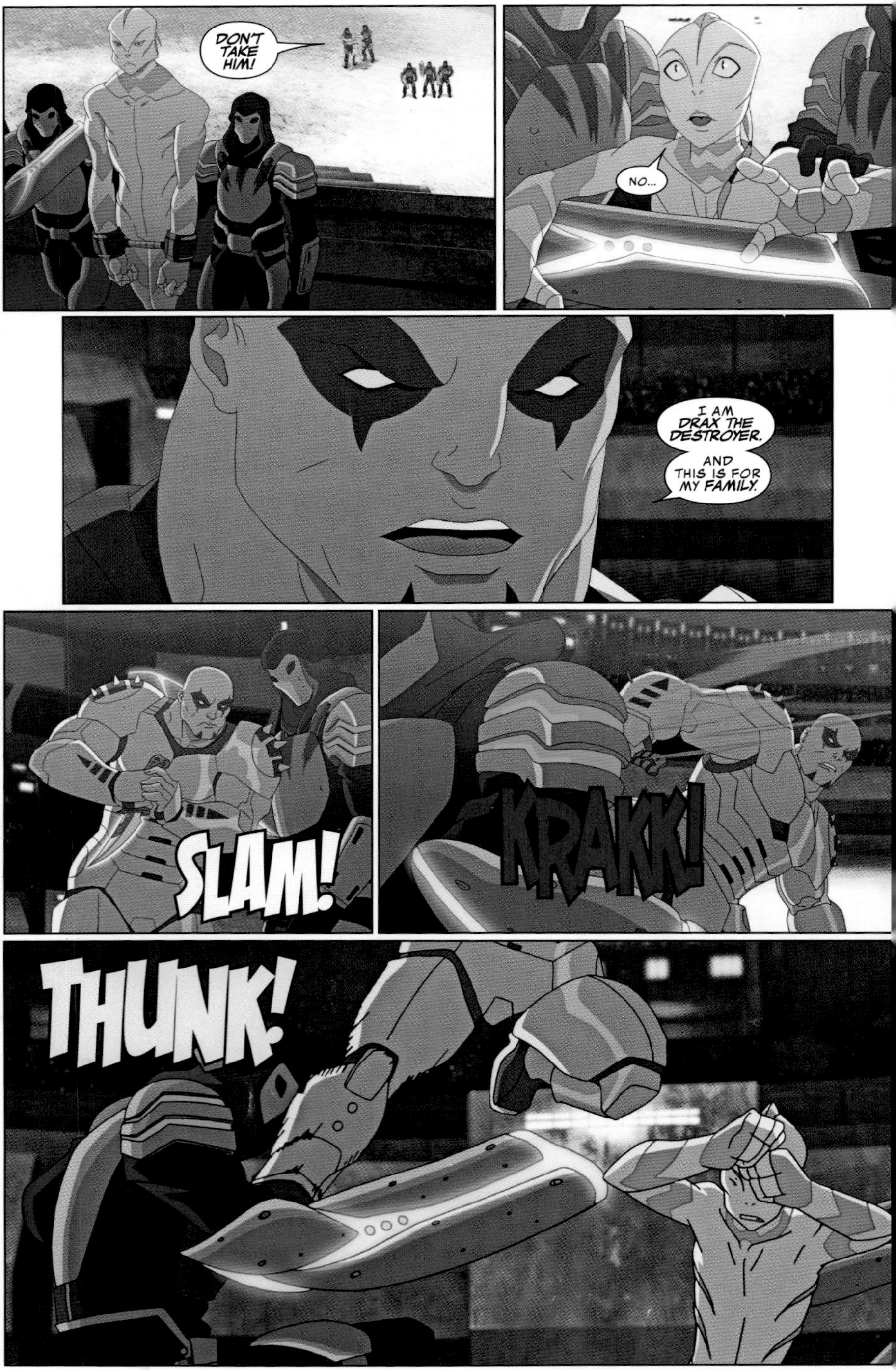
DON'T TAKE HIM!
NO...
I AM DRAX THE DESTROYER.
AND THIS IS FOR MY FAMILY.
SLAM!
KRAKK!
THUNK!

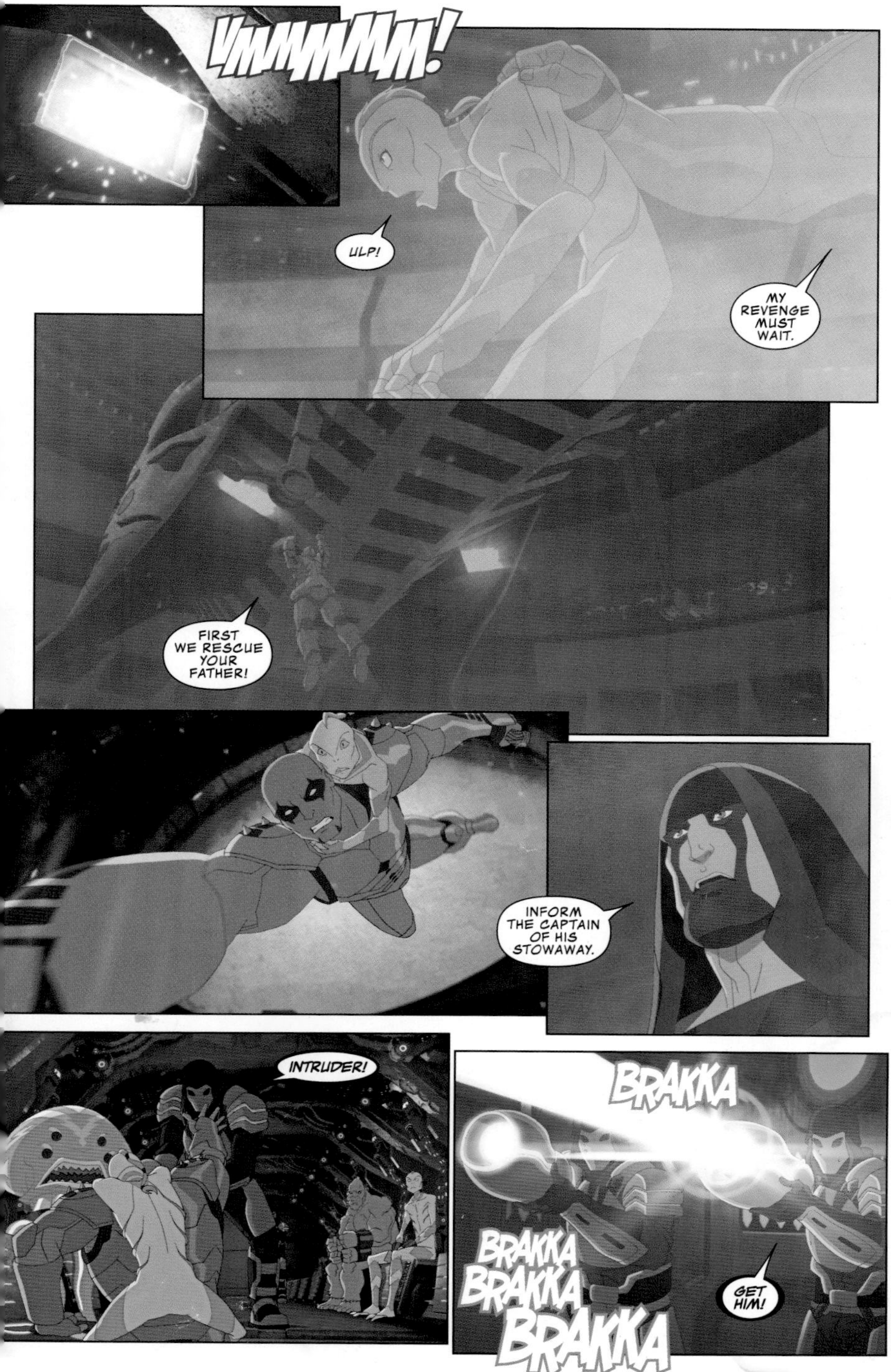
VMMMMMM!
ULP!
MY REVENGE MUST WAIT.
FIRST WE RESCUE YOUR FATHER!
INFORM THE CAPTAIN OF HIS STOWAWAY.
INTRUDER!
BRAKKA
BRAKKA
BRAKKA
BRAKKA
GET HIM!

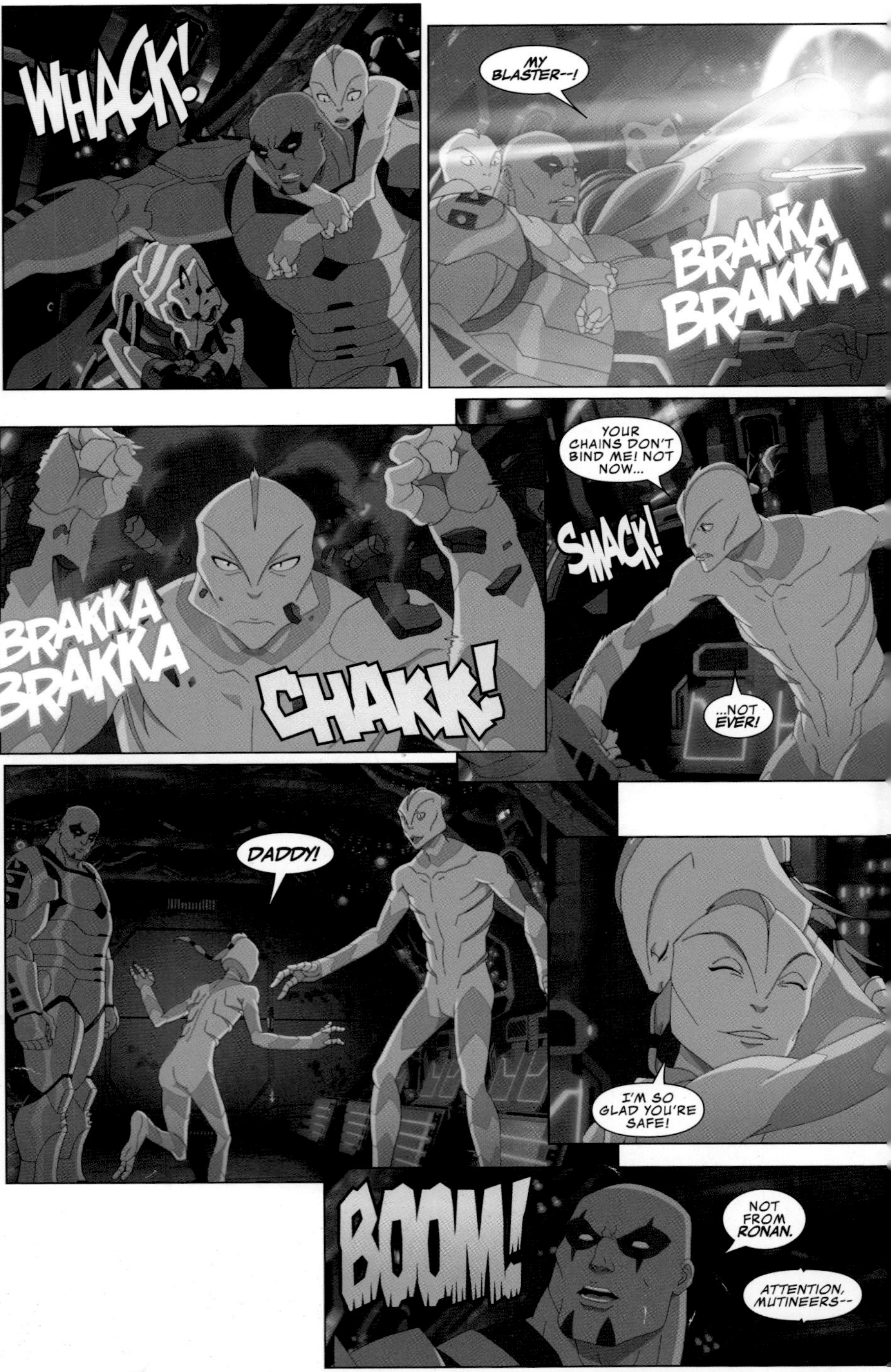
WHACK!
MY BLASTER--!
BRAKKA BRAKKA
BRAKKA BRAKKA
CHAKK!
YOUR CHAINS DON'T BIND ME! NOT NOW...
SMACK!
...NOT EVER!
DADDY!
I'M SO GLAD YOU'RE SAFE!
BOOM!
NOT FROM RONAN.
ATTENTION, MUTINEERS--

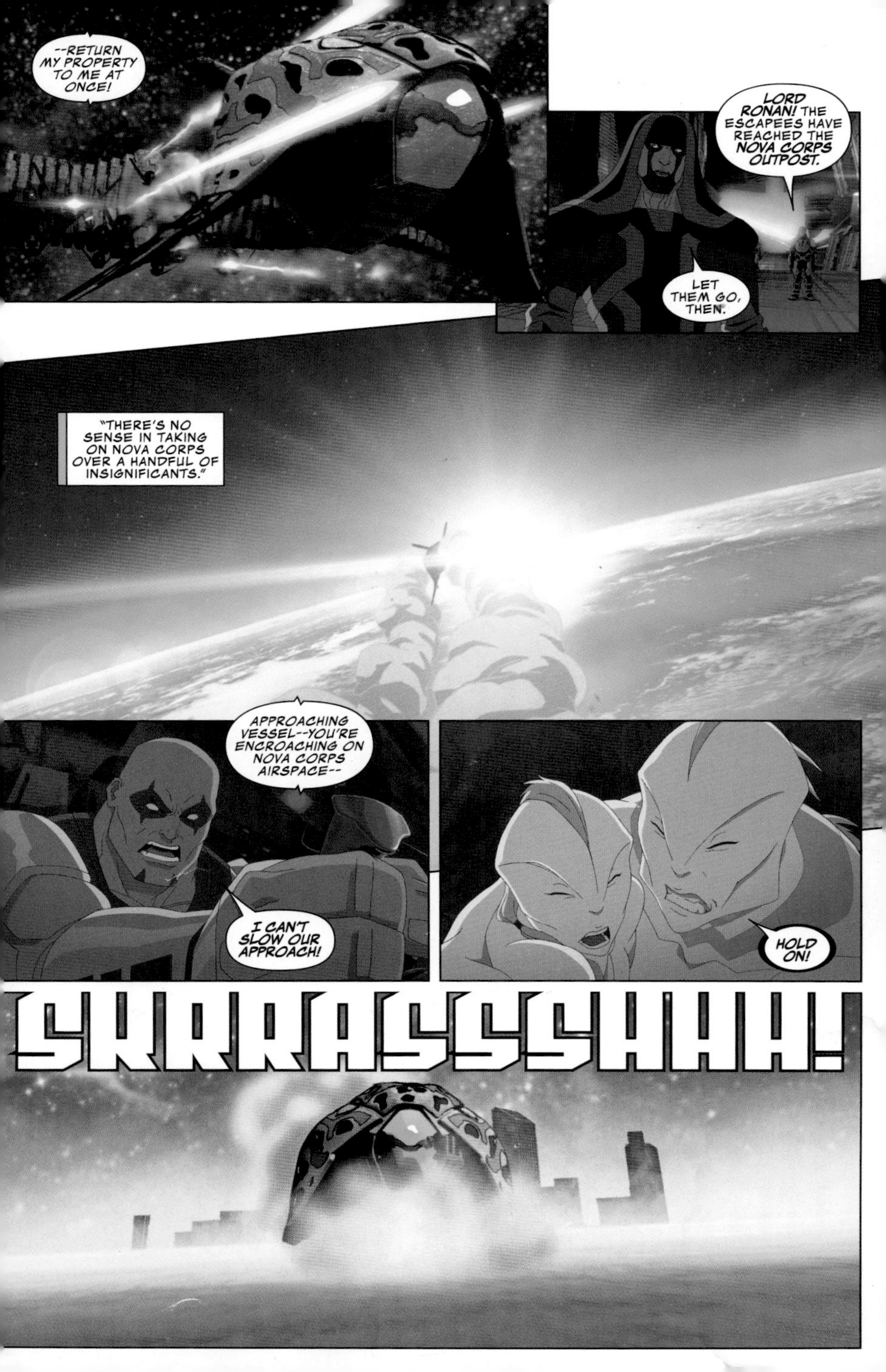
--RETURN MY PROPERTY TO ME AT ONCE!
LORD RONAN! THE ESCAPEES HAVE REACHED THE NOVA CORPS OUTPOST.
LET THEM GO, THEN.
"THERE'S NO SENSE IN TAKING ON NOVA CORPS OVER A HANDFUL OF INSIGNIFICANTS."
APPROACHING VESSEL--YOU'RE ENCROACHING ON NOVA CORPS AIRSPACE--
I CAN'T SLOW OUR APPROACH!
HOLD ON!
SKRRASSSHHH!

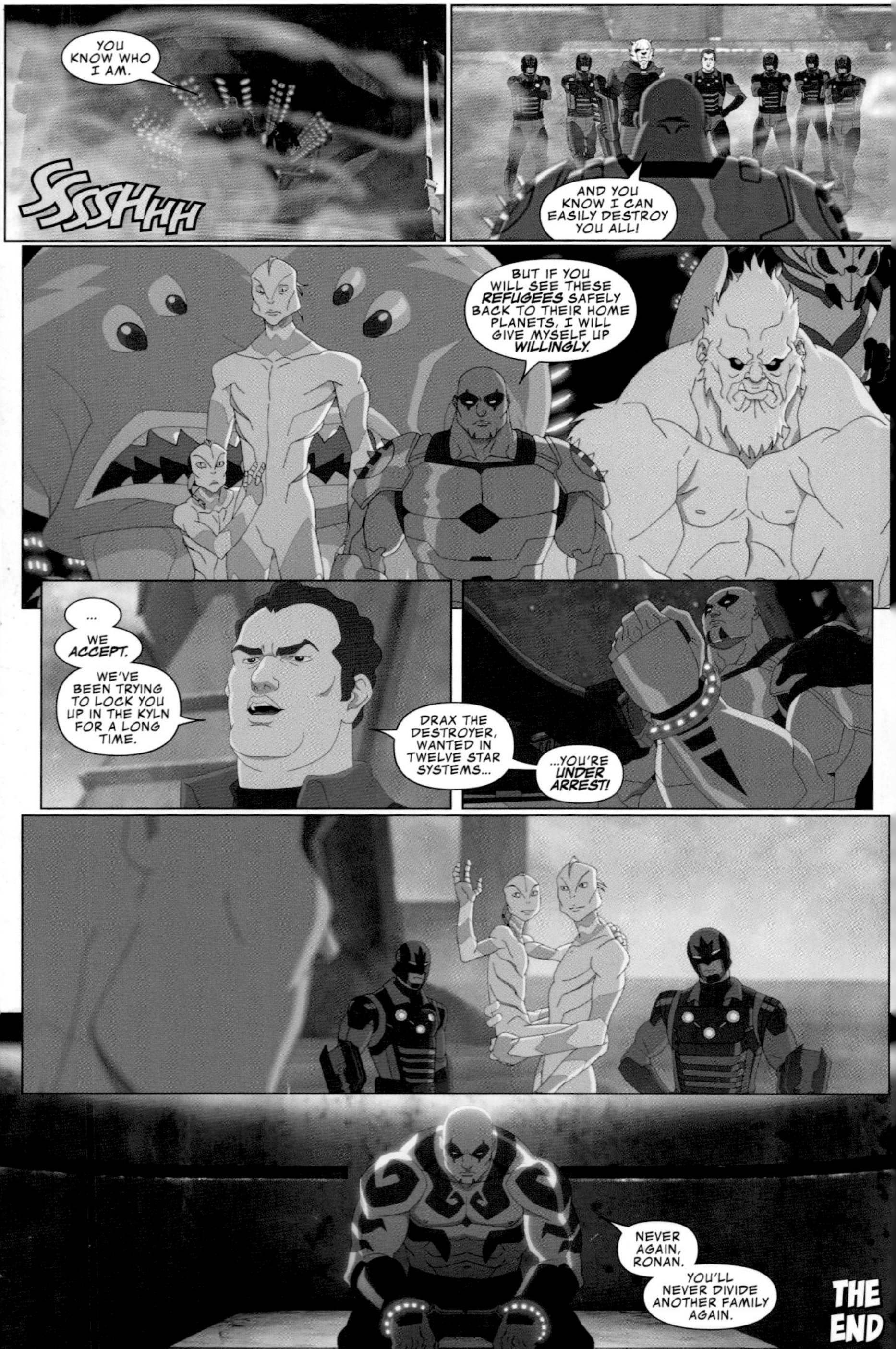

YOU KNOW WHO I AM.
SSSSHHH
AND YOU KNOW I CAN EASILY DESTROY YOU ALL!
BUT IF YOU WILL SEE THESE REFUGEES SAFELY BACK TO THEIR HOME PLANETS, I WILL GIVE MYSELF UP WILLINGLY.
...
WE ACCEPT.
WE'VE BEEN TRYING TO LOCK YOU UP IN THE KYLN FOR A LONG TIME.
DRAX THE DESTROYER, WANTED IN TWELVE STAR SYSTEMS...
...YOU'RE UNDER ARREST!
NEVER AGAIN, RONAN.
YOU'LL NEVER DIVIDE ANOTHER FAMILY AGAIN.
THE END

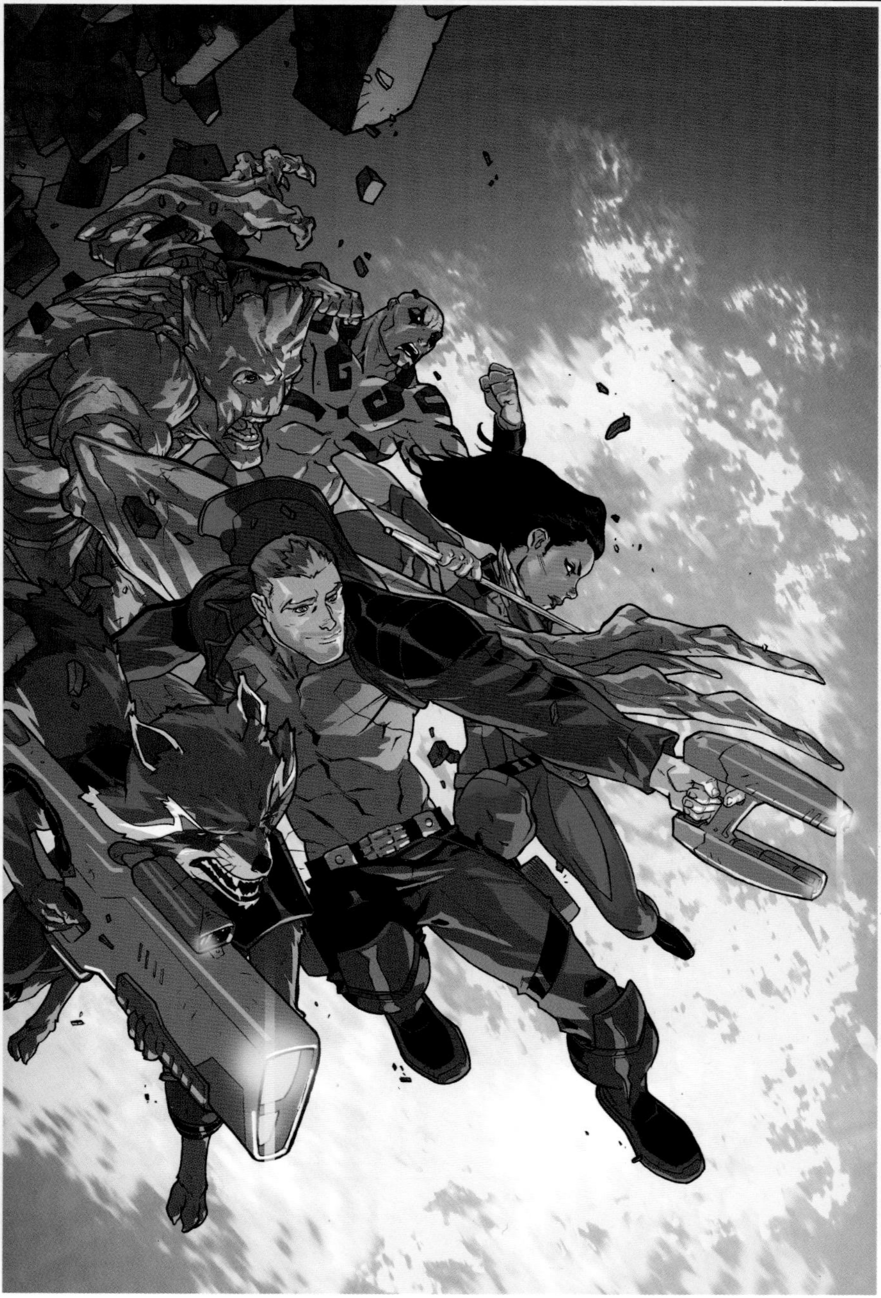

4

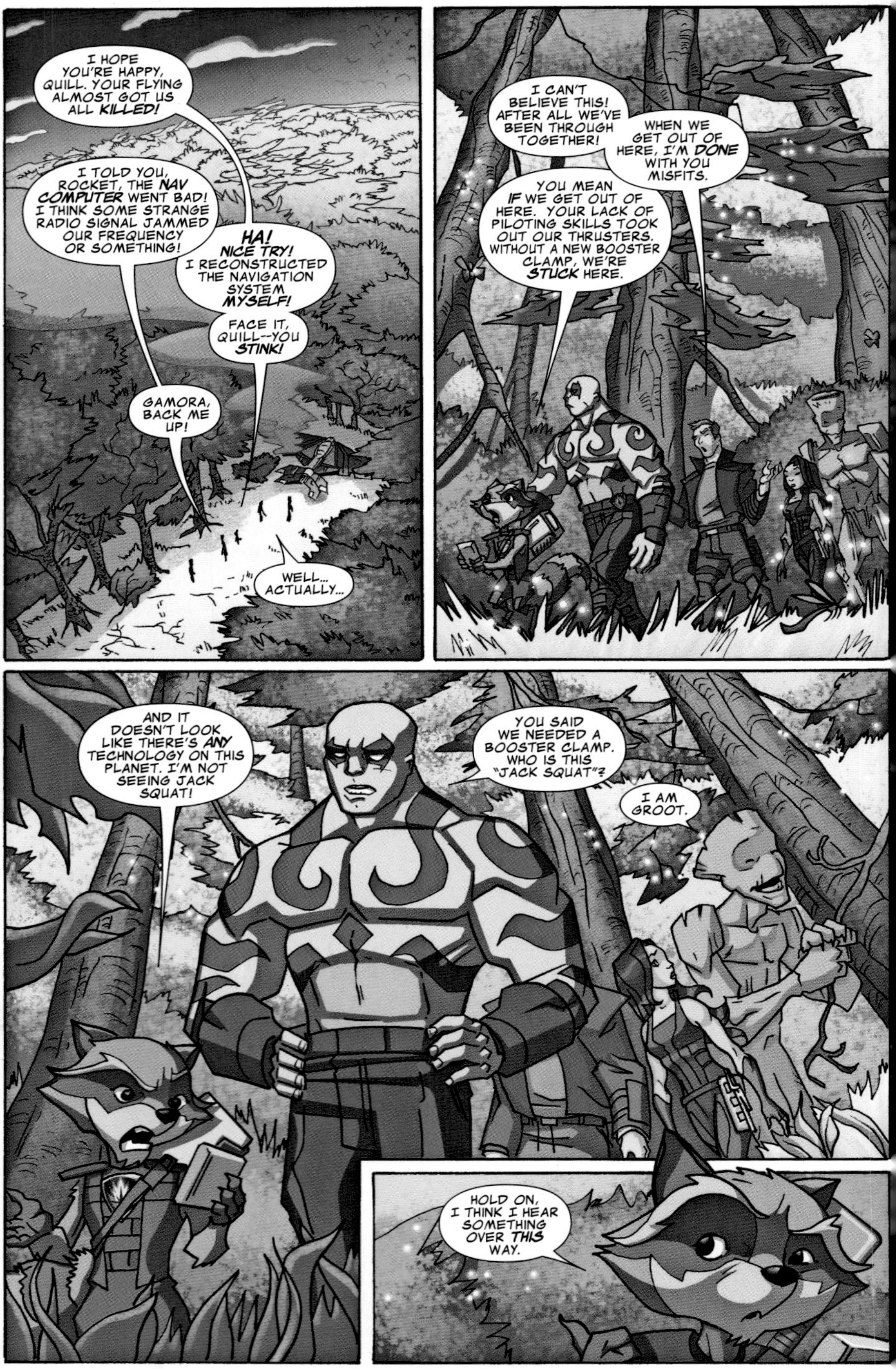
I HOPE YOU'RE HAPPY, QUILL. YOUR FLYING ALMOST GOT US ALL KILLED!
I TOLD YOU, ROCKET, THE NAV COMPUTER WENT BAD! I THINK SOME STRANGE RADIO SIGNAL JAMMED OUR FREQUENCY OR SOMETHING!
HA! NICE TRY! I RECONSTRUCTED THE NAVIGATION SYSTEM MYSELF!
FACE IT, QUILL--YOU STINK!
GAMORA, BACK ME UP!
WELL... ACTUALLY...
I CAN'T BELIEVE THIS! AFTER ALL WE'VE BEEN THROUGH TOGETHER!
WHEN WE GET OUT OF HERE, I'M DONE WITH YOU MISFITS.
YOU MEAN IF WE GET OUT OF HERE. YOUR LACK OF PILOTING SKILLS TOOK OUT OUR THRUSTERS. WITHOUT A NEW BOOSTER CLAMP, WE'RE STUCK HERE.
AND IT DOESN'T LOOK LIKE THERE'S ANY TECHNOLOGY ON THIS PLANET. I'M NOT SEEING JACK SQUAT!
YOU SAID WE NEEDED A BOOSTER CLAMP. WHO IS THIS "JACK SQUAT"?
I AM GROOT.
HOLD ON, I THINK I HEAR SOMETHING OVER THIS WAY.

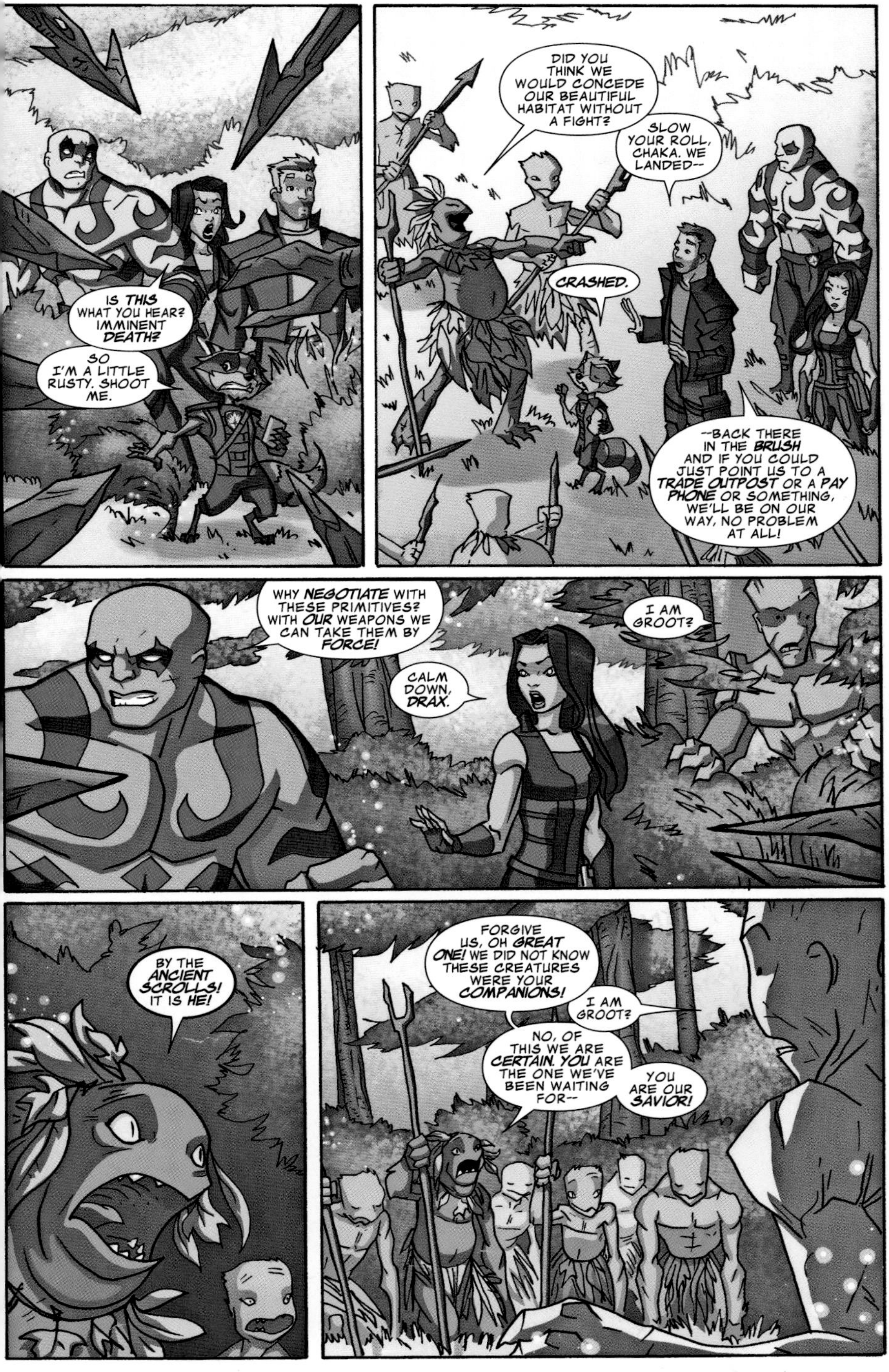
IS THIS WHAT YOU HEAR? IMMINENT DEATH?
SO I'M A LITTLE RUSTY. SHOOT ME.
DID YOU THINK WE WOULD CONCEDE OUR BEAUTIFUL HABITAT WITHOUT A FIGHT?
SLOW YOUR ROLL, CHAKA. WE LANDED--
CRASHED.
--BACK THERE IN THE BRUSH AND IF YOU COULD JUST POINT US TO A TRADE OUTPOST OR A PAY PHONE OR SOMETHING, WE'LL BE ON OUR WAY, NO PROBLEM AT ALL!
WHY NEGOTIATE WITH THESE PRIMITIVES? WITH OUR WEAPONS WE CAN TAKE THEM BY FORCE!
CALM DOWN, DRAX.
I AM GROOT?
BY THE ANCIENT SCROLLS! IT IS HE!
FORGIVE US, OH GREAT ONE! WE DID NOT KNOW THESE CREATURES WERE YOUR COMPANIONS!
I AM GROOT?
NO, OF THIS WE ARE CERTAIN. YOU ARE THE ONE WE'VE BEEN WAITING FOR--
YOU ARE OUR SAVIOR!

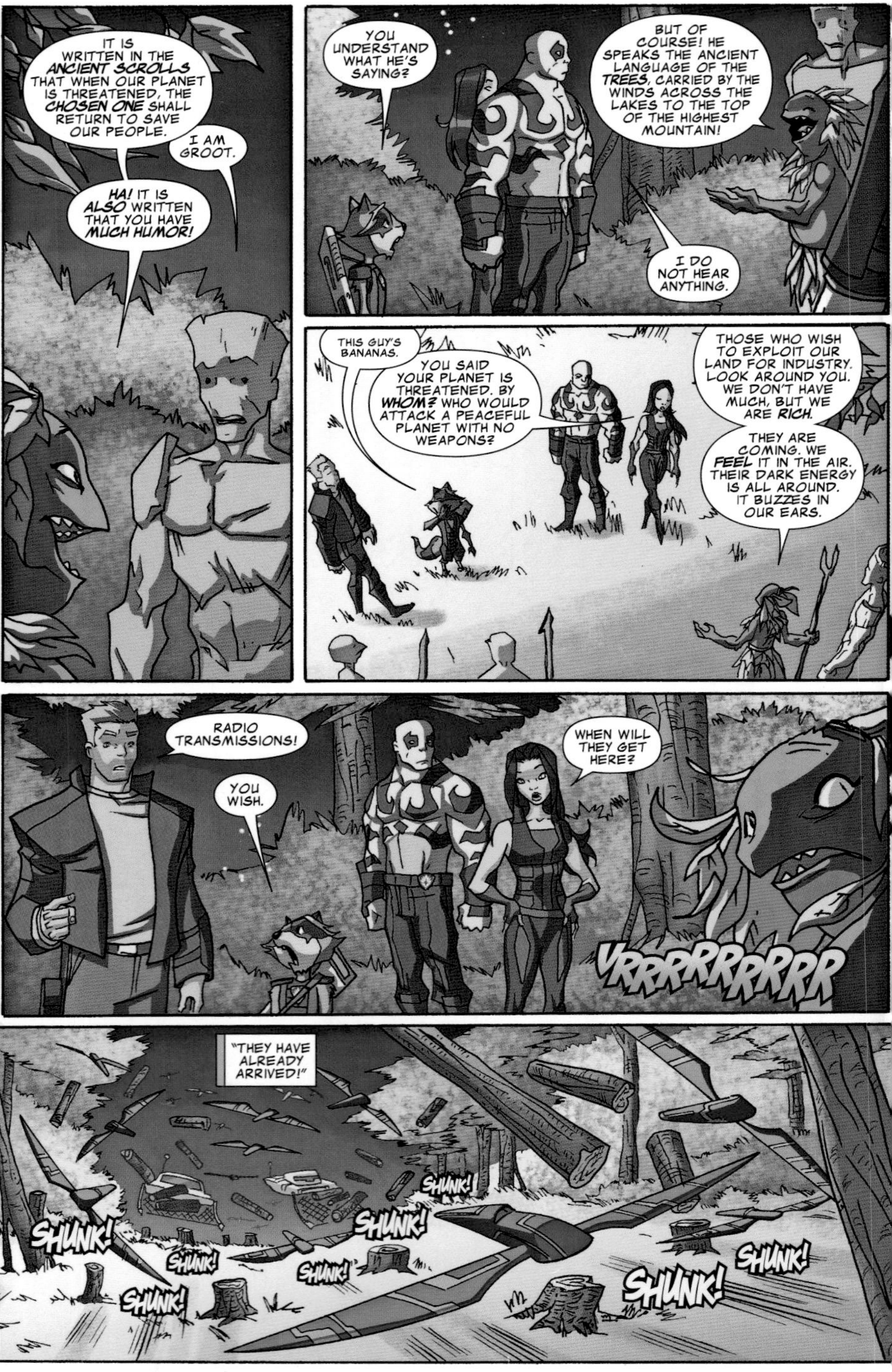
IT IS WRITTEN IN THE ANCIENT SCROLLS THAT WHEN OUR PLANET IS THREATENED, THE CHOSEN ONE SHALL RETURN TO SAVE OUR PEOPLE.
I AM GROOT.
HA! IT IS ALSO WRITTEN THAT YOU HAVE MUCH HUMOR!
YOU UNDERSTAND WHAT HE'S SAYING?
BUT OF COURSE! HE SPEAKS THE ANCIENT LANGUAGE OF THE TREES, CARRIED BY THE WINDS ACROSS THE LAKES TO THE TOP OF THE HIGHEST MOUNTAIN!
I DO NOT HEAR ANYTHING.
THIS GUY'S BANANAS.
YOU SAID YOUR PLANET IS THREATENED. BY WHOM? WHO WOULD ATTACK A PEACEFUL PLANET WITH NO WEAPONS?
THOSE WHO WISH TO EXPLOIT OUR LAND FOR INDUSTRY. LOOK AROUND YOU. WE DON'T HAVE MUCH, BUT WE ARE RICH.
THEY ARE COMING. WE FEEL IT IN THE AIR. THEIR DARK ENERGY IS ALL AROUND. IT BUZZES IN OUR EARS.
RADIO TRANSMISSIONS!
YOU WISH.
WHEN WILL THEY GET HERE?
VRRRRRRRRRR
"THEY HAVE ALREADY ARRIVED!"
SHUNK!
SHUNK!
SHUNK!
SHUNK!
SHUNK!
SHUNK!
SHUNK!

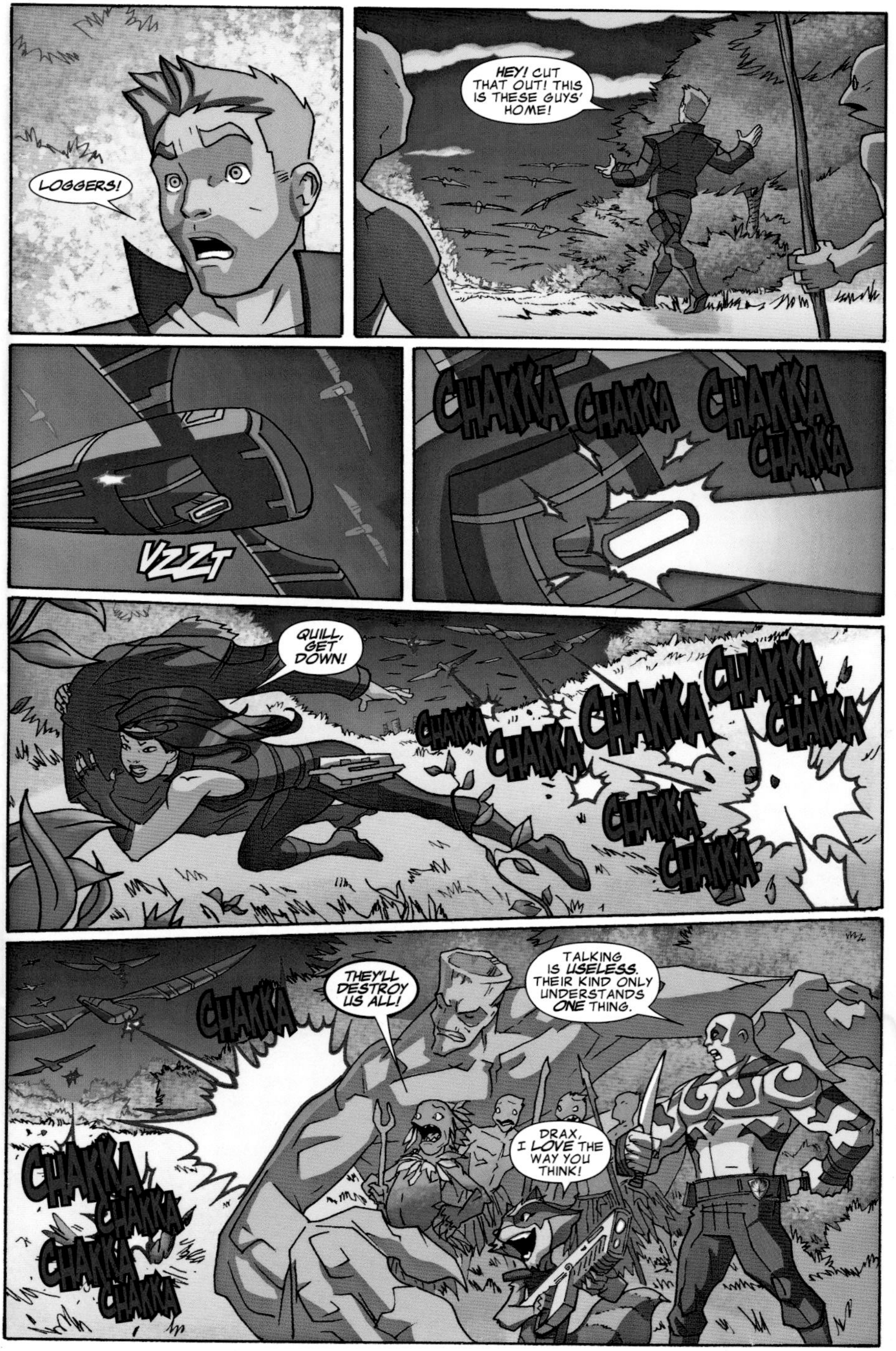

LOGGERS!
HEY! CUT THAT OUT! THIS IS THESE GUYS' HOME!
VZZT
CHAKKA CHAKKA CHAKKA CHAKKA
QUILL, GET DOWN!
CHAKKA CHAKKA CHAKKA CHAKKA CHAKKA CHAKKA CHAKKA
CHAKKA
THEY'LL DESTROY US ALL!
TALKING IS USELESS. THEIR KIND ONLY UNDERSTANDS ONE THING.
DRAX, I LOVE THE WAY YOU THINK!
CHAKKA CHAKKA CHAKKA CHAKKA

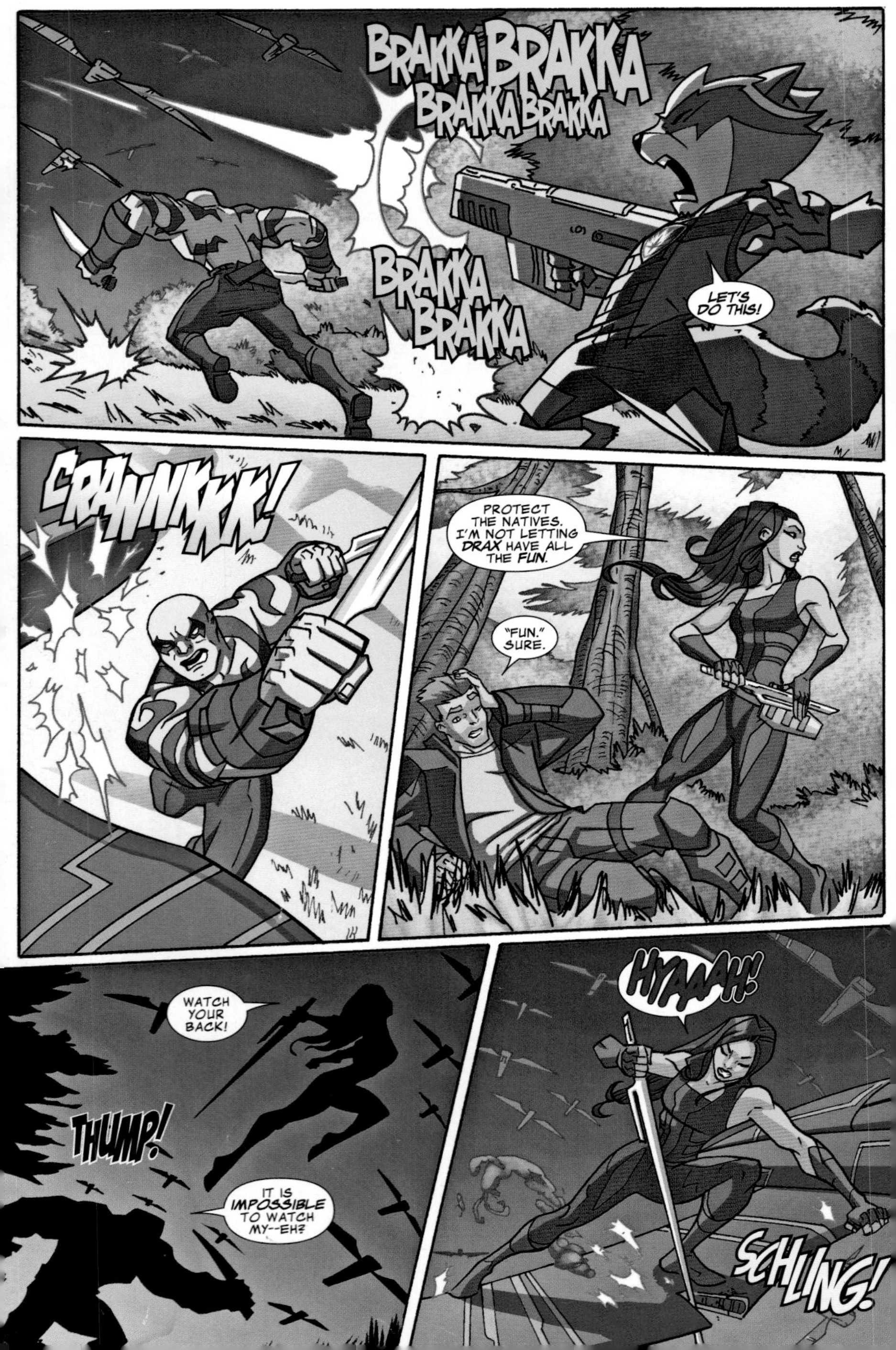
BRAKKA BRAKKA
BRAKKA BRAKKA
BRAKKA
BRAKKA
LET'S DO THIS!
CRANNKKK!
PROTECT THE NATIVES. I'M NOT LETTING DRAX HAVE ALL THE FUN.
"FUN." SURE.
WATCH YOUR BACK!
THUMP!
IT IS IMPOSSIBLE TO WATCH MY--EH?
HYAAAH!
SCHLING!

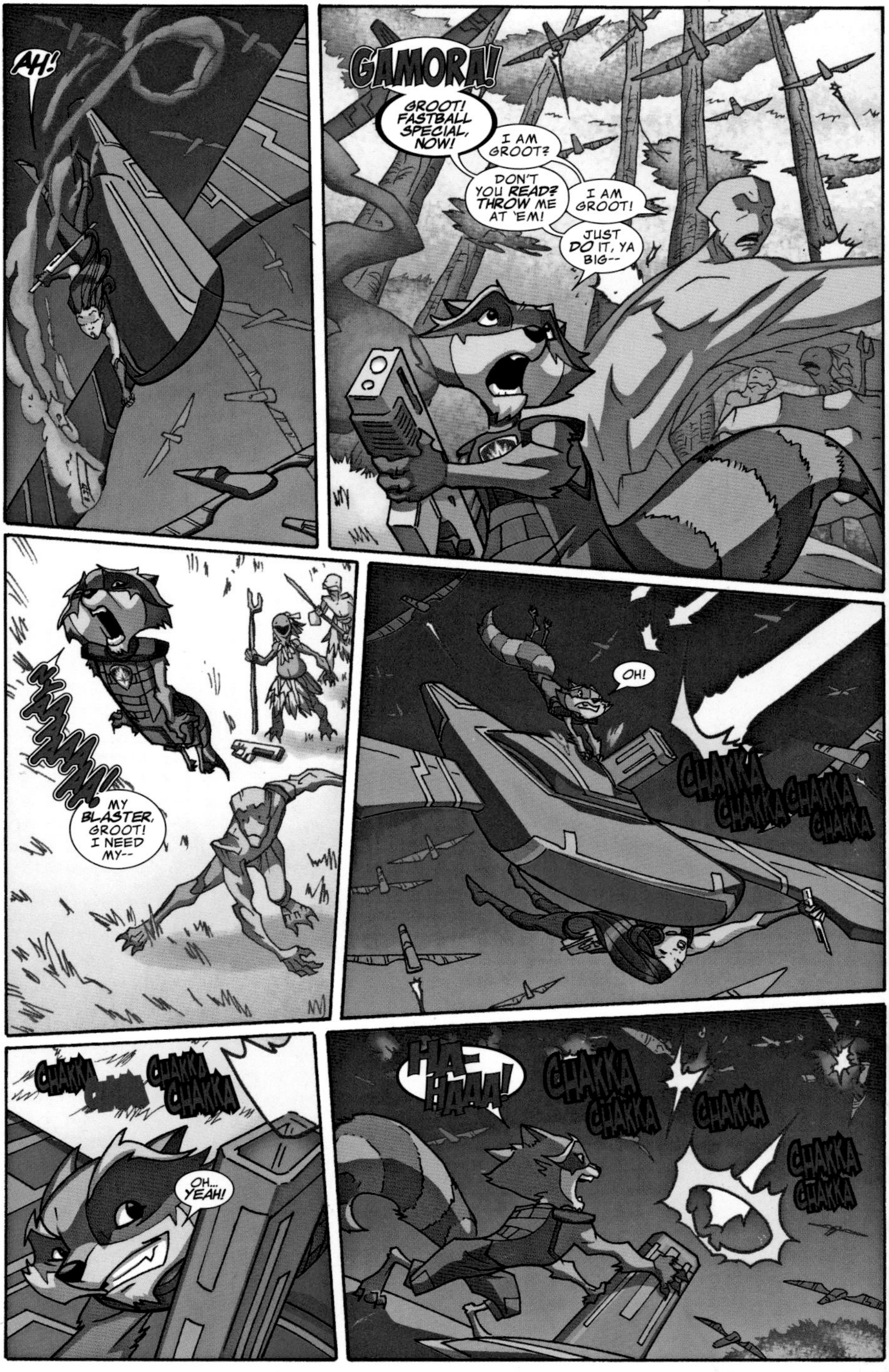
AH!
GAMORA!
GROOT! FASTBALL SPECIAL, NOW!
I AM GROOT?
DON'T YOU READ? THROW ME AT 'EM!
I AM GROOT!
JUST DO IT, YA BIG--
NYAAAAAAH!
MY BLASTER, GROOT! I NEED MY--
OH!
CHAKKA CHAKKA CHAKKA CHAKKA
CHAKKA CHAKKA CHAKKA
OH... YEAH!
HA-HAAA!
CHAKKA CHAKKA
CHAKKA
CHAKKA CHAKKA

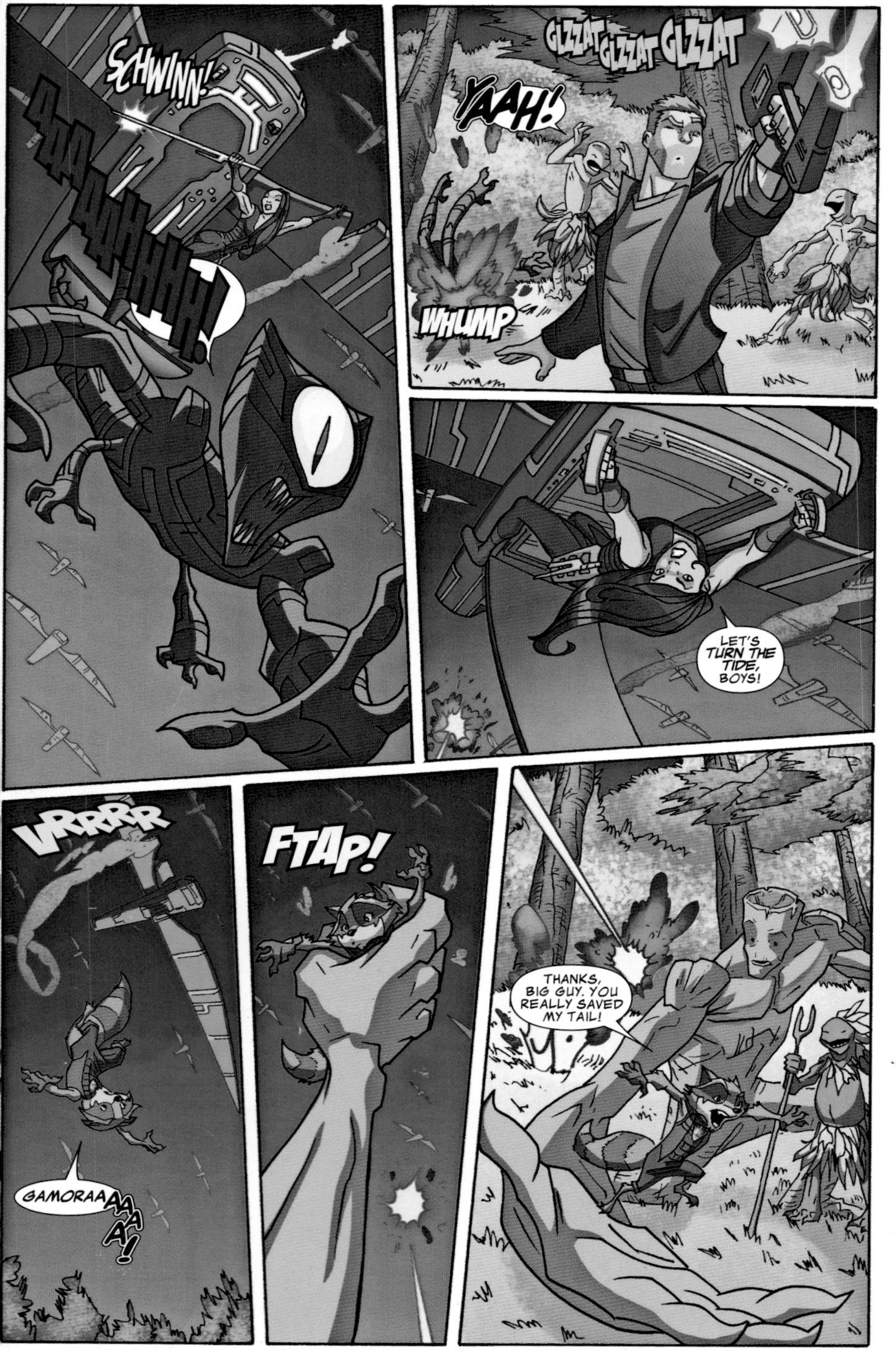
SCHWINN!
AAAAAHHHH!
GLZZZAT GLZZZAT GLZZZAT
YAAH!
WHUMP
LET'S TURN THE TIDE, BOYS!
VRRRR
GAMORAAAAAA!
FTAP!
THANKS, BIG GUY. YOU REALLY SAVED MY TAIL!

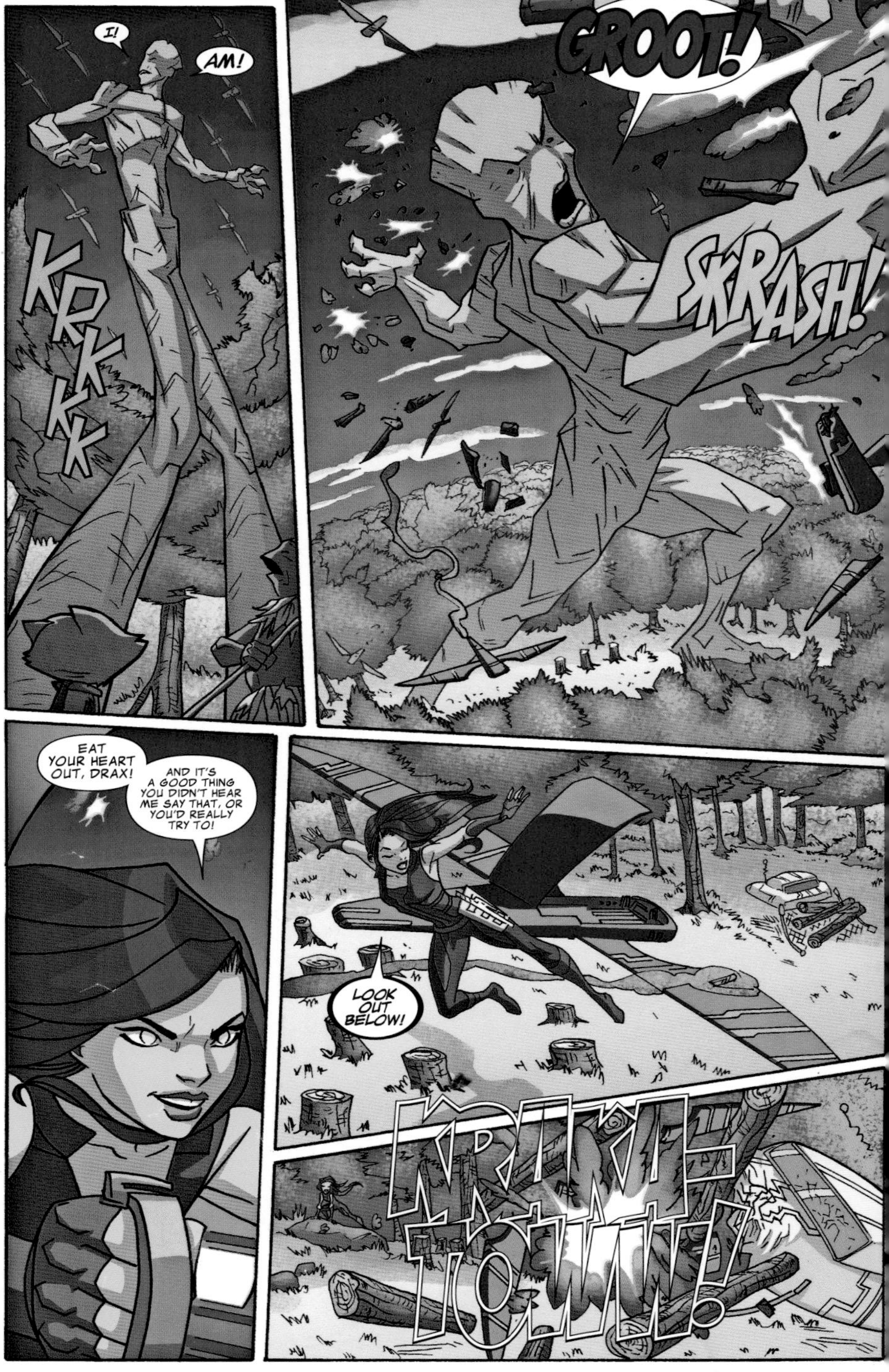
I!
AM!
KRKKKK
GROOT!
SKRASH!
EAT YOUR HEART OUT, DRAX!
AND IT'S A GOOD THING YOU DIDN'T HEAR ME SAY THAT, OR YOU'D REALLY TRY TO!
LOOK OUT BELOW!

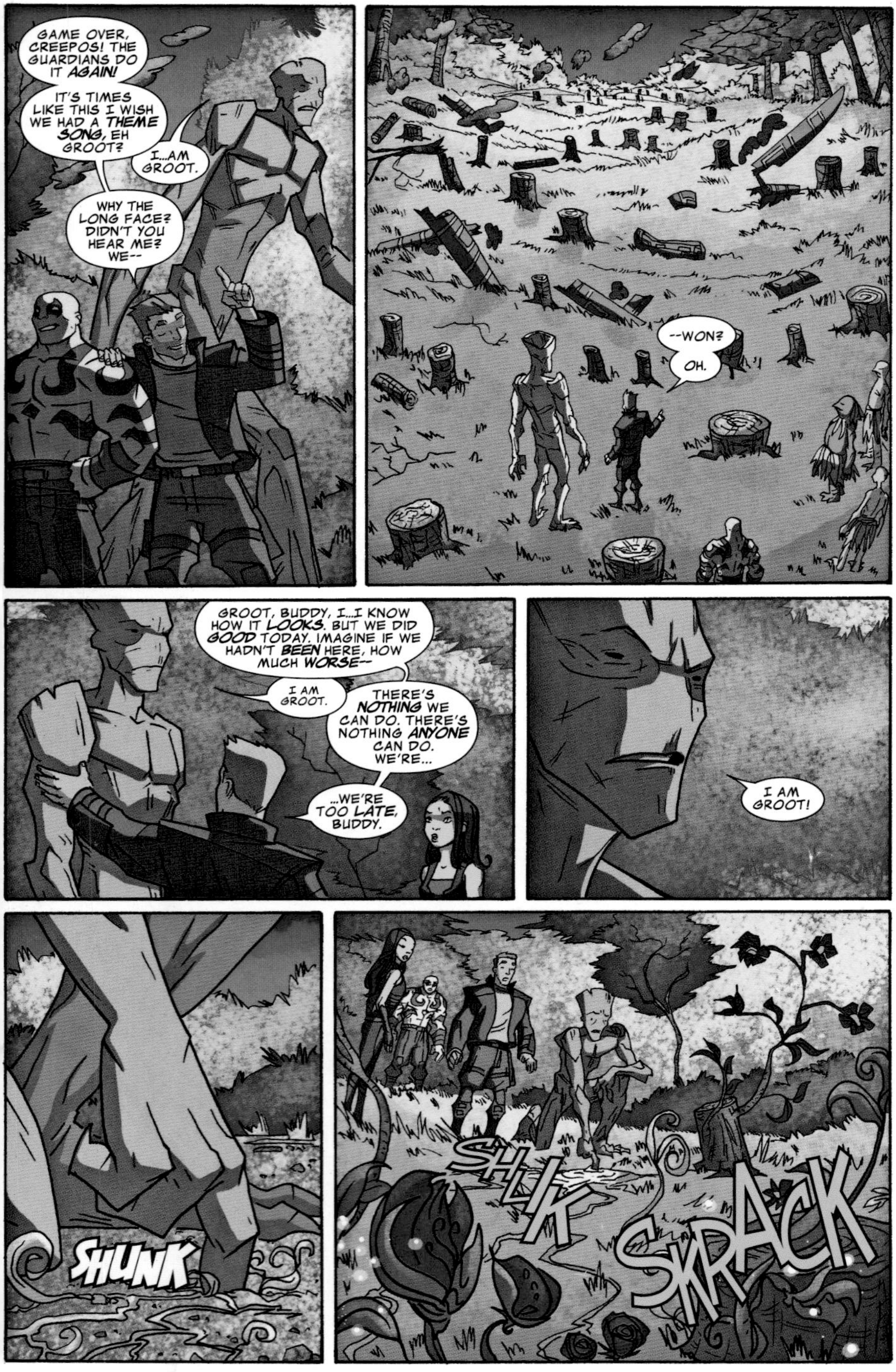
GAME OVER, CREEPOS! THE GUARDIANS DO IT AGAIN!
IT'S TIMES LIKE THIS I WISH WE HAD A THEME SONG, EH GROOT?
I...AM GROOT.
WHY THE LONG FACE? DIDN'T YOU HEAR ME? WE--
--WON?
OH.
GROOT, BUDDY, I...I KNOW HOW IT LOOKS. BUT WE DID GOOD TODAY. IMAGINE IF WE HADN'T BEEN HERE, HOW MUCH WORSE--
I AM GROOT.
THERE'S NOTHING WE CAN DO. THERE'S NOTHING ANYONE CAN DO. WE'RE...
...WE'RE TOO LATE, BUDDY.
I AM GROOT!
SHUNK
SHLIK
SKRACK

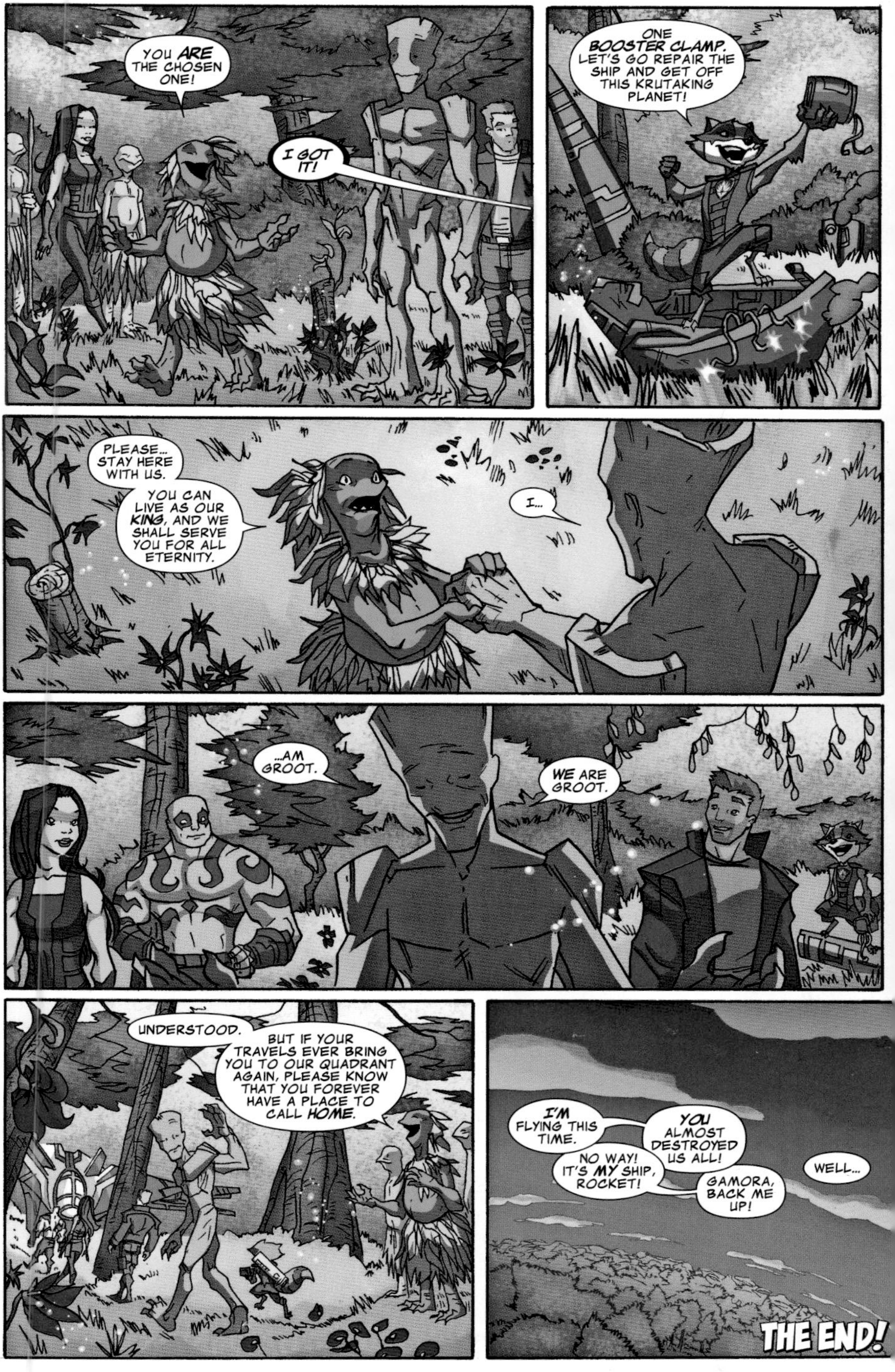
YOU ARE THE CHOSEN ONE!
I GOT IT!
ONE BOOSTER CLAMP. LET'S GO REPAIR THE SHIP AND GET OFF THIS KRUTAKING PLANET!
PLEASE... STAY HERE WITH US.
YOU CAN LIVE AS OUR KING, AND WE SHALL SERVE YOU FOR ALL ETERNITY.
I...
...AM GROOT.
WE ARE GROOT.
UNDERSTOOD.
BUT IF YOUR TRAVELS EVER BRING YOU TO OUR QUADRANT AGAIN, PLEASE KNOW THAT YOU FOREVER HAVE A PLACE TO CALL HOME.
I'M FLYING THIS TIME.
YOU ALMOST DESTROYED US ALL!
NO WAY! IT'S MY SHIP, ROCKET!
GAMORA, BACK ME UP!
WELL...
THE END!

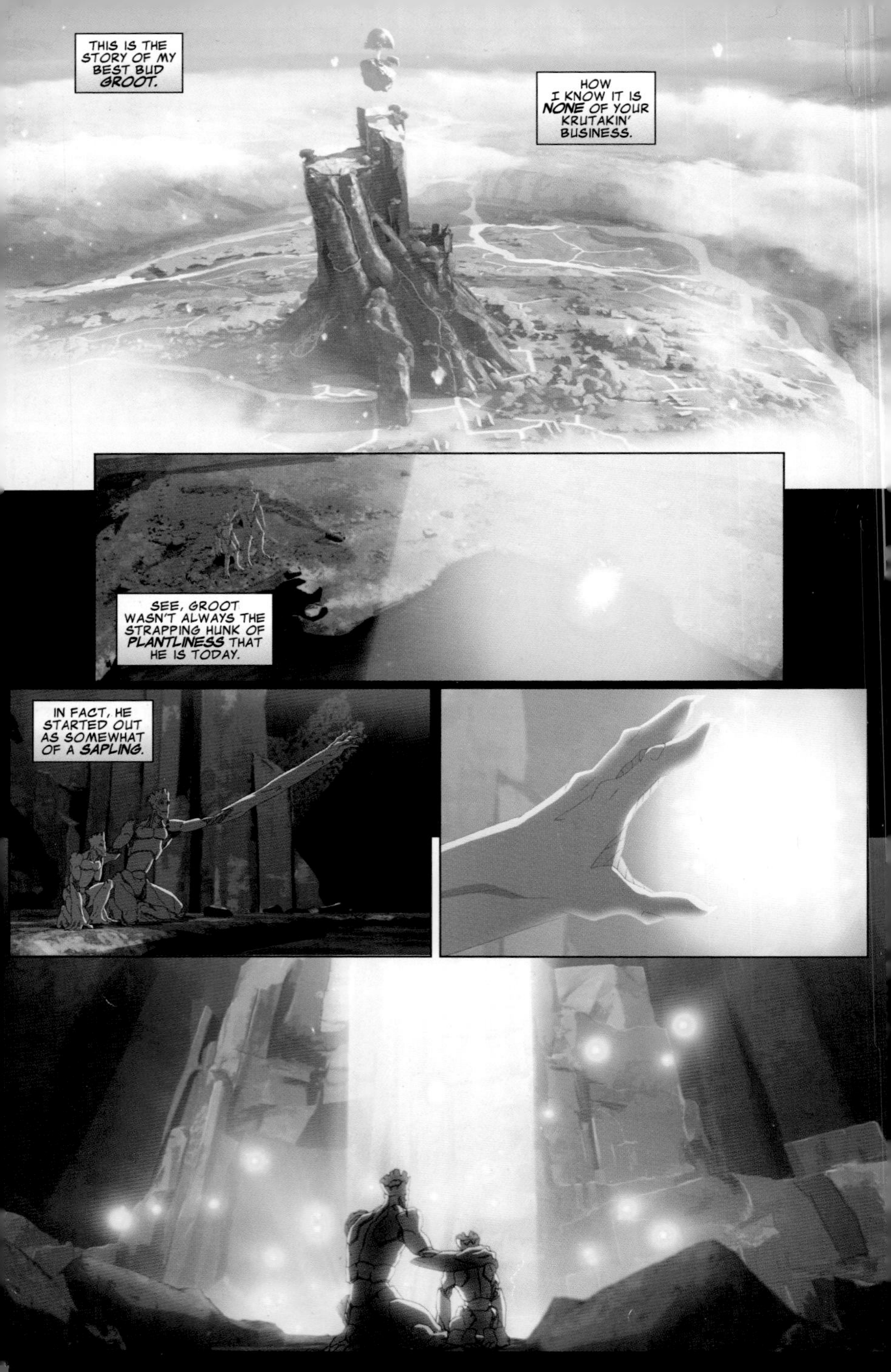
THIS IS THE STORY OF MY BEST BUD GROOT.
HOW I KNOW IT IS NONE OF YOUR KRUTAKIN' BUSINESS.
SEE, GROOT WASN'T ALWAYS THE STRAPPING HUNK OF PLANTLINESS THAT HE IS TODAY.
IN FACT, HE STARTED OUT AS SOMEWHAT OF A SAPLING.

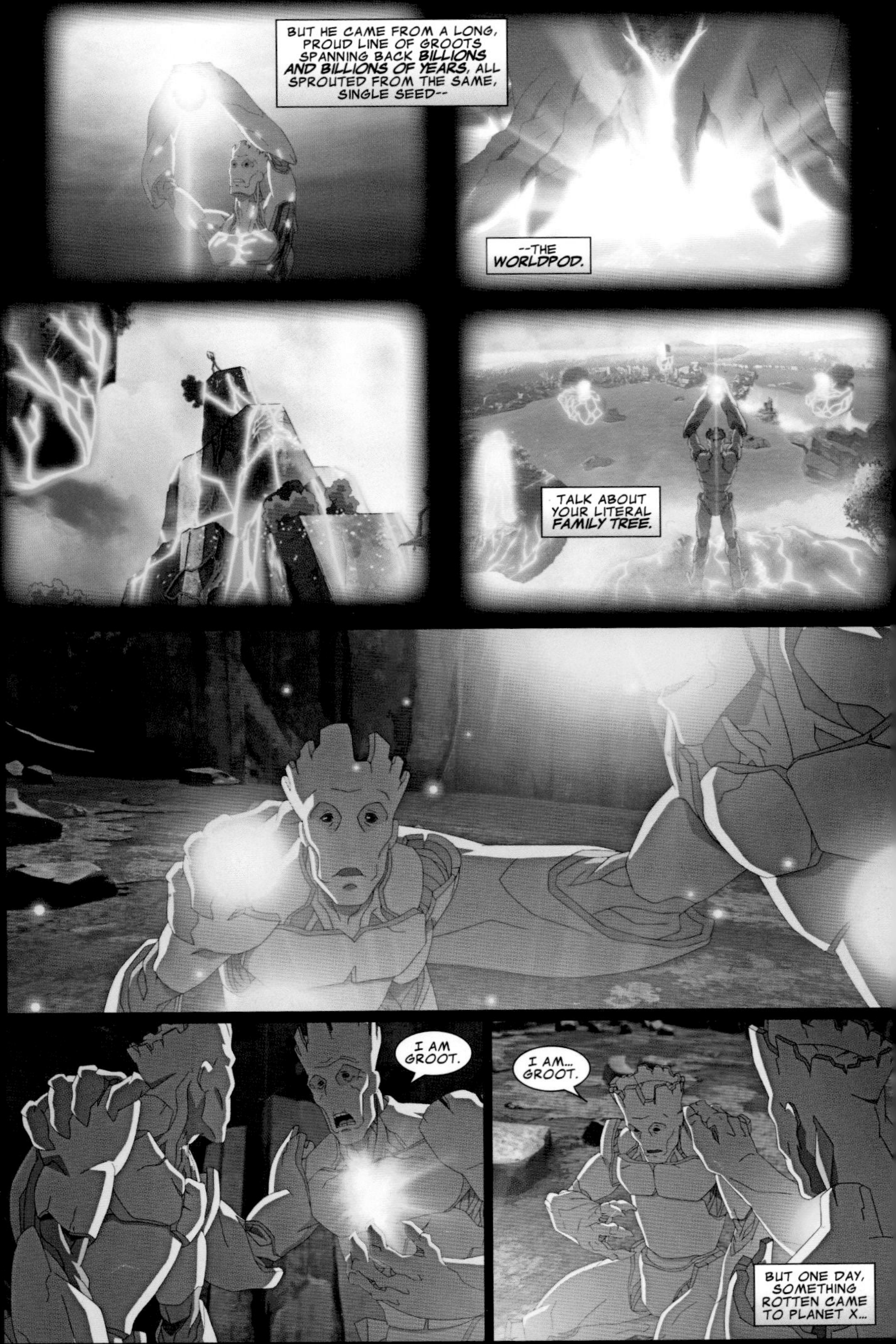
BUT HE CAME FROM A LONG, PROUD LINE OF GROOTS SPANNING BACK BILLIONS AND BILLIONS OF YEARS, ALL SPROUTED FROM THE SAME, SINGLE SEED--
--THE WORLDPOD.
TALK ABOUT YOUR LITERAL FAMILY TREE.
I AM GROOT.
I AM... GROOT.
BUT ONE DAY, SOMETHING ROTTEN CAME TO PLANET X...

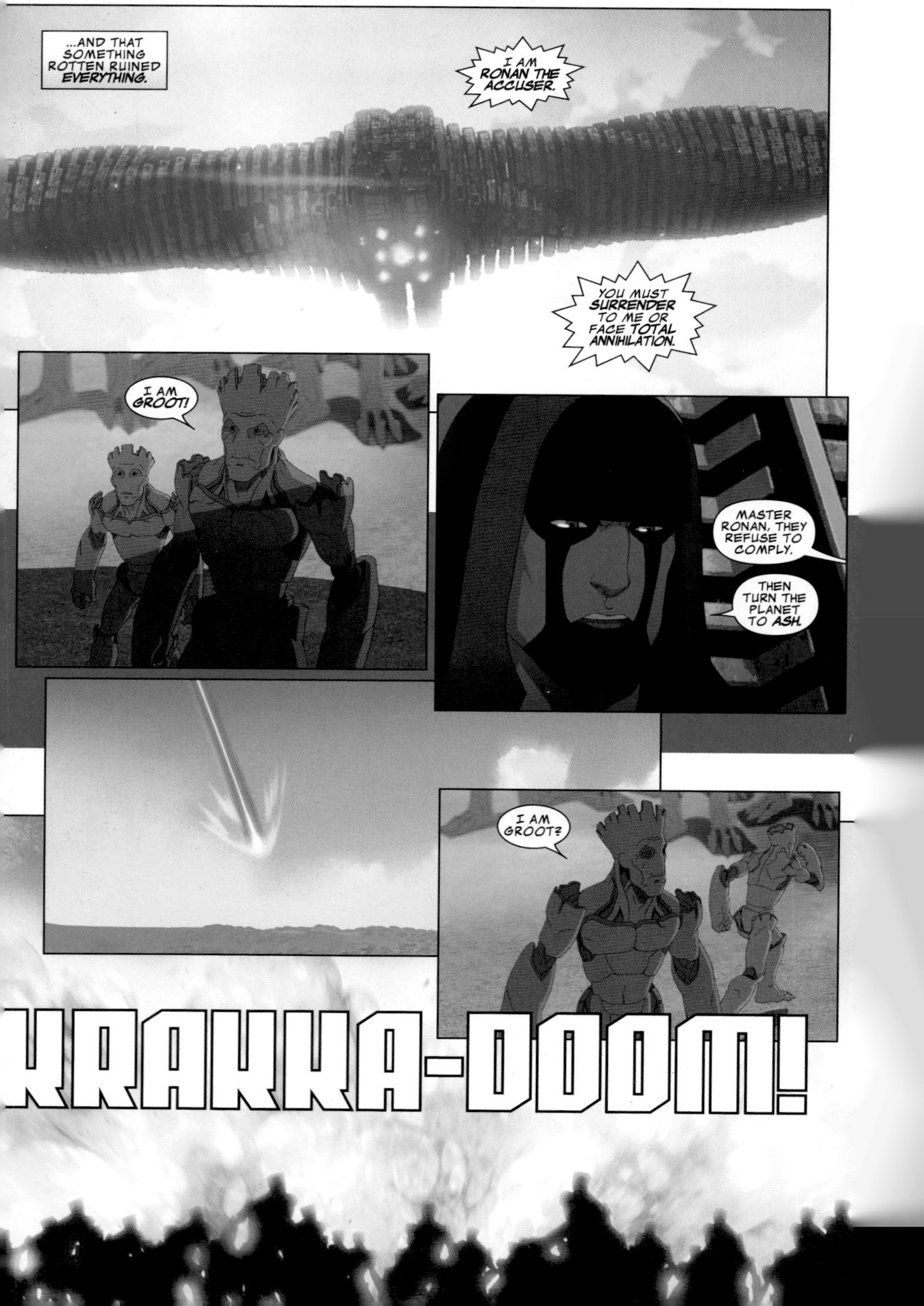
...AND THAT SOMETHING ROTTEN RUINED EVERYTHING.
I AM RONAN THE ACCUSER.
YOU MUST SURRENDER TO ME OR FACE TOTAL ANNIHILATION.
I AM GROOT!
MASTER RONAN, THEY REFUSE TO COMPLY.
THEN TURN THE PLANET TO ASH.
I AM GROOT?
KRAKKA-DOOM!

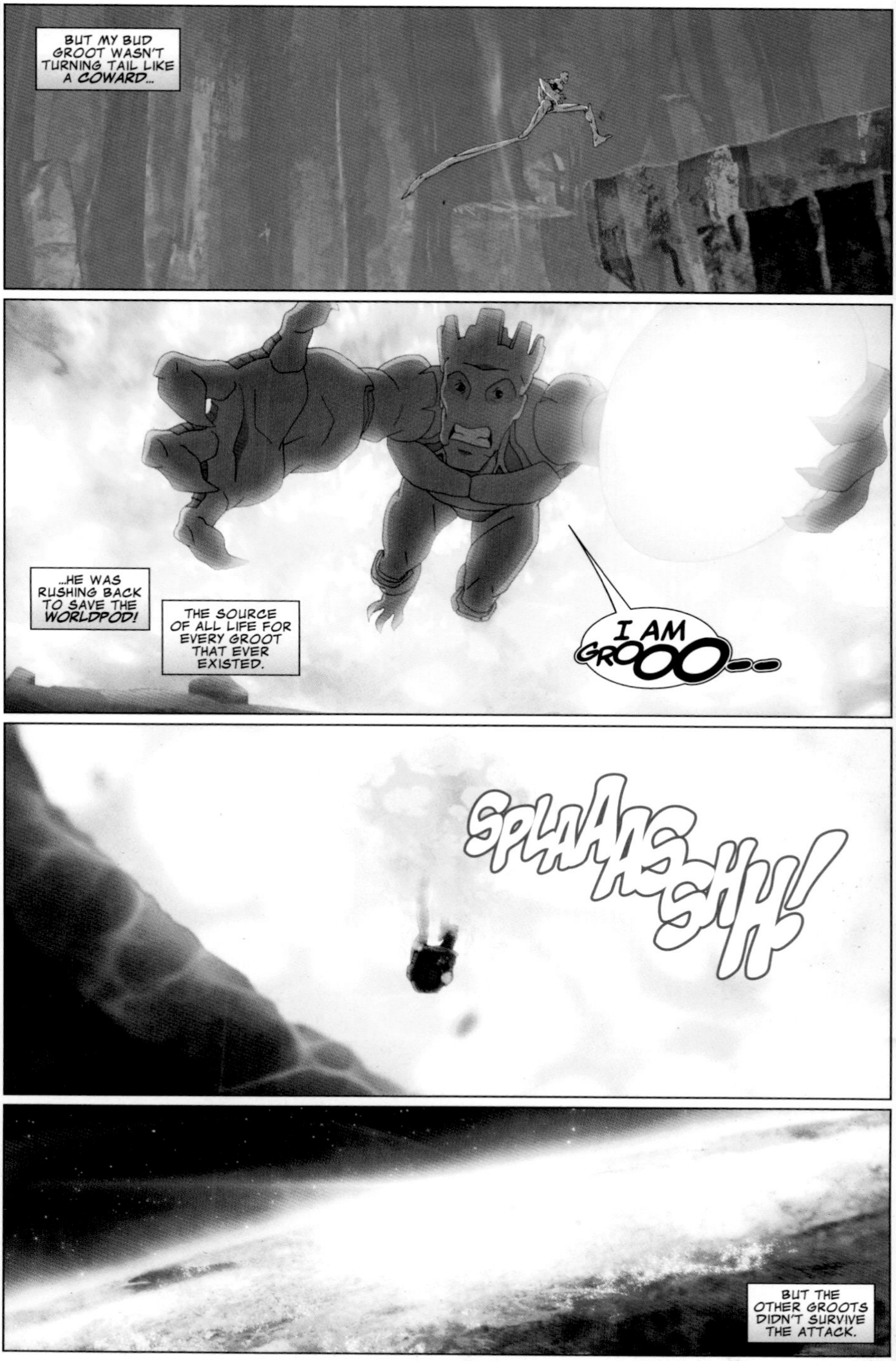
BUT MY BUD GROOT WASN'T TURNING TAIL LIKE A COWARD...
...HE WAS RUSHING BACK TO SAVE THE WORLDPOD!
THE SOURCE OF ALL LIFE FOR EVERY GROOT THAT EVER EXISTED.
I AM GROOOO--
SPLAAASSHH!
BUT THE OTHER GROOTS DIDN'T SURVIVE THE ATTACK.

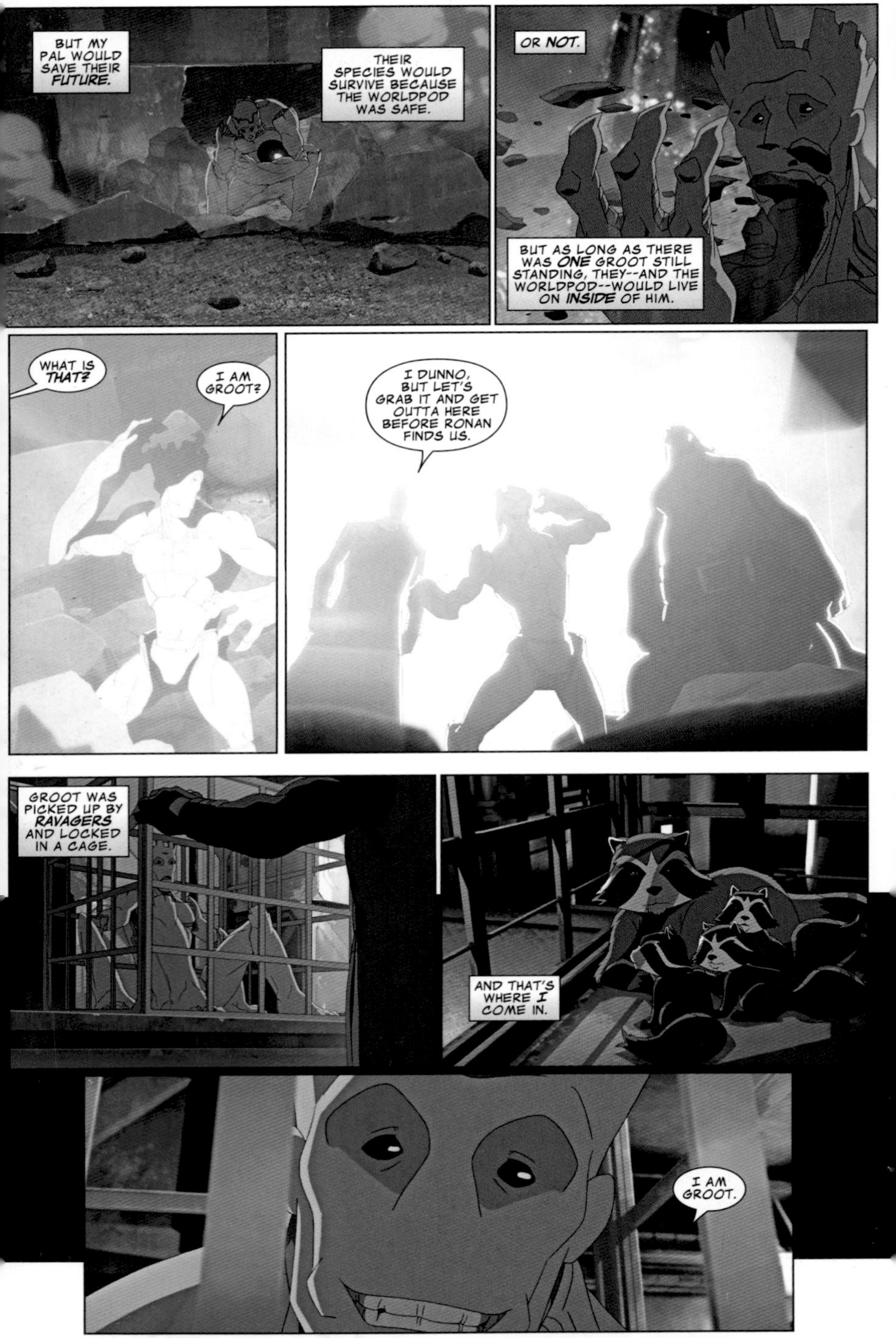
BUT MY PAL WOULD SAVE THEIR FUTURE.
THEIR SPECIES WOULD SURVIVE BECAUSE THE WORLDPOD WAS SAFE.
OR NOT.
BUT AS LONG AS THERE WAS ONE GROOT STILL STANDING, THEY--AND THE WORLDPOD--WOULD LIVE ON INSIDE OF HIM.
WHAT IS THAT?
I AM GROOT?
I DUNNO, BUT LET'S GRAB IT AND GET OUTTA HERE BEFORE RONAN FINDS US.
GROOT WAS PICKED UP BY RAVAGERS AND LOCKED IN A CAGE.
AND THAT'S WHERE I COME IN.
I AM GROOT.

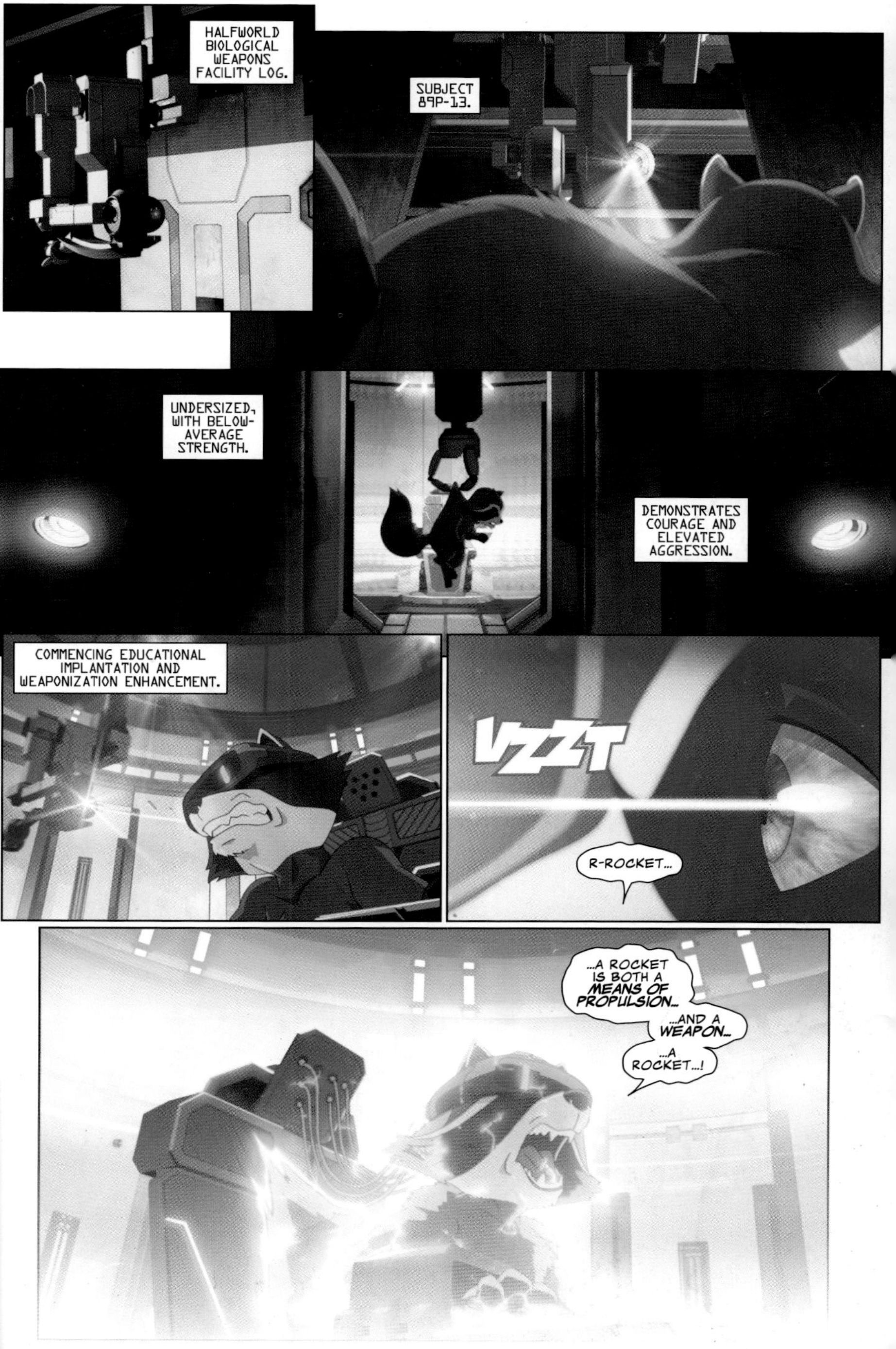
HALFWORLD BIOLOGICAL WEAPONS FACILITY LOG.
SUBJECT 89P-13.
UNDERSIZED, WITH BELOW-AVERAGE STRENGTH.
DEMONSTRATES COURAGE AND ELEVATED AGGRESSION.
COMMENCING EDUCATIONAL IMPLANTATION AND WEAPONIZATION ENHANCEMENT.
VZZT
R-ROCKET...
...A ROCKET IS BOTH A MEANS OF PROPULSION...
...AND A WEAPON...
...A ROCKET...!

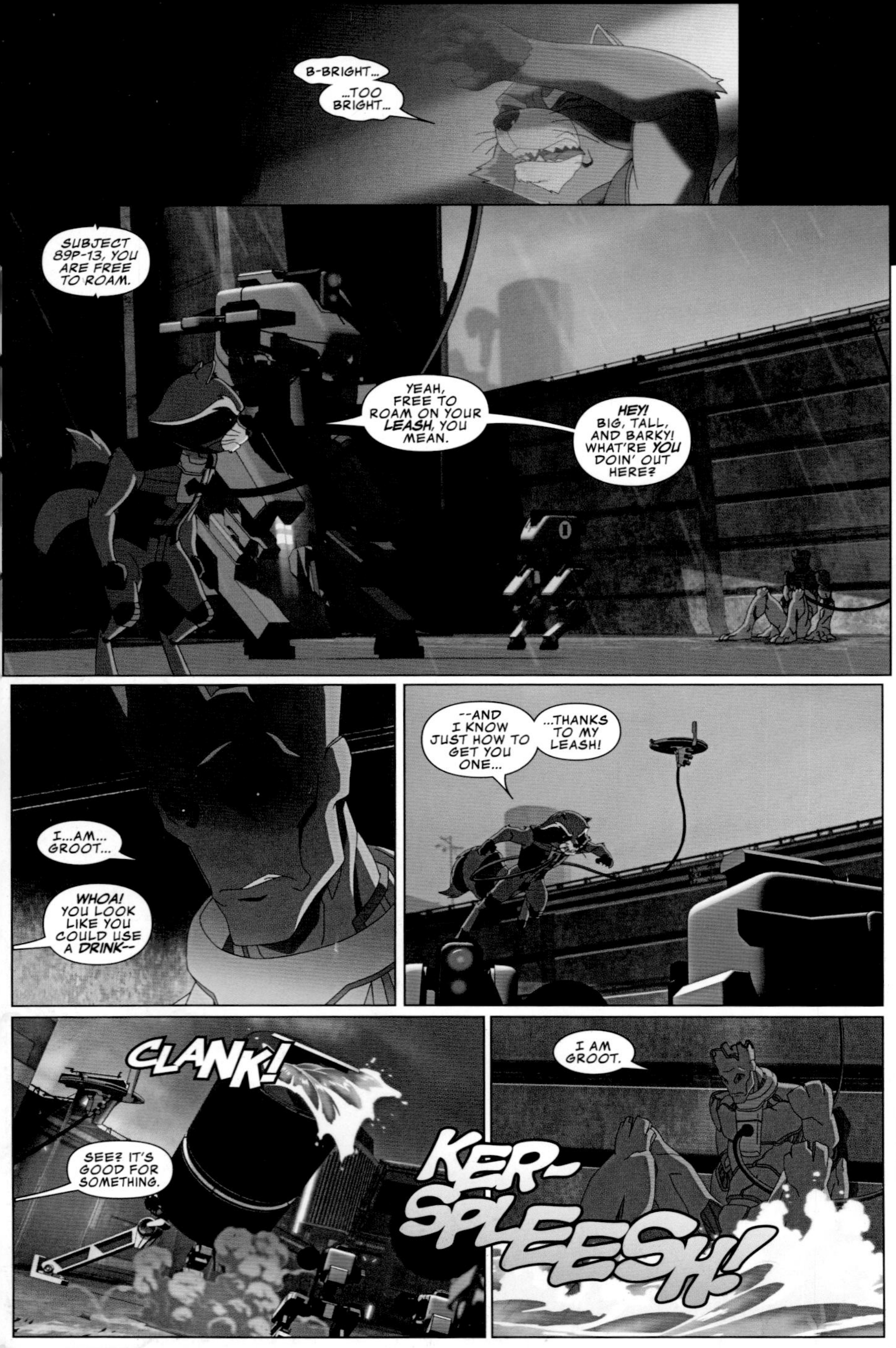
B-BRIGHT...
...TOO BRIGHT...
SUBJECT 89P-13, YOU ARE FREE TO ROAM.
YEAH, FREE TO ROAM ON YOUR LEASH, YOU MEAN.
HEY! BIG, TALL, AND BARKY! WHAT'RE YOU DOIN' OUT HERE?
I...AM... GROOT...
WHOA! YOU LOOK LIKE YOU COULD USE A DRINK--
--AND I KNOW JUST HOW TO GET YOU ONE...
...THANKS TO MY LEASH!
CLANK!
SEE? IT'S GOOD FOR SOMETHING.
KER-SPLEESH!
I AM GROOT.

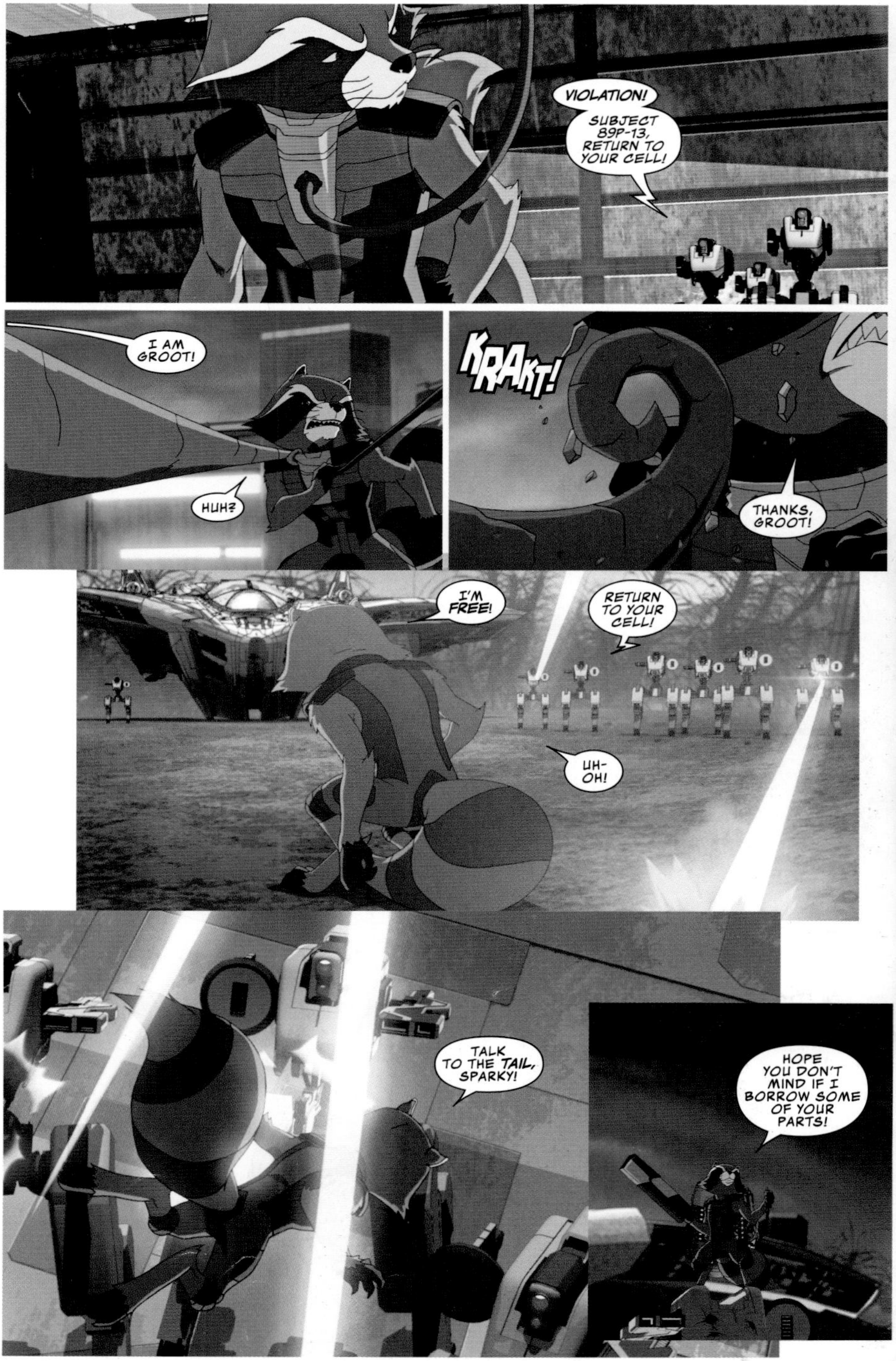
VIOLATION!
SUBJECT 89P-13, RETURN TO YOUR CELL!
I AM GROOT!
HUH?
KRAKT!
THANKS, GROOT!
I'M FREE!
RETURN TO YOUR CELL!
UH-OH!
TALK TO THE TAIL, SPARKY!
HOPE YOU DON'T MIND IF I BORROW SOME OF YOUR PARTS!

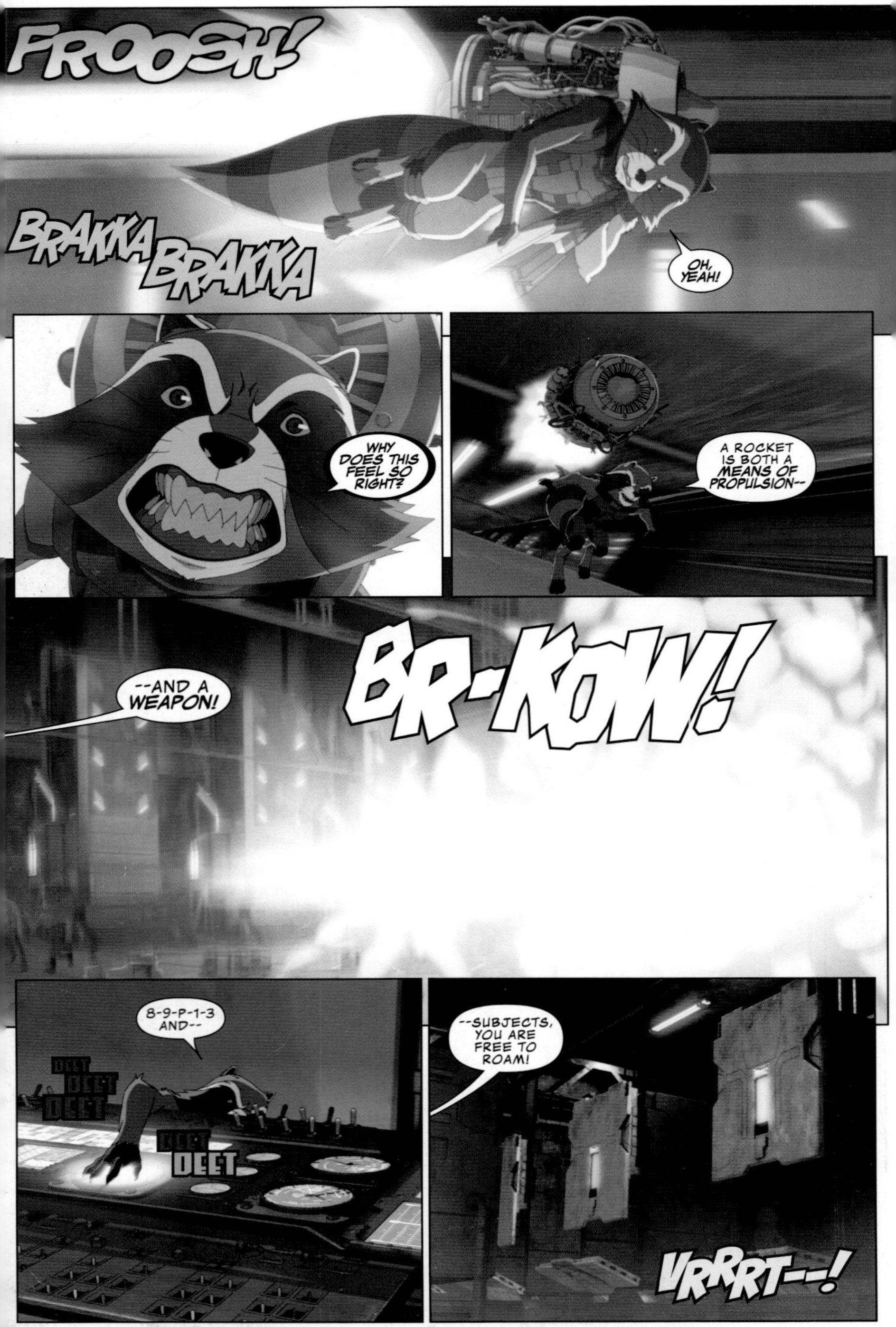
FROOSH!
BRAKKA BRAKKA
OH, YEAH!
WHY DOES THIS FEEL SO RIGHT?
A ROCKET IS BOTH A MEANS OF PROPULSION--
--AND A WEAPON!
BR-KOW!
8-9-P-1-3 AND--
DEET DEET DEET
DEET DEET
--SUBJECTS, YOU ARE FREE TO ROAM!
VRRRT--!

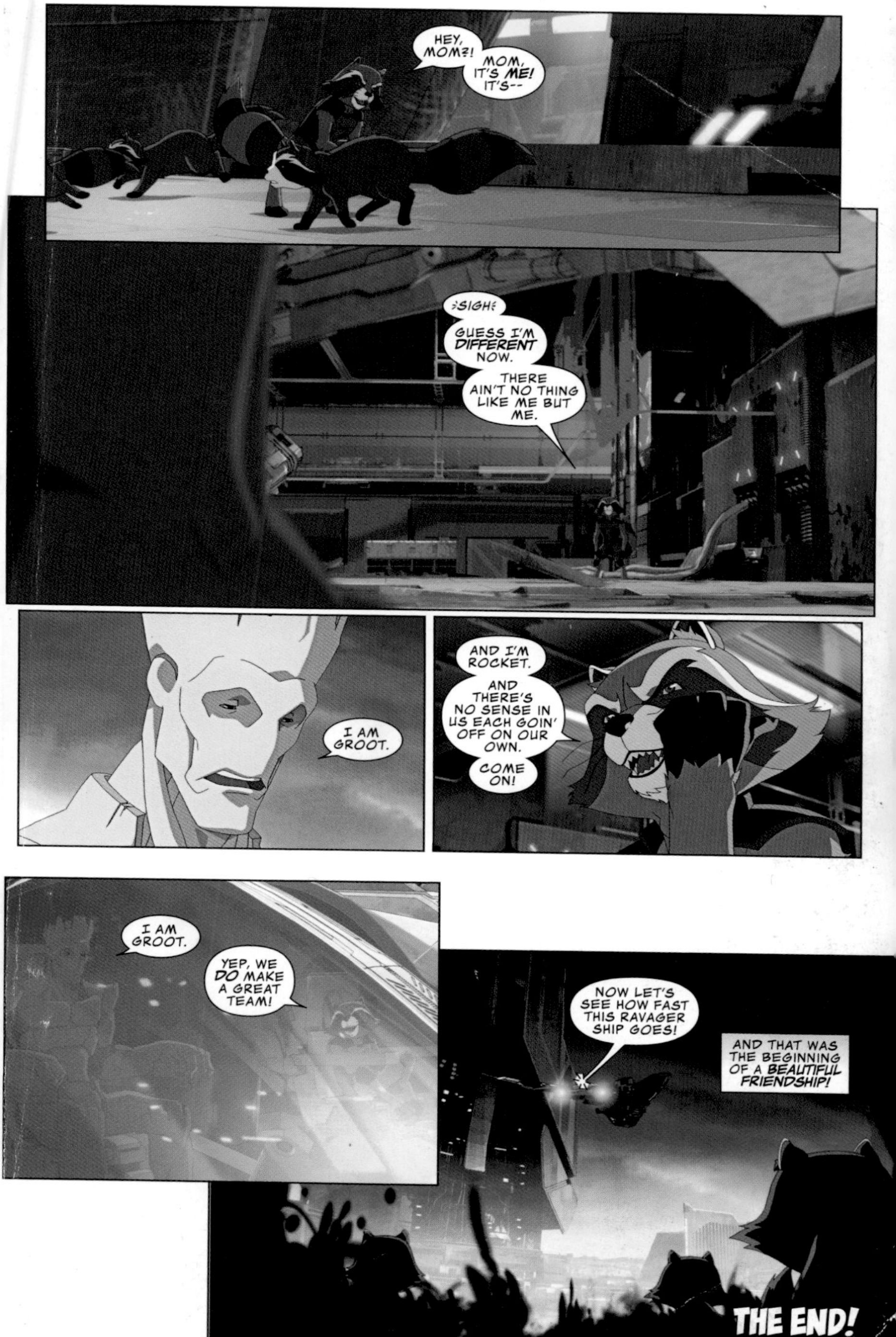
HEY, MOM?!
MOM, IT'S ME! IT'S--
SIGH
GUESS I'M DIFFERENT NOW.
THERE AIN'T NO THING LIKE ME BUT ME.
I AM GROOT.
AND I'M ROCKET.
AND THERE'S NO SENSE IN US EACH GOIN' OFF ON OUR OWN.
COME ON!
I AM GROOT.
YEP, WE DO MAKE A GREAT TEAM!
NOW LET'S SEE HOW FAST THIS RAVAGER SHIP GOES!
AND THAT WAS THE BEGINNING OF A BEAUTIFUL FRIENDSHIP!
THE END!

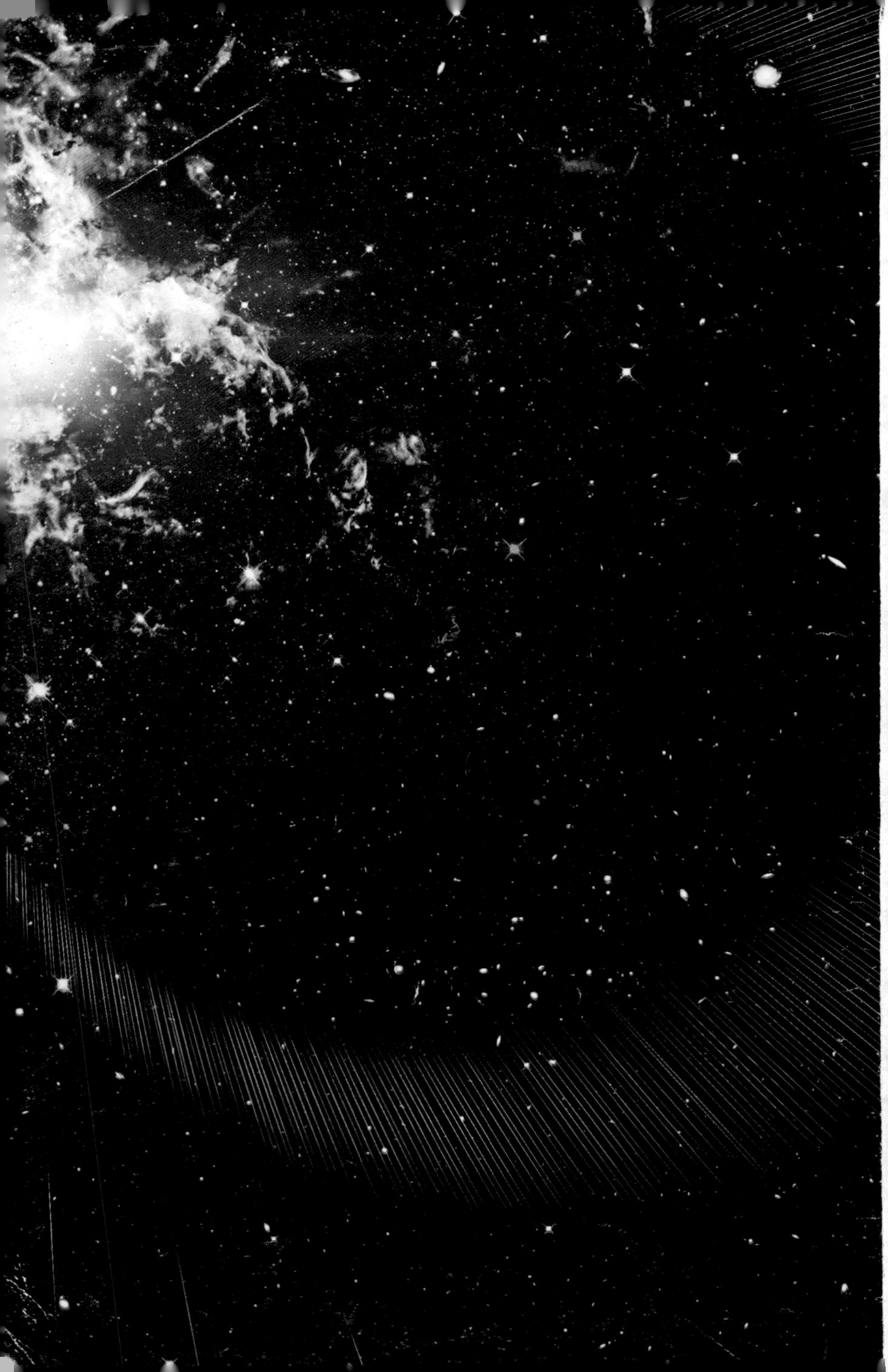